T0355851

Sweet Escape

ALSO BY MEREDITH WILD

Hacker Books

Hardwired

Hardpressed

Hardline

Hard Limit

Hard Love

Bridge Books

On My Knees

Into the Fire

Over the Edge

Blood of Zeus Books

Blood of Zeus (With Angel Payne)

Heart of Fire (With Angel Payne)

Fate of Storms (With Angel Payne)

Bridge of Souls (With Angel Payne)

Red Ledger Books

Reborn

Recall

Revenge

ALSO BY JILLIAN LIOTA

Cedar Point Series (Small Town Romance Series)

The Trouble with Wanting

The Opposite of Falling

The Start of Someday

The Problem with Perfect

The Truth About Regret

The Downside to Forever

Hermosa Beach Series (New Adult Romance Series)

Promise Me Nothing

Be Your Anything

Give My Everything

We Were Something

Holidays in Hermosa (New Adult Romance Novella Series)

Nowhere Like This

Anywhere But Here

Sandalwood (Small Town Romance Series)

Solo

Sure

Like You Series (Contemporary Romance Series)

Like You Mean It

Like You Want It

A Gift Like You

Keeper Duet (New Adult Romance)

The Keeper

Keep Away

Additional Works

This Vulnerable Heart (Poetry)

Who You Used to Be (Anthology, short)

Birthday Girl (Anthology, short)

Distraction (Anthology, short)

Sweet Escape

MEREDITH WILD
AND JILLIAN LIOTA

 Montlake

Published by Montlake, Seattle

www.apub.com

Amazon, the Amazon logo, and Montlake are trademarks of Amazon.com, Inc., or its affiliates.

ISBN-13: 9781662523977 (paperback)
ISBN-13: 9781662523984 (digital)

Cover design by Caroline Teagle Johnson
Cover images: © Wander Aguiar Photography; © Pattadis Walarput, © Spondylolithesis / Getty

Printed in the United States of America

For any girl who has ever been considered "too much."
You're never too much for the right person.

Chapter One

Memphis

I close my eyes and lean back in my chair, feeling a sense of exhaustion deep in my bones after another long day of trying to hold everything together.

Another day of feeling like I've given all that I have.

Another day of wondering if it will end up being enough.

Before I can take even a few minutes for myself, my phone beeps with a text, and I groan, sure that it's another emergency that demands my attention.

Murphy: Cory called in sick. Can you cover the bar so I can cut Mira?

Letting out a sigh, I consider for just a moment the idea of telling my sister no. Saying I need a night to myself. A chance to go out and blow off some steam for the first time in who knows how long. Or even to hole up in my room, have a long shower, and collapse into my bed.

But I can't say no.

I would never say no.

All of this . . . everything . . . rests on my shoulders.

And as much as I'd like to check out and run away sometimes, I can't do that to my family. To our employees who rely on this business for their livelihoods. To the legacy I'm trying to preserve.

Me: I'll be over in fifteen.

I drop my phone on my desk and close my eyes again, attempting to give myself those few minutes I desperately need before I push on.

I can't ever really be sure of what the future holds, but the way things have been over the past few years has wrung me dry. In more ways than one.

And now, the future of this vineyard seems to rest on the success of the restaurant.

God, that fucking restaurant.

Part of me thinks it was equal parts the best decision I've made *and* the worst.

The best because it's doing exactly what I hoped it would do: bring in more profit so the vineyard doesn't continue digging a deeper hole of debt.

The worst because it's doing the other thing I knew it would do: more than double my workload and open a whole other can of worms that I have to keep on top of.

But it feels wrong for me to resent the very thing that might save us.

Especially when it was my idea in the first place.

I put my computer to sleep and push out of my chair, stretching my arms above my head and rotating my head and neck, trying to work out the muscles that get so fatigued from the tense way I sit at my computer.

My aunt Sarah told me I need to set it up ergonomically, whatever that means, and she made all these recommendations for how to change the monitor and adjust my chair that would supposedly help. But I don't have time to deal with that kind of woo-woo bullshit.

Hell, I barely have time to get in a full night of sleep.

I grab my phone off the desk as I leave my office, pulling up our marketing coordinator's number and hitting call.

"Hey, it's Memphis," I say when I get her voicemail. "Sorry for the last-minute notice, but I need to reschedule our meeting. I've got a fire to put out at the restaurant. Just shoot me a message with a good time for you in the next few days, and I'll make it work. Thanks."

I hate marketing. It was my least favorite part of my business degree, and always the area I struggled with the most. Thankfully, we have employees to handle some of that, and I get to focus on other things that are more important.

At least to me.

I hit end as I head out the french doors to the back patio, taking the path through the vines toward where the restaurant sits on the northeast corner of the property. My eyes scan the netted vines as I walk, assessing the nearly ripened bunches and stopping every so often to take a closer look.

My family has owned and operated this vineyard for four generations . . . five if I include myself, though it hasn't officially passed over to me yet. We work the land, harvest and crush the grapes, ferment the wine, bottle and distribute the vintages, and manage the business. It truly is a family-run production.

We're not too shabby, either. Hawthorne Vines is a wine recognized for excellence. We've won several awards over the past few decades, and we're regularly kept on the wine lists of some of the best hotels and restaurants in Napa and Sonoma.

And we're still struggling.

Which is why I've been on an endless quest to find every single extra cent I can.

Most of the decisions I've made are small. Things that don't have a huge impact on how we operate, just on what resources we use.

Except for the restaurant. It was my biggest, riskiest idea, and pretty much altered everything about how things work around here.

I round the corner at the end of the last row of vines, my gaze falling on the crowd of customers on the back patio of the restaurant, enjoying themselves. Their laughter and chatter and the sound of utensils and glasses clinking fill the air. I pause and watch for a few moments as servers bustle around, taking orders and refilling wineglasses.

I want to smile, because it means that there are people here, drinking and eating and contributing toward the bottom line that is an ever-present, looming shadow in the back of my mind.

We opened the doors four months ago—my last-ditch effort to keep things going. Business seems to be moving smoothly so far, but I'm not sure when I'll truly feel like the venture has accomplished everything I hoped.

Maybe when I don't feel choked by debt.

Because even though the restaurant is doing its job, the decisions I've made in order to get us here . . . I'll be living with the consequences of those choices for longer than I like to think about.

But that's why I can't allow myself to revel in the good. There is just . . . too much at stake. And it feels like there is still too far to go before the wrongs have been made right. Before the legacy that is supposed to be bestowed upon me no longer feels like an anchor wrapped around my neck, dragging me under.

When I finally slip through the front door, I give the hostess, Enid, a tight smile before scanning the room. I take in the smattering of guests at the tables and the wine bar, the guitarist in the corner strumming something lightly, and the waitstaff moving about the room.

I should feel amazing when I survey everything going on. Especially in this space, when my own blood, sweat, and tears went into every single element of this restaurant's creation. I oversaw each intricate detail, ensuring its perfection.

It's my baby, my project, my brainchild.

The sacrifices I made to make sure this place became what it is will be something I live with for quite a while.

But even though I feel like I'm drowning in everything that's still going wrong, I give myself just a second to be thankful. Because the restaurant seems to be a well-functioning operation instead of the money pit it could have been if even just a little bit of bad luck had come our way.

"Thank you so much for stepping in."

I turn, spotting my sister, Murphy, as she walks toward me carrying a tray of wineglasses and a bottle of merlot.

"Can you cut Mira when you head over there? Her daughter is sick, and she needs to get home as soon as possible."

She doesn't wait for me to respond, instead striding past me and slipping easily between tables, heading for whatever table ordered the wine.

"Can I get you anything, Mr. Hawthorne?"

I glance at Enid, who is looking at me with wide eyes and a bright smile on her face.

"I'm fine. Shouldn't you be cleaning something instead of standing around?"

Her face pinches, and she spins immediately to survey the host stand before grabbing a rag and a bottle of spray from underneath.

I don't wait around to watch what she does with it, choosing to leave her to her responsibilities and crossing to the wine bar along the far wall, where Mira is pouring a bottle of chardonnay into a glass for a customer.

"Mira, you're cut."

The brunette bartender grins at me gratefully.

"Thanks for covering for Cory so I can dip out," she says, finishing up her pour and setting the bottle back in the fridge. "Farrah's caught a bug or something, otherwise I would have offered to stay later."

I shake my head. "You're fine. I was going to be over here eventually anyway, so . . . happy to step in," I lie.

As Mira closes out, I take a few minutes to scan through the bottles we have behind the counter and in the fridge.

I've only worked the bar a few times since we opened—on most nights that we're open, I'm helping out with service or something in the dining room, the wine bar being a fairly well-contained area—but I'm the one who created the protocol and organizational system we use. So it doesn't take long for me to assess that we're low on reds, and that the bar staff needs to do a better job of cleaning out the wine cooler at the end of each shift.

But even though a handful of things need tending to, it's still easy to see that the bartenders are doing their jobs. In fact, *everyone* is doing their jobs. From the kitchen to the waitstaff to the hosts. I might have given Enid a little bit of shit when I walked in, but Murphy has praised her work ethic multiple times.

Still, though. I can't seem to let the little things slide, my hypervigilance a reflection of my fear.

And my frustration.

For as long as I can remember, I was told that this vineyard would be mine one day. That someday, I'd be the one in charge, and I'd be leading Hawthorne Vines into the future. But when I envisioned my life living that future, I imagined it being . . . different.

More of the feeling I remembered my grandpa talking about when I was a kid.

A sense of pride.

Of accomplishment.

But I don't feel those things.

Instead I'm just . . . angry.

Angry at my father for the mess he made that I'm having to clean up.

At my grandfather for failing to teach my dad the things he needed to understand in order to keep this business in the black.

At the stupid economy, even the weather, for never seeming to do what I need it to do at the right time.

And mostly, I'm furious at myself. Because no matter what I do, it still feels like the right choices for how to solve the problems we face—problems that I had zero hand in creating—are barely out of reach.

But I can't dwell on that anger. And I can't dwell on what I wish was different. There's no point in spending time thinking about what I originally thought my life would be.

Because whatever that vision was doesn't matter.

Not anymore.

"Have a good night," Mira says, sliding next to me and clocking out at the register.

"Hope your daughter feels better."

She waves, then disappears from my line of sight, and I take a few more minutes after she's gone to survey the equipment and look through the open tabs. Then I turn to check in with the customers seated at the bar.

Which is when my eyes lock on the most . . . exquisitely beautiful woman I've ever seen.

Copper hair and hazel eyes and a smattering of freckles, all of which sit above lips that are tilted into a little smirk that has something twisting inside my stomach in the best way.

I blink twice, then clear my throat and give her a friendly smile, my mind leaving the stresses of the vineyard behind and instead focusing on the beauty before me.

"Good evening," I say, leaning forward and bracing my hands wide against the bar, nodding my head. "Can I get you another glass?"

Only then do I spot the chardonnay in front of her, the one that Mira poured seconds before she clocked out.

The redhead's smirk grows, and it's easy to spot the humor dancing behind her eyes.

"I think I'm okay," she answers. "I'd look a little ridiculous sitting here with a glass filled to the brim."

My chuckle comes easily as I step back, leaning against the counter behind me and crossing my arms. "Well, I can guarantee that you wouldn't be the first if you did."

She laughs, and I can't help the way that thing inside me twists tighter at the sound of her voice.

Melodious and playful and warm.

Unlike anything I've heard before.

"Oh, I don't doubt it in the slightest. I had a brief but informative stint as a bartender at a nightclub a few years back." She leans forward and dips her voice. "I felt officially scandalized after one night."

"I can only imagine."

I stare at her for a long moment, unable to look away.

Unusual for me. I'm rarely distracted from the things I need to get done just because a beautiful woman looks my way.

But for whatever reason, my focus is glued to her.

And she stares right back, her eyes never leaving mine as she takes a sip of her wine.

It feels brazen.

Or maybe *defiant* is a better word.

Like she refuses to look away just because etiquette would suggest that she should.

I like everything about it.

"What brings you here tonight?" I ask her, my eyes scanning the room only briefly. "Waiting on a date?"

She scoffs and rolls her eyes, but the playful energy is still there. "Definitely not. I have no interest in dating right now, I assure you."

"Oh?" I step forward and brace my hands on the counter again. "And what *do* you have interest in?"

It's been a while since I've intentionally flirted with someone. Sure, I've had a run in the past of hooking up with tourists or people coming through The Standard, our local watering hole. But the past few months have been a lot, and I've not had the time or the inclination to head out for more than a beer with some friends at our monthly pool night.

This woman, though . . . gives me the inclination.

Her smirk returns at my playful comment. "I have many interests, though I'm certain some of them would scandalize you."

I should be checking in with other customers. Or cleaning. Or making a list of the things the bar staff needs to work on.

But instead, I find myself drawn to her. Like a moth to a flame.

"And what if I wouldn't mind being scandalized?" I ask her.

She leans forward again, and this time I find myself doing the same.

"Tell me, Mr. Bartender," she replies, her voice dipping low, "when you picture being scandalized, am I on my knees or on my back?"

I swallow thickly, shock ricocheting through my body. I don't know what I expected her to say, but it wasn't something like that. Something outlandish and wild that has me beginning to grow hard inside my jeans like a goddamn teenager.

Her eyes twinkle, and my imagination takes the reins, picturing her in the very positions she just mentioned as she lifts her glass to her lips and takes a long sip.

Something delicious skitters down my spine when she winks at me, and it occurs to me how much I've been missing out on by relying on my imagination and my own fist. In seconds, this woman has set my entire body on fire. Has me ready to close down the wine bar and take her to the tasting room, where we have a massive couch and a fireplace and stone walls that would echo as she cried out in pleasure.

It's equal parts the best feeling and the worst.

The best because it's a reminder of how incredible it feels to want someone like this.

The worst because it's also a reminder of the fact I don't have the time to have even just a bit of fun.

One night couldn't hurt, though, right?

The little voice comes from somewhere in the depths of my mind, telling me that I'm already here, stationed at the bar until we close for the night. And that once we close, I would just be heading to bed. No responsibilities or fires to put out until tomorrow morning.

It couldn't hurt to take a tiny break. Give myself a night of something good to balance out all the bad. Maybe have some fun for the first time in far too long.

"Told you I'd scandalize you," she teases. "Though I'll be honest, it's fun watching your thoughts skip across your face and wondering if I'm guessing them correctly."

My lips tilt up and I lean even closer, my own voice dipping low. "I doubt you know the things I was thinking about. Maybe *I* would have scandalized *you*."

She laughs. "There's not much that does that anymore, I promise you."

I lick my lips, her eyes tracking the movement, and I can tell she's not lying.

"Let me check in with the other customers," I tell her, keeping my voice low. "Then I want to hear at least one story from that nightclub you worked at. If you say working there scandalized you, I can only imagine the things you've seen."

Her smile widens, and her fingers tap gently on the base of her glass.

"Sounds like a plan."

I try to make quick work of it, stopping at each taken seat at the wine bar and offering top-ups and wine lists and beverage suggestions.

Normally I don't mind the monotony of it. If anything, in the past, I've wished I could be the only person pouring because I know that I'm the most dedicated to making the sale, every single time.

But I find myself breezing through it, uninterested in closing the deal on a second—or third, or fourth—glass. And it only takes me about ten minutes to get through the five or six other customers.

After closing out a tab and leaving a receipt and a pen with the elderly couple at the opposite end, I'm finally able to make my way back to . . .

"What was your name?" I ask her, setting an empty wineglass in the sink and tucking a rag into my back pocket.

"Vivian."

It suits her. Something both refined and wild. Like she seems to be.

"Well, Vivian," I say, extending a hand. She slips hers into mine, and I enjoy the way her skin feels warm and smooth against my palm. "It's nice to meet you. I'm Memphis."

I wait for the inevitable question. The one *everyone* asks when they hear my name.

Like the city?

It can be annoying sometimes, but I've gotten used to it over the years.

Besides, my mother picked my name. Apparently, she and my father argued about it for months before he finally relented. It's one of the few things I have left of her, and that's enough for it to be important.

Only, Vivian doesn't say what I think she's going to say.

In fact, she doesn't say anything at all.

Instead, I see a sour expression flicker across her face, like she tasted something bitter and unpleasant. All traces of the flirtatious vixen are wiped away, replaced by a look that can only be described as . . . disappointed.

Then she slowly pulls her hand from mine and laughs, though there isn't any humor in it.

"Why am I not surprised?" she says, reaching out and swirling her wine in her glass. "Of course *you* would be Memphis."

I furrow my brows in confusion, unsure what she means. It's like she's thinking out loud rather than speaking to me.

"Because that's my luck, right? You couldn't be anyone else? Or be you, but not be"—her hand comes out, and she gestures to me where I stand—"all of that."

I blink a few times, completely lost.

"I'm sorry, did I miss something?" I ask, keeping my tone even.

"Lots of things."

It feels like whiplash, swinging from the flirtation just moments ago to . . . whatever this is.

Gone is the woman who looked at me with a twinkle in her eye, like we were sharing a secret, and in her place is someone who apparently can't stand the sight of me.

And I can't for the life of me figure out what changed.

Before I can say anything in response, my sister slides in right next to the woman across from me, wrapping an arm around her shoulder. Standing a few feet away is Wes, our head chef and the man Murphy's been seeing for the past few months.

"Thanks again, Memphis," she says. "It's been busy tonight, and normally I would have found a way to cover it myself, but sometimes it's so much better to have the extra hands."

My eyes flick back and forth between my sister and Vivian, wondering what's happening.

"Besides! Vivian is here and I'm so excited!" She waves a hand between the two of us. "V, this is my brother, Memphis. Memphis, this is Vivian Walsh. She's my closest friend from Santa Monica. And Vivian, *this* is Wes."

Vivian looks away from me, her genuine smile returning when she greets Wes, the two of them exchanging that "nice to meet you" that most people share when they're introduced to someone important.

Very unlike the way she looked at me when she realized I'm Murphy's older brother, which feels incongruous.

Murphy, unaware of my discomfort, launches into a story that I only half listen to . . . something about how the two of them first met at her old waitressing job and Vivian slapping the manager. I barely hear it until I catch the very end of what Murphy says.

". . . will be staying with me tonight."

My head jerks, and I unlatch from where my eyes had been locked on Vivian, turning toward my sister.

"Did you clear that with Dad?"

Murphy rolls her eyes. "It's just one night, Memphis. It's not a big deal."

"Maybe not, but some of us don't like being surprised by strangers wandering around our houses in the middle of the night."

Wes laughs, but Murphy pins him with a glare before she returns her attention to me.

"Jesus, Memphis, what crawled up your ass?" she demands. "Stop being a prick." Then she looks at her friend. "Sorry, Viv."

"You don't have to apologize for him," she responds. "His behavior matches with everything I've heard about him."

My entire body bristles at that, and I pin Vivian with a look. "*Excuse* me?"

"You're not excused," she replies, then hops off her stool and digs into her purse. She looks at Murphy as she drops some cash on the bar. "I'll finish my glass outside. Come get me when you're off for the night. Nice to meet you, Wes."

Then without looking my way again, she strides to the door that leads out to the back patio and pushes outside, leaving me and Murphy behind.

My gaze follows her as she goes, and I wish there was a way to rewind the past five minutes and return to the way we interacted before she knew who I was.

Not that I understand her sudden attitude change. At all.

"What the hell was that about?" my sister hisses.

Wes dips forward, his lips pursed, and I can tell he's trying not to smile or laugh or something.

"I'm gonna head back to the kitchen," he says, glancing between us both. Then he plants a kiss on Murphy's forehead and gives me a wave, before returning to his domain.

"Seriously, Memphis, I know you can be a grouch, but you couldn't be nice to one of my best friends for five seconds?"

I grit my teeth and stay silent, because honestly, I'm not sure how to answer her.

One minute Vivian and I were flirting, and then suddenly she looked like she wanted to light me on fire.

"And since when is it a problem to have friends stay the night?"

"What did she mean when she said 'everything I've heard about him'?"

Murphy crosses her arms. "She's the person I talk to about almost everything, Memphis. You think I moved away and didn't shit on you and Dad a little bit in the nine years I was gone?"

I grab the cash off the bar and give Murphy a glare. "Oh, thanks. That feels great."

My sister lets out a long sigh, one I've heard aimed my way many times. "Look, I don't have the mental capacity for this right now. I need to get back to work, and I'd rather not continue arguing in front of anyone. Can I trust that if Vivian comes back inside, you're not going to be an ass?"

Glancing to the side, a bit of relief rushes through me when I see that the people at the bar are all enthralled in their own conversations. It's rare for me to lose my cool like that in front of customers, and I'm even more irritated that Vivian was able to crawl so easily under my skin.

"Yeah. Fine."

Murphy spins and heads over to the host stand, and I turn my gaze through the large windows, out where I can see Vivian sitting alone in an Adirondack chair looking over the property.

Clearly, my sister's friend has a few choice thoughts about me. Though I'll be honest, I can't imagine anything I've done or said to my sister warrants a reaction like that one.

The only conclusion I can make is that Vivian must be a drama queen. Someone who latches on to things that are none of her business.

I shift my attention to greet two new customers as they take a seat at the bar, and I push the redhead as far out of my mind as I'm able to do.

Murphy said Vivian is just staying one night.

Hopefully, our exchange tonight is the extent of our interactions.

Judging by the way she talked to me, I'm assuming she wants the same.

Chapter Two

Vivian

"He's not so bad, you know."

I turn my head, looking to where Murphy lies next to me, staring up at the ceiling.

"Who?"

"Memphis."

I snort.

"I'm serious, V. I might have complained a lot about him and Dad, but . . . I don't want you to get the wrong idea."

"It doesn't matter what I think," I reply, kicking one leg out from underneath the sheet, trying to get comfortable. "It matters what *you* think."

"I know, and I'm telling you, I think Memphis is actually pretty great. Most of the time, at least."

"A rave review," I reply, my tone dripping with sarcasm.

Murphy laughs into a yawn, then turns on her side to face me. "I'm just saying . . . If you see him or my dad around while you're in town, feel free to tone down the guard dog in your soul. I appreciate it, but really, things are pretty good."

"Okay so . . . maybe I *do* have a flair for the dramatic."

"Just a little."

I reach out and take her hand, squeezing it gently.

"Just making sure your brother sees that you have someone in your corner."

Murphy leans over and plants a kiss on my cheek. "I never doubted it for a second." Then she turns onto her other side, facing away from me. "Night, Viv."

"Night, Murph."

She's softly snoring within a few minutes. I, unfortunately, am not so lucky. Instead, I stay awake, lost in my thoughts, my mind racing and unable to be quieted, no matter what I do.

I wasn't honest with her about the real reason I'm here. The last thing I want is to rehash the past few days of my life. With anyone. Even with someone I trust as much as Murphy.

So I told her I'm here to write. That my manager sent me on a trip to work on the last few songs for my album. A little writing retreat to stoke the creative juices.

Technically, it *will* be true. Probably. I'm scheduled to go into the studio soon, and there is plenty that I need to work on between now and then to make sure I'm ready.

But in truth, Todd has no idea I've even left LA. He has no idea that my life has blown apart. I'm sure if he knew, he'd be upset for me on all counts, because that's the kind of manager Todd is. The kind that actually cares about his talent for more reasons than just dollar signs.

He *is* my manager, though, and as much as I appreciate that he cares, I don't want to talk to him about it, either. Because he'll try to wax poetic about it and turn everything into a positive, at least where my music is concerned.

So, instead of facing what happened, instead of dealing with reality, I ran.

I had Theo's things boxed up and removed from my condo. I changed the locks. I avoided his calls and texts.

I haven't been ready to face it all.

My phone vibrates with a text message. The light pierces through the darkness of Murphy's bedroom, casting everything in a cool glow. I let out a long, frustrated sigh. Then I grab my phone off the nightstand and finally read through the messages I've been ignoring all day.

Theo: I've tried calling you for two days, Vi. TWO.

Theo: You're absolutely overreacting. She means nothing to me.

Theo: This is ridiculous. I'm coming home after work. You can't kick me out forever.

Theo: You seriously left town?

Theo: Where the hell is all my stuff?

And the one that just came through.

Theo: Come on, Vi. Are we ever going to talk this out?

Maybe for some women, his constant messages and calls are enough to at least respond once. Enough to warrant giving the man a chance to provide an explanation that's as much truth as it is lies.

But I'm not "some women," and honestly, it doesn't matter what Theo has to say.

I am absolutely *not* overreacting, and there is nothing he can tell me that will get me to forgive him for cheating on me after three years together. Nothing.

What Theo did . . . It robbed me of something important. Something that was sacred, and precious, and can never be replaced.

My trust.

When it lights up again, I power my phone down, not wanting to be bothered anymore tonight.

Not that shutting off my phone will allow me to get any sleep.

Eventually, I push myself out of bed and grab a sweater from my bag, then slip quietly from Murphy's room. Making my way through the darkened house, I tiptoe across the cool terra-cotta tiles and out through the french doors that lead from the living room to the covered patio that faces the vineyard.

The moon is bright, lighting up the vines that stretch out before me as I take a seat on the stone steps. Pulling my sweater snug around my body, I tilt my head back and breathe in deeply, my eyes closed.

The air here smells so different. It's damp and earthy and tinged with a little bit of sweetness.

And it's quiet. *So* quiet. I can hear crickets chirping and the breeze rustling the trees that line the edge of the property.

I can't imagine growing up in a place like this. Not that there's anything wrong with it. It's just so different from the city I've known most of my life.

For me, nights are filled with the sound of crashing waves in the distance, the occasional sirens, and people out on the streets until early hours of the morning. The briny smell of the ocean mixes with warm concrete and the gardenia plant that my neighbor kept on her balcony.

Now that I'm here, experiencing how peaceful my friend's home is, it makes sense why Murphy has always claimed she had a hard time falling asleep for the first year she lived in Santa Monica.

I laugh quietly to myself and shake my head.

Murphy hated growing up here, but the one positive thing she repeated over and over is how beautiful it is. And damn was she right.

Rosewood is a beautiful place. I enjoyed sitting out on the patio at the restaurant earlier, looking at the vines as the sun was setting, the rolling hills and trees stretching out in the distance in a way that's so picturesque, it doesn't feel entirely real.

She told me that if I ever wanted to plan a girls' weekend trip or just get away, that this town was a great place to do it. So, in my moment of need, this is where I came.

And something tells me I made the right choice.

I sit for a few more minutes before pushing to my feet and heading back inside. I'd been hoping to go outside to distract myself from my thoughts, but it's so quiet all I can hear are the very thoughts I'm trying to avoid.

Instead of returning to Murphy's room for more of that riveting staring contest I've been having with the little stars all over her ceiling, I wander into the kitchen and tug open the freezer, thinking maybe some ice cream might be the cure for my mental funk.

A small carton of mint chocolate chip is sitting front and center, and I snatch it with glee, smiling when I peek inside and see that there are more than a few bites left.

Perfect.

After hunting down a spoon, I dig in, closing my eyes and moaning quietly when the cool mint explodes on my tongue.

There is nothing better than a sneaky ice cream in the middle of the night to take your mind off things.

"What are you doing?"

My eyes fly wide, my entire body jerking with surprise at the dark figure standing in the doorway, and I drop the carton and spoon on the floor.

Pressing my hand to my chest, I take a deep breath, trying to quiet my racing heart.

Then I pin Memphis with a glare, only staring at his shirtless chest for a brief second. "Sneaking ice cream, which would be a lot easier if you didn't appear out of the darkness like a serial killer."

Bending, I pick my mess up off the floor, then turn to rinse the spoon in the sink. Once I'm done, I spin back around and look Memphis right in the eye.

"What are *you* doing?" I take another bite. "Besides scaring the shit out of me."

"I was planning to sneak some ice cream," he replies, crossing the kitchen in my direction and tilting the carton in my hand. He glances inside, sighs, then lets it go. "But it looks like an unwanted houseguest stole my last bites."

Part of me wants to slam the carton on the counter, storm from the room, and leave him to eat the final two or three scoops all by himself.

But that might be a bit of an overreaction. And Murphy *did* say I should cool the guard dog in me a smidge.

So instead, I spoon a tiny bit and bring it to my mouth, looking him right in the eyes as I place it on my tongue. And then I moan around the cool metal, enjoying this bite even more knowing that Memphis had wanted it.

He narrows his eyes at me, irritation evident even in the darkness.

"What is your problem?" Memphis's question is gritted out at me, filled with frustration.

I don't answer right away. Instead, I take another spoonful and bring it to my mouth, moaning again.

"You know, I was having trouble falling asleep," I eventually say, "but now that I've had this delicious ice cream, all to myself . . . well, I should sleep like a baby."

I'm being a little too caustic. I know that.

But I've been plotting his demise for the better part of ten years.

Okay, so maybe I wasn't actually plotting his demise. And sure, I've never interacted with him before tonight, and that might make my feelings a little . . . much.

Murphy shared a lot over the years about her struggles with her family. And even though most of her frustration has been directed at her father, feeling that her older brother seemed completely content without her in his life caused her a lot of hurt, too. I witnessed her tears plenty of times, and that was enough for me to add him to my shit list.

Which made it *such* a disappointment earlier tonight when Memphis introduced himself at the restaurant bar.

Theo and I haven't had sex in months, which was mildly frustrating while we were dating, and I was horny and very unsatisfied but just assumed we were facing a lull in our sex life. But now that I know he's been stepping out? That he's been getting his dick wet with other women?

I'm infuriated. Infuriated and adamant that I find someone to sleep with so that I can officially move on from Theo and place him squarely in the past, where he belongs.

I thought I'd found the perfect opportunity with Mr. Bartender. By the way he'd been watching me as I teased him, I was almost positive we'd be closing down the bar together and heading . . . somewhere.

And let's be honest, I would have let a man who looks like Memphis take me *anywhere*.

It's been a long time since I've been ravaged, and he seemed like he could be just the man for the job.

My eyes scan him up and down in the darkness of the kitchen, appreciating the firm cut of his jaw and the way his hair is a little bit too long, possibly tussled from a restless sleep. His broad shoulders and toned arms are crossed against his chest, and his basketball shorts hug his trim hips below that sexy-as-fuck pelvic muscle that I want to lick.

Memphis Hawthorne is a treat and a half.

If only he wasn't my best friend's older brother.

And a bossy asshat.

"I guess it shouldn't surprise me that my sister went to LA and befriended a crazy lady. I hear that place is filled with lunatics."

My nostrils flare at the jab.

"God, you are everything I assumed you would be," I tell him, stabbing my spoon into a chunk of ice cream.

"Oh yeah? And what did you assume?"

"Judgmental, for one."

"Me?" His voice rises, but then he lowers it again. "Says the woman who hung me on a cross when she doesn't even know me."

"Bossy."

"That's not a critique. That's a fact, and one I don't apologize for."

I growl with irritation. "Ugh. And arrogant. Cocky. Certain you're always right about everything. Men like you are infuriating. Especially when you look the way you do because you think you can do whatever and say whatever and never face any accountability for the damage you cause."

Memphis's head jerks back, and there's a beat of silence. Suddenly I realize I've said too much. Half of that wasn't even about Memphis, and a thread of embarrassment ripples through me at the knowledge that I've pushed too far.

Especially because . . . maybe this brittle and irritated feeling is less about Memphis than I thought it was, and more about my own bullshit.

"I'm sorry, that was . . ." I trail off, staring down at the last bite of ice cream at the bottom of the carton in my hand.

Maybe he's right. Maybe I am crazy.

"Don't apologize," Memphis says. "Not when you meant what you said."

Then he surprises me by plucking the carton out of my hand, and I watch with unblinking eyes as he grabs my spoon and scoops out the last bite to eat himself.

I let out a quiet chuckle and shake my head, all my bluster and bravado leaking out of me like a deflating balloon. "I might have meant what I said, but . . . it definitely wasn't all about you."

He hums softly but doesn't say anything else. Instead he just stands there, one arm crossed, the other holding the spoon in his mouth, watching me.

And even though it's dark in the kitchen, the moonlight cascading through the windows is enough that I can see that his eyes are assessing me. Taking me in and trying to figure me out.

It's not unfamiliar, having a man watch me.

Maybe it sounds bold, but I know what I look like. My red hair and curvy figure attract attention, mostly from men.

But what *is* unfamiliar is *wanting* to be watched.

From the moment our eyes connected at the bar, something in the back of my mind said that I wanted his gaze on me at all times.

Which is a bit infuriating considering how certainly I believed I would despise him.

"I'm sorry I ate the last of your ice cream," I finally say, extending an olive branch. "That was rude of me."

Memphis shrugs. "It would have been rude if it was the last of the ice cream."

I blink, confused, and I watch as he walks to the fridge and opens the freezer door, digging around for a second before pulling out another carton.

My mouth drops open. "You knew that was in there this whole time?"

He grins, shrugs, and closes the door. "You're not the only person in the world who eats ice cream in the middle of the night."

I cross my arms as he tugs off the lid and peels off the protective seal. And when he takes a big bite, mischief clear on his face, my eyes narrow.

But there's no real heat behind it.

No, the heat is in my belly as he scoops out another bite and puts it in his mouth, watching me the entire time. It's almost sinful, and I can't help the way I get distracted by his mouth. It happened earlier, at the bar too, and I'd found myself unable to look away as he spoke, as he licked his lips, as the edges tilted up with a smile.

It made me wonder what it would be like to kiss those lips.

Among other things.

We stand in silence as he takes a second bite. But then he jabs his spoon into the dairy confection and extends the carton my way.

I pause only briefly before accepting his offer.

"I'm surprised you're willing to share this with me, considering the stink you made when I was eating it before," I tease, scooping a small spoonful.

He shrugs a shoulder. "I figured if there's a way to appease the crazy lady rummaging through my kitchen in the middle of the night, I better take advantage of it."

I snort and roll my eyes, but I don't address his "crazy lady" comment, just enjoy another bite before passing the carton back.

"You never told me any of those scandalizing stories from the nightclub."

He's kind to not mention why: because I had declared him the enemy the second he told me his name.

Nibbling on the inside of my cheek, I think it over, trying to decide what story to share.

"Well, there were the many times I caught people having sex in a bathroom stall," I say, testing the waters with a story that could be any nightclub on any night.

Memphis scoffs. "Oh, come on, I thought you were going to scandalize me." He sets the ice cream on the counter and leans back, crossing his arms. "Isn't sex in a bathroom stall like . . . an intro to what happens at a nightclub?"

I laugh at how directly he'd echoed my own thoughts. "All right, that's fair."

I reach out and grab the carton, digging in for another bite as I think back, trying to find a different story. A better one that might be more likely to shock him.

After taking another spoonful, I return the carton to the island counter.

"I only worked at the club for six months," I start, bracing my hands behind me and lifting myself up so I'm seated on the edge. "Toward the end, I moved from the main bar to the private bar, which was in a room that overlooked the dance floor. And on my first night, this guy came in with a big entourage. We chatted for a little bit when he took a seat at the bar, but I left him alone when this girl came and sat in his lap."

As the memory flits through my mind, I still can hardly believe it really happened.

"When I checked in a few minutes later to refill his drink, the girl was like . . . gyrating against him. Which isn't the craziest thing in the world. I figured she was grinding against him like people do at a club."

Pinning Memphis with a look that says I was wrong, I finish the story.

"They were having sex. Right there at the bar. And by the time I realized what was happening, it was too late. Both of them were watching me as they finished." I shake my head. "It was outrageous and wicked, and it totally freaked me out."

It was also kind of hot, but I don't say that part out loud. Because who thinks that?

I smile at Memphis's shocked expression.

"So, Mr. Bartender . . . Are you officially scandalized?"

He rubs his palm along the faint hint of stubble at his chin, his own mischievous smile creeping out. "Maybe."

"If you want another dirty story," I tease, "I might be able to find something else. In exchange for more ice cream, of course."

He smirks. "Of course."

Memphis steps forward and hands me the carton, but when I expect him to take a step back, he doesn't. Instead, his hands brace the counter on either side of my hips, his face dipping toward mine as he steps between my legs.

It's a flirtatious move. I know that. *He* knows that.

The only thing neither of us could possibly know is whether the flirtatious move will become something else entirely.

And as much as I've promised myself to despise him, my body doesn't seem to be on the same page.

Not looking away, I scoop a tiny bit of ice cream from the carton and lift it between us, placing the spoon gently against his mouth. His eyes search mine for a second, but he parts his lips, and I feed him a bite.

"Oh, look." I say, my voice quiet as I wipe away a bit of cream at the edge of his mouth. "You've got a little something . . ."

But Memphis's patience has disintegrated, and before I can continue with whatever little game I was considering, his lips are on mine.

Surprise blisters its way through my body, but so does lust, and I clumsily set the ice cream down beside me, not even caring when I hear a loud *thunk* as it falls onto the counter.

Then my arms are wrapping around his neck as I open my mouth against his, the taste of mint chocolate chip exploding on my tongue as we begin to explore each other. Memphis's arms wrap around my waist, tugging me tightly against his body, pressing hard and hot between my legs.

My stomach swoops, and I think back to earlier tonight, when I asked him if he pictured me on my knees or on my back.

I need this. Desperately. Something raw and sordid, right here in the kitchen. Bent over the counter or laid out on the table.

I moan when he shifts against me, and then my head falls back as he kisses and licks at my neck.

The light in the kitchen turns on, and we both freeze at the sound of a throat clearing on the other side of the room.

Slowly, slowly, ever so slowly, I turn my head, embarrassment splashing like a bucket of cold water all over my body when I see who I can only assume is Murphy and Memphis's father standing in the archway between the kitchen and the hallway that leads to the front of the house.

"Thought I'd get myself a little late-night snack," he starts, "but I can see someone else had the same idea."

The joke surprises me, considering everything Murphy has ever told me about her father, but I can hardly concentrate on that when I'm too busy wishing I could fall through the floor and disappear forever.

Memphis clears his throat and releases me, though he doesn't move away, and I can only assume it's because he's hard as a rock.

"Dad, I . . ."

"Don't." Mr. Hawthorne holds his hands up. "Just . . . head back to your room, okay? Murphy's friend is visiting, and I don't want one of them to stumble upon"—he waves his hand in our direction—"this."

Mortification begins to creep through my body at his assumption that I'm *not* Murphy's friend—because Murphy's friend could *never* be the horrible human hooking up with Memphis in the kitchen, obviously—and I'm thankful when he finally leaves the kitchen.

But he doesn't flip the light back off, and in the harsh brightness of the fluorescent lights, I'm struggling to make sense of what happened.

Memphis finally backs off, and my eyes dip for a second, finding the hard length of him tenting his shorts and confirming my earlier suspicions.

I hop off the counter, then turn my back to him, giving myself a moment to collect my thoughts. I reach into the sink and pull out the slightly melty carton of ice cream.

"That was . . . less than ideal," Memphis says, and I can hear the mixture of amusement and embarrassment in his tone.

Licking my lips, I chuckle awkwardly. "Yeah. Can't remember the last time I was walked in on by someone's dad," I reply, trying to push back my own mortification. "Maybe that's the universe saying this isn't a good idea."

Memphis says nothing as I put the lid back on the ice cream and then slip the container into the freezer, and when I turn to look at him, I find him watching me with an easy expression.

"At least tonight," I add, drinking him in where he stands, his body now on display to me in the brightness. "I mean, I don't know what we were thinking . . ."

"We weren't," he says, a contrite look on his face. "But thankfully, nothing happened."

His voice sounds hollow, though, no true conviction behind what he's said.

And I get it.

Because I'm *not* thankful nothing happened, even though I probably should be.

Sighing, I grab the spoon off the counter and place it in the sink.

"I'm gonna . . ." I jerk a thumb in the direction of the hallway. "Head back to bed. I guess I'll see you around?"

He nods.

"Hopefully things won't be weird for the rest of my trip."

His entire body seems to freeze in place. Except for his nostrils. They flare, which is plenty of indication that he's displeased about something.

"I thought you were just staying one night."

"I am. Here. But I'll be in town for two weeks."

His chin juts up and he shakes his head, barely.

"How inconvenient."

His words fall from him in a grumble, and my lips part in shock. But before I can say anything else, he's left the room.

I blink a few times, my eyes staring at the empty space he left behind for far longer than is warranted.

What the hell was that about?

I slap off the kitchen light and then return outside. I plant my butt on the cold tile of the porch, with my feet on the steps. Staring into the moonlight, I try to make sense of what happened. To reconcile Memphis's quick shift from charming tomcat to irritable grouch.

The longer I sit in the cool, damp night air, though, the more exhausted I feel. The last thing I want to do is try to decipher what is going on in that brain of his when I have my own bullshit to figure out.

And as much as I wish having blistering chemistry and a little bit of fun was enough to take my mind off the drama I left behind in LA, clearly, it's not.

Chapter Three

Memphis

The shower soothes my aching muscles as the hot water hits my back. It drips down over my body, providing some much-needed relief.

I haven't worked out that intensely in quite some time, keeping most of my energy and attention on the goings-on of the vineyard and all the moving parts that I have to tend to. I actually had to dust off the weight set that sits in the makeshift gym in the back corner of the garage, which makes me think it's been at least a few months.

This morning, for the first time in who knows how long, I flew out of bed at six o'clock with a scrambled mind and enough energy to power the new generator we just installed on the west side of the property. I'm not a gym bro by any means, but keeping fit used to be a regular part of my routine. As exhausted as I am right now, it also feels amazing to get back to something I used to love so much.

The mental strength required to push myself. The physical fatigue in my muscles. The ability to take out my emotional stress.

Of course, what *didn't* feel amazing was how my mind was seemingly incapable of staying on topic. I'd intended to spend the time mentally going over the list of final tasks I need to complete before the harvest season begins next weekend.

Did I think about that at all?

No.

Instead, I was too busy fuming over everything that happened with Vivian last night. From her whiplash behavior at the bar, to the way she seemed to tease me in the kitchen, and then my dad showing up and flipping the lights, exposing us making out like horny teenagers.

I think the most irritating part of it all is that now I'll have to see her again, when that's the exact opposite of what I want.

When Murphy said she was staying with us for one night, I assumed she was stopping through town before heading somewhere else. Not that she was bunking with my sister for a single night before . . . what? Finding a room somewhere?

I'd thought maybe a one-night hookup might relieve some of the tension that has been living in my every muscle. In the past, it's been fairly cut-and-dried with women I meet out in town who are passing through for wine tastings or some other event. There was no risk of needing to see anyone ever again.

Now, I'm facing potentially *weeks* of dealing with the regret of having even talked with her in the first place.

Not that talking was the only thing that happened.

I grit my jaw, the memory of her sweet mouth on mine something that has been hovering on the edge of my subconscious since our 3 a.m. rendezvous.

The truth is that it's a problem of my own making. Walking out to the kitchen in the middle of the night had been my first real mistake. I knew it was probably our houseguest snooping around, and I'd still given in to the urge to head out there.

When I first walked in, she'd been leaning back against the counter in the dark in a little pair of shorts and a T-shirt that read FASHION IS MY SECOND FAVORITE F-WORD. I almost wanted to stand quietly in the dark and watch her as she scooped my ice cream into her mouth. But I couldn't keep my mouth shut. I felt like poking the bear.

Among other things.

I groan in irritation at myself, lathering up my body as the ebb and flow of our conversation replays in my mind. First feisty. Then calm. Then flirty.

It's wild to me how quickly the mood shifted. Though maybe I can attribute that to the fact I didn't want to be fighting with her in the first place.

No, I'd much rather have been doing something else. Evidenced by the equally foolish mistake I made when I leaned into her as she sat on the bar.

My hand dips, gripping my shaft between soapy fingers, and this time when I groan, it's not irritation I feel. It's pleasure.

And then she fed me that bite of ice cream . . .

I thrust into my fist, my mind creating an alternate reality where we didn't get interrupted. Where she put ice cream on my lips and then sucked it off and then sucked *me* off. Where I could have tugged off her clothing and slid into her right there, on the counter, the perfect height for me to fuck into her tight heat. Where I could have bent her over the kitchen table and taken her from behind, my hand over her mouth to keep her quiet.

It's the last image that sends me over the edge, my body vibrating with my release.

Fuck.

I lean forward and brace myself against the shower wall, my forehead flat against the tile as I catch my breath.

Jerking in the shower is how I handle my stress more often than I care to admit, but normally my mind scatters across all my memories and desires to bring me over the edge. That was . . . different. Specific. Singularly focused on Vivian and this one encounter.

The woman is . . . something. Though I'm not sure exactly what.

Beautiful, obviously.

A spitfire, absolutely.

But there's something else there as well. Something I don't fully understand.

As much as it turns me on, though, my attraction to her is also a horrible complication.

I slap the shower handle and step out, making quick work of drying off and slipping on a pair of jeans and a vineyard polo—my normal work attire.

The reality is that I don't have time to be standing in the shower, thinking about some woman and what my fantasies about her mean. I don't have space among the rest of the mental load I'm carrying to figure out whether my attraction to her is anything more than inconvenient.

I meant what I said as we stared at each other in the harsh light of the kitchen after my father left the room. Her presence in town is going to be exactly what I said—inconvenient for me. A nagging thing in the back of my mind, distracting me from the very important, complicated shit on my plate.

Thankfully, our interaction wasn't all the sordid things I'd imagined doing to her. It was, in full truth, just a kiss.

And that's all it needs to be.

Once I've finished getting ready for the day, I head to my office on the opposite end of my family's ranch-style house.

When my great-great-grandfather arrived in Rosewood and purchased the first forty acres of this property, he built four small cabins on the west edge. One was a single-bedroom house that was just big enough for him and my great-great-grandmother and their baby to live in, and the other three were for the hands he hired to bunk in during the busy part of winery life—the harvest.

My eyes flick briefly to the photos on the wall of our family over the years, from the shot of my grandfather and my dad and me, to the aged and fading image of my great-great-grandparents standing in an empty field all the way back when Hawthorne Vines was just an idea. A hope and a dream.

Over the years, the property has changed a lot, each generation of Hawthornes putting their own stamp on what the vineyard was to grow into. We acquired another forty acres, doubling the property size, but also tripling the number of vines and expanding us into new varieties of grape. That first single-bedroom home was converted to an equipment shed after my great-grandfather had our current house built in the southeast corner of the expanded property.

I power up my computer and an aerial shot of the property fills the screen, the background image on my desktop and more proof that this place has grown so much.

It's not just the acres of vines that have grown. There's also a wine cellar and testing facility. A warehouse and an office building. And now a restaurant. The handful of employees that have full-time office positions work out of the building on the back side of the warehouse, and sometimes I head over there and work in the conference room.

But for the most part, I keep to my office here in the house, preferring the quiet and solitude. It's nice to live and work in the same place, especially considering how often I'm sitting at this desk or roaming around the property handling things or putting out fires.

Although, every so often, I wish I was able to leave my office at five, head home, and completely check out from work. Put my feet up and enjoy some baseball for once. Or hang out in town with friends.

That's not the way things look right now, though.

I haven't watched a baseball game in years, and the best I can do when it comes to keeping up with the few friends I still have in town is a monthly pool game and beers at The Standard.

It's not ideal, the fact that I have almost no life outside of this vineyard. But that's the reality of the mess my father has all but dropped in my lap, and there's no use dwelling on it when there are far more pressing issues.

I'm in my office for an hour before I hear movement in the house, and my entire body tenses as I imagine Vivian strolling into my office. Or worse . . . Murphy, ready to confront me for putting the moves on her friend.

But it's my father who walks through the doorway instead. Which, I quickly realize, isn't any better.

"Morning, Memphis," he says, giving me an easy smile and crossing the room. He sets a mug of coffee down before me, then turns and takes a seat in one of the two armchairs facing my desk.

"Morning." I eye the coffee briefly, then decide it's probably a necessary evil considering the piss-poor sleep I got.

"Figured you could use a little caffeine boost this morning," he says, his thoughts echoing mine.

Inwardly I groan, but I raise it to my mouth all the same, taking a sip and then placing it on a coaster.

"I've been thinking about the fact that we outsource printing our labels," I tell him, changing the subject. "You know I'm a big fan of using local work, and Tony has always printed our labels, but maybe we ought to look into printing them ourselves."

Dad bobs his head. "All right."

I wait, hoping that he'll contribute something . . . anything. An opinion, an idea, even just some encouragement.

But he doesn't. He takes another sip of his coffee and looks out the window, his eyes focused on the vineyard just beyond the walls of this room.

I'm not surprised, but it doesn't mean I'm not disappointed.

I'm disappointed every time I try to engage with him about running this business and he seems checked out and disinterested. This vineyard is supposed to be my legacy, and it feels like he couldn't care less about creating a smooth transition as it begins to pass into my hands.

But that disappointment is my own fault. I can't expect him to be different today than he was yesterday, or the day before, or on any other day over the past few years as he's been less and less involved and more and more disinterested in the goings-on around here.

Still, though . . . I can't help wishing it was different.

"We typically spend a few thousand dollars every quarter on printing labels," I continue, still pressing. "But I found this company that creates wine label printers. And if we buy our own, it's a one-time cost of a few thousand bucks. But in each subsequent bottling batch, we're only out the cost of the labels and the ink, which would save us a lot if we . . ."

"I think you should do what you think is best."

My father's interruption is, again, not surprising. But again, disappointing.

He gives me a pinched smile, then slaps his knee and pushes out of his chair. "Welp, I better get my butt out there. I can see Naomi already driving through the vines. I don't want her to think I'm still lazing around."

I nod, then turn my attention back to the computer screen. "Sounds good, Dad."

I think he gives me a wave before he heads out the door, but I'm not watching for it so I don't know for sure. Instead, I take the retreating sound of his footsteps echoing gently on the terra-cotta tile as proof, the noise fading as he moves through the house and away from my office.

Sighing, I lean back in my chair and rub my palm against the stubble I didn't take the time to shave off this morning.

It's hard not to notice the weird place my father has been in recently. Scratch that. Not recently. For years, at least.

It's just become a lot more obvious in the past year or so.

I've been working this land and this business as my father's right-hand man since I was a teenager, back when my grandfather was technically still in charge of the operations and my dad was *his* right-hand man. We were a team, the three of us.

And then, when my grandfather passed away when I was nineteen, everything changed.

My father was finally thrust into the role his father had been preparing him for.

But Dad wasn't prepared.

He was a mess.

They'd had issues, the two of them. And I don't think they'd resolved them by the time my grandfather passed unexpectedly. So when it came time to take the reins, my dad choked.

Maybe that sounds harsh. I don't like thinking about my dad not living up to the responsibilities placed into his hands.

But it's the truth.

Now, years later, I'm desperately trying to make sure that the damage he's caused while he's been in the top spot doesn't reverberate outward and destroy everything our family has worked on for generations.

His recent attitude—the one he has affected over the past year or so—makes it seem like he's finally completely checked out from the operational side of things. He's been acting more like an employee than an owner and leaving most of the decisions in my hands—big ones, small ones, ones that could have a long-term effect on how things run around here.

The only thing he hasn't done is actually sign the business over to me on paper, which I'm grateful for. Because I'm not sure I'm ready for that additional burden.

Not yet.

Not when we're still struggling to climb out of this hole and I have so much to learn.

Still, most things do end up being my responsibility.

For better or worse, I'm the one making most of the decisions around here.

And my greatest fear is that a choice I make is going to be the final nail in this vineyard's coffin.

Two quick knocks on the doorjamb pull me from my work hours later. I grin when I spot my baby brother.

"Hey, Memphis. Got a second?"

I nod. "Yeah, let me finish this up."

Micah takes a seat in the armchair where my father sat earlier and waits silently as I wrap up an email. When I finally turn to look at him, I'm hit with a stark reminder of how similar he and my father actually are.

Murphy and I take after our mother, both in looks and temperament. Lighter hair, paler skin. Maybe a little obstinate, if I'm being honest.

Micah, with his quiet nature and olive tones, is all my dad.

Even the way he's sitting, with his ankle resting casually on his other knee, his elbows on the armrests and his hands clasped loosely against his middle . . . It's uncanny.

"What's up?"

"Did you have a chance to talk with Dad about staffing for the harvest?"

I rack my brain, trying to place when Micah and I might have talked about this before.

"I haven't. Can you remind me what the issue is?"

"I think we need to bring in some additional hands—more than we normally do. And you said you wanted to talk with Dad about it first."

I wince, not even remembering us having this conversation, and hating that I'll need to be the bearer of bad news.

"I didn't talk to Dad, but I'll be honest, Micah. I don't think we have the budget to hire additional temp workers," I say, mentally combing through our employees. "I'm trying to keep a budget for fifteen temporary hands . . ."

"Fifteen!" Micah interjects. "The last few years we've had twenty."

"Well, we can't afford twenty this year if we want to keep paying salaries to our full-time staff and not have to lay anyone off."

He slumps back in his chair, dejection evident on his face.

"I was hoping we could have closer to thirty," he says, though I can hear in the tone of his voice that he knows that would be far outside the realm of reality.

I haven't shared much with my brother about the truth of our finances, but I doubt he's completely in the dark about the situation. He's a smart kid, and even though most of his attention is on the physical labor side of operations, his hands always in the dirt, I'm sure he's noticed the way things have been getting trimmed back over the past seven or eight months.

Murphy and my aunt Sarah have been the only two who have really gotten any insight into the truth of what our budget looks like, but they're pretty hush about it, encouraging me to guide things how I see best.

So even though Micah might not understand the why behind the recent changes, he doesn't fight me when it comes to things that affect the bottom line. He knows how desperately I want this vineyard to return to its former glory.

Back when I was a kid, my grandfather talked about this place with pride. Even into my teenage years, Hawthorne Vines was winning prestigious awards and selling out of select vintages each year.

I want to get us back to that. Return us to a successful and thriving operation that all of us can be proud of. So I appreciate that he doesn't push me on a lot of shit.

"It's less than ideal. I get that. One day, I hope we can hire more again. But for now, you'll have to trust that I'm doing the best thing."

Micah gives me a smile. "I'm bummed, sure. But I get it. I'm sure we'll be able to figure it out with just fifteen." He pauses. "And I *do* trust you."

My shoulders ease slightly at his words.

I appreciate that faith he has in me.

Or, at least, that he pretends to have faith in me.

All I can hope is that it pays off. That his trust is well placed. And that I don't let everyone down in the end.

Chapter Four

Vivian

The Firehouse Inn is a truly unique brick building on a tree-lined block at the very end of Main Street. It's three stories, and even though it seems like great care has gone into preserving a lot of the original detailing on the exterior, the largest, most obvious change is the conversion of the fire truck garage door into a set of massive double doors leading inside.

My eyes scan over the building, taking in the old signage that says Rosewood Fire Station before I round to my trunk to grab my bag and guitar case.

The interior is just as beautiful as the outside, the exposed brick walls and high wooden ceiling giving off a feeling that is rustic and warm. I pause, wanting to take a moment to look at every detail, but when I see an elderly gentleman smiling at me from behind a desk in the corner, I decide a lazy snoop around can wait until later.

"Are you Vivian?" he asks, standing and stepping out to greet me.

I nod. "I am."

"Welcome to the Firehouse Inn. I'm so glad we were able to accommodate you at the last minute. Normally we're all booked up around this time of the year, but lucky for you, our suite was still available."

Grinning, I dig my wallet out of my purse. "Oh yes, lucky for me."

"I'm Errol, the owner. I'll most likely be the one to help you if you have any issues or need anything." He clicks around on his computer. "Where are you visiting from?"

"LA."

"Oh, fun. We get a lot of people looking to escape the big cities for a little bit of a slower pace. There's really nowhere better than Rosewood. It's got all the amazing amenities like Napa and Sonoma, but in my opinion, a whole lot more charm."

I laugh internally at Errol's enthusiasm, but also understand exactly what he means. I've done plenty of trips to Napa before, and it feels very curated. Like everything is designed to accommodate people who want to spend a few days or a week visiting a spa and drinking bottles of wine.

Not that there's anything wrong with either of those things. I love a good girls' weekend.

But as I drove through the adorable little downtown on my way over here, I got a different vibe. Like this is the kind of place that is filled with locals. The people here actually live here, they're not just visiting. And based on the bustling busyness of Main Street and all the signs I saw sharing community events, I'd wager that they love the town, too.

Which is funny considering how long Murphy hated it before deciding to move back.

"I see you're staying for two weeks! Anything in particular you're looking to do while you're in town?" Errol asks, looking up at me briefly before returning his eyes to the screen.

"I haven't really looked into it yet. But for now I'm hoping to take a nice long shower, and then I'm heading to that café I saw as I was driving in to do a little work. It looked like it might be a good place to set up shop."

"Our water pressure is amazing, and we installed those fancy water heaters that never run out, so I don't doubt you are in for quite a treat. But I'd recommend Rosewood Roasters if you're looking for a place to sit and work. It's on the opposite side of the street, all the way at the end. The Carlisle—that's the café—well, they can be a bit persnickety about customers who linger for too long."

Then he jumps into explaining the hotel building, pointing out the stairs and the coffee machine in the lobby and the little take-one-leave-one library in the corner with a couple of cozy armchairs and cute decor.

"Your suite is on the top floor, so it's an extra flight of stairs, but it does have a soaking tub that all our guests rave about." He hands me my room key, which is a real, actual brass key instead of those plastic cards everyone uses.

I'm obsessed with the quaintness of it all.

"That soaking tub is why I booked the suite," I tell him with a wide smile. "Thanks so much for your help."

"Call down if you need anything!"

I head for the stairs, lugging my too-large bag and guitar case behind me, and making slow work of hauling it up. I wasn't imagining a situation where I'd need to lug my belongings up several flights of stairs, but it'll sure be good for my glutes.

And now that I'm single, keeping my ass in amazing shape suddenly feels a bit more important than it did a few days ago.

When I finally make it to the top, I turn down a long hallway before finding the door to my room. And when I shove it open, any doubts about walking up to the third floor disappear.

Because this place is gorgeous.

The room features the same kind of exposed brick and high wooden ceilings as downstairs, with beautiful contemporary furniture. The linens, in shades of cream and dusty rose, bring a light, breezy quality that I wasn't expecting, and a massive king-size bed sits right in the center of the room, facing gorgeous windows that are letting in the glowing midday sun.

It's the exact kind of place that I had hoped for—beautiful, bright, and comfortable.

A perfect place to escape.

I set my guitar case on the ground, hoist my bag onto a chaise lounge in the corner, and rummage through to find my toiletries.

When I step into the bathroom, I let out a dreamy sigh at the sight of the soaking tub. I wasn't kidding when I told Errol it's the reason I grabbed this suite when I saw it was available. It's incredible, and I know I'm going to spend hours in it during this trip.

Candles. Bubbles. A little me-time to release some of the sexual tension that's been brimming inside me for the past few months.

I am *all* about self-care, in all its forms.

But unfortunately, that will have to wait.

Right now, I want a long, hot shower, and then I want to wander around downtown Rosewood to scope out the little shops and find a good cup of coffee.

"Soon," I whisper to the tub, and then I get about my business.

It doesn't take long for me to get ready, and barely an hour passes by the time I've showered, shaved, and done my hair and makeup. Then I'm strolling out the front door of the Firehouse and onto the streets of Rosewood.

I take in as much as I can, from the strong oak trees lining the sidewalk, to the little benches scattered here and there, to the streetlamps with signs announcing the final night of the Summer Movies in the Park. I make a mental note to ask Murphy if she wants to attend.

I pass a bakery and a boutique. An exercise studio and a health food market. A music store and a flower shop. A bar, a café, a bookstore. And then . . .

I smile.

The coffee shop.

I breathe in deeply as I push inside, the familiar scents of roasted coffee beans and pastries swirling together in a way that is simply magical.

And as I stand in line behind other patrons, I revel in my new surroundings.

It's quaint and adorable, and I love that it's walking distance from the inn. There are a few couches and armchairs in the middle, and plenty of tables along one wall where several others have set up shop with their laptops and headphones.

I'm not normally a scheduled worker—writing tends to be an organic process for me. But this looks like the type of place I could use as a home base. Maybe a spot at which to kick off my day and make a plan, even if I don't end up doing the majority of my creative work here.

Even though I'm in town to get away from the drama of what happened with Theo, there's still a deadline looming in the not-so-distant future. I still have obligations to my manager and my record label. And as nice as it would be to check out from all of that and disappear, the last thing I want to do is squander my dream just because I decided to waste three years of my life on a cheating asshole.

"What can I get you?"

The barista is a smiley brunette in her teens, and I offer her a returning smile before ordering a flat white and a croissant.

It only takes a few minutes for my order to come up. I take my drink and snack back outside to sit at one of the outdoor tables in front of the windows.

Then I tug out my notepad and pen and just . . . sit and watch. Waiting for inspiration to strike.

I've been writing my own music since I was old enough to hold a pen, and my first song was a jolly little thing about our neighbor's dog, Lily.

> Lily, Lily, why are you so silly?
> You love to sniff everything you see.
> Lily, Lily, why are you so silly?
> I'll pet you all day for free.

I smile at the memory. It might not be my best stuff, but I was only five.

Even back then, I loved to write about what I saw.

As a five-year-old, I saw my neighbor's dog. I saw my friends at school doing secret handshakes. I saw Christmas lights and the beach and Popsicles. So I wrote about those things.

Now, what I see is different. More nuanced.

Like now, sitting at this table and watching the slow calm of a lazy afternoon in Rosewood, what I see is . . .

An elderly woman walking her dog.

A mother struggling to get her son into his car seat.

A little girl begging her dad to go into the bakery.

And while I might not write about those particular things, specifically, they might inform something I *do* write.

I write down a few key words and then play around in a thesaurus online.

Help. Comfort. Guide. Save.
Care. Protect. Trust. Guard.

The words get crossed out or erased or circled with arrows pointing in different directions, until I'm left with a few messy lines.

I thought you could save me.
Oh how I was wrong.
Instead you betrayed me.
Now my trust is gone.

It's not the best. Far from it, actually. And I don't even have my guitar. It's tucked safely away in my room back at the inn. But every bit of music starts somewhere, is inspired by something.

I'm hoping Rosewood will provide me with that inspiration. That creative spark that can't be forced.

What I *don't* want is for this bullshit with Theo to be the only thing I think about when I'm writing. There are plenty of artists who use their bad breakups to inform their music, and I don't judge them for it. I get it. It's traumatic and emotional and can create a wealth of content.

But it can't be my only inspiration. Not when there is so much that can guide the creative process.

My mind briefly flickers over the memory of my kiss with Memphis, and my neck grows warm. I wonder if our midnight moment can prompt something . . . *anything* . . . in my creative psyche.

With that thought, I flip to the next page, and start again.

I spend over an hour in front of Rosewood Roasters, letting my mind wander. Giving myself the chance to catch that inspiration. But in the end, apart from the few lines I wrote when I sat down, I only make a few notes about idle hands and what it means to sit around waiting for something to happen.

It feels very meta, and I'm worried that my initial desire to find inspiration in this town might have been half-baked. Most of the time, I have full faith in myself, but I wouldn't be an artist if I didn't face at least a *little* bit of impostor syndrome. Though I didn't expect it to rear its ugly head during the collapse of my relationship *and* a period of intense creative block.

I can't help the little prickle in the back of my mind that I won't make my deadline. That I'll have let this perfect storm of personal struggles ruin the most incredible opportunity I've ever had.

Just as I'm thinking it might be time to accept defeat and head back to the inn, my phone rings. And when I see my manager's name on the screen, I groan, knowing I need to answer.

Reluctantly, I answer the call and put the phone to my ear.

"Hey, Todd."

"Hey, Viv. How's the writing coming?"

"Good. I'm actually sitting in front of a coffee shop with my notepad right now," I tell him, honestly.

"Nice. Anything good coming to you?"

"Oh yeah. I'm really in the zone," I tell him, not so honestly.

"Great. Glad to hear that. Especially with your studio time right around the corner. I'm thinking you should come in to the office and we can go over your songs, create a priority sheet for what we'd like to focus on first."

My heart launches into my throat.

Shit.

"Well . . . there might be a problem with me coming in."

Todd's silent for a beat. "Okay," he eventually says, drawing out the end of the word. "What kind of problem?"

I sigh. "I'm not in LA right now."

"Vivian. We talked about your schedule for this month, and you said you didn't have any trips planned. 'I won't be going anywhere, I'll be sitting at home, writing and focusing on getting ready for the studio.' Those were your exact words."

"I didn't think I would be. I . . ." The words are like tar on my tongue. "I caught Theo cheating, and I decided I needed to get out of town for a little while."

He makes a sympathetic noise. "I'm sorry to hear that, Viv."

"It's been a lot, and I wanted a break. From everything." Then a thought occurs to me. "I'm visiting Murphy, though. So it's not completely unrelated to work."

Murphy is an incredibly talented songwriter and is responsible for several of the songs we're considering for my album. She also writes music for my label, Humble Roads, so it isn't totally outside the realm of work-related travel for me to be here, even if writing with Murphy hadn't actually been the original plan. But Todd doesn't need to know that.

"Oh! Well, tell her I said hello. You guys planning to write while you're up there?"

I nod, then remember he can't see me. "Yeah. Yes, we're meeting up tonight, actually."

A lie right now, but something I can turn into the truth if I reach out to my friend like I had already planned to do.

"Great. Listen, if you're really working, I guess it's not such a big deal for us not to meet. We can handle the priority list over the phone. Maybe next week?"

"That would be great, Todd. I just got here yesterday, so coming home right now . . . I'd really like a chance to take a break and focus on myself." I pause. "And my work, of course."

"I get it. I'll keep you posted."

"Sounds good."

"Talk soon."

We get off the phone, and I drop it crankily on the table.

It never even occurred to me that I might be blindsided by my manager wanting an in-person meeting. I'd assumed that fitting in this last-minute trip right before I go into the studio would be a chance for me to spend two weeks writing and fully purging myself of Theo so that when I get back, I'm prepared.

I'm glad I don't have to fly back to LA just yet. I don't want to have to face the reality of returning home to a condo that is now tainted with the memory of what I saw.

And I definitely don't want to have to go into the studio and bare my soul without getting a chance to sort through some things in my mind. Because I'll have to sing those few songs that were written about a man who ripped my life apart, before he did. That music was written about someone I thought I loved. A man I thought loved *me*.

Though I doubt that was ever really true.

I collect my shit and tuck it into my purse, then begin the short walk back to the Firehouse, my mind scattered and unfocused.

It's normal to rethink everything after a breakup. I think most people do. There's a place your mind goes to after you realize you're not going to be with someone for forever, after you realize they're not at all who you thought they were.

Every action is scrutinized.

Every word recounted.

Every mistake rehashed.

Suddenly, the most important thing in the world is figuring out all the ways that you were never truly compatible. Because the real terror is realizing the person you thought was your soulmate *isn't*.

Though even as I think it, I know the words aren't true.

I never thought Theo was my soulmate. I'm not even sure I believe in such a thing.

He was a man who I connected with.

Physically, sometimes.

Emotionally, on occasion.

Apart from decent sex, though, toward the end of our relationship, it felt like we were existing around each other and nothing more. We had overlapping friends, a condo we shared, and the same taste in music, but I'm pretty sure that's it.

And being with someone forever simply because you both enjoy jamming out to a shared playlist as you get ready for work in the morning does *not* a relationship make.

Errol gives me a wave as I walk through the front door of the Firehouse, but thankfully, he's on the phone and I quickly pass him by and jog up the stairs. My bright and sunny mood from earlier has been officially soured by all these thoughts of Theo and our relationship, and I'm not in the mood for chitchat.

Instead, I flee to the privacy of my suite and crawl into bed.

I haven't had much time to really grieve. I've mostly oscillated between rage and irritation or shock, clinging to this good riddance kind of attitude.

Right now, though, I feel less resilient than I've been since I found him naked in our bed five days ago with another woman. A bed I had promptly removed from the condo with the rest of Theo's things.

We loved each other once. In the beginning, I know we did.

Or at least, I thought we did.

But now I can't help but wonder if that was ever really true.

Maybe that's the actual hardest part of breaking up.

Dissecting that love, and facing the fact that it was never as real as we believed it to be.

Chapter Five

Memphis

The crowd outside the restaurant makes me smile, and I slip through the couples and families waiting to be seated. Saturday nights have been our busiest nights since we opened, but I can feel the difference as we begin to creep into harvest season.

Every year as we begin to pluck the grapes—first the whites, then the reds—the vineyard gets an influx of visitors. More tours are scheduled. We do a handful of those foot-crushing sessions, catering to those wanting to recreate that old *I Love Lucy* episode. We sell more bottles during September and October than we do during the entire rest of the year.

Even though I hoped for that business to translate to the restaurant, I wasn't sure what would happen. So it's encouraging to see that the wave of guests wanting to visit the property are interested in spending time dining with us as well.

When I walk through the front door, everything looks clean and organized. The hosts are seating new guests, and the servers are bustling around with trays of food. Not wanting to get in anyone's way, I only poke my head into the kitchen for a second. The hustle and bustle looks like the controlled chaos I've come to expect as several chefs move about with efficiency. I spot Wes in the corner, arranging plates on a tray, then giving directions to a server as she hoists it on her shoulder.

All in all, it seems like a smooth operation tonight, and I slip back into the dining room, tucking my hands in my pockets, just watching.

Until my eyes lock on the redhead at the wine bar.

I huff out an irritated breath as she smiles and says something to Mira.

Does she really plan to be here every day? Because two nights in a row is too much.

Too much of her little smiles and her sass and her distracting laugh.

Before I can think better of it, I stride toward the bar without a clue as to what I intend to do once I get there.

It's evident when Vivian sees me. Her eyes flash and her chin tilts up in obstinance, bringing my attention to her long, graceful neck.

The same neck that I placed a long, wet kiss on less than twenty-four hours ago.

She's sexy as fuck, and it's infuriating.

"I'm surprised to see you back here," I say, coming to a stop next to where she sits at the end.

"I don't know why," she replies, a smile on her face that is nowhere near as genuine as the one she was giving Mira seconds ago. "I told you I was in town for a couple of weeks."

"Yes, you *did* say that. But I didn't think that 'in town' meant you'd be setting up a tent in our restaurant. Surely there are other places far more interesting for you to spend your time."

My eyes briefly connect with Mira's. She's standing completely still, frozen in the act of uncorking a bottle, watching us with curiosity.

"Mira, I think the gentleman in the green jacket needs a top-up."

She blinks, then gives me a sheepish grin before stepping away toward the other end of the bar and giving us at least the false impression of privacy.

"That was rude."

"It was rude of me to point out that my bartender was neglecting her job? I disagree."

"She was hardly neglecting her job, though it's unsurprising that you disagree with me, since that seems to be all you're capable of."

My eyes narrow as she swirls her glass of wine against the oak wood of the bar top, one of her eyebrows higher than the other as she stares right back, her lips tilted up at one side.

"Instead of gracing us with your presence every evening, I'd be happy to have a crate of wine delivered to wherever you're staying," I say, redirecting us entirely. "If you'll let me know where, I can have it dropped off with you tomorrow."

Her smirk grows, and I want to kick myself when I realize how long I've been watching her mouth.

"You know, I *could* do that. But what fun would that be when I could be here instead. Gracing you with my presence, as you so *kindly* referred to it."

I take a step closer to her, dipping my voice low to make sure the woman two seats over can't hear me. "You really plan to blow hundreds of dollars a night sitting at this bar just in an attempt to rattle my cage?" I ask. "Because I'm sure there are better ways to waste your money."

"Oh, honey. I have bottomless pockets and a tendency to provoke. You have no idea the lengths I'm willing to go to *rattle your cage.*" Then she reaches out and adjusts the collar of my shirt, her finger gently tracing along the skin of my neck. "Nothing about flustering you the way I so obviously do could ever be a waste."

The touch of her skin on mine sends a shiver down my spine, and my nostrils flare. And when her eyes flick to my lips for barely a second, almost faster than I can even record that it's happened, the back of my neck grows hot.

God, she's exasperating.

I want to kiss that fucking smirk right off her face.

"You end up at the Firehouse?"

The sound of my sister's voice is like nails on a chalkboard, and I take a step back, belatedly realizing how close I was hovering to Vivian.

As much as I hate being interrupted, my family's ability to intrude on every single interaction I've had with Vivian is actually appreciated.

"Yeah," Vivian responds, her shoulders relaxing, the smirk on her face morphing back into that smile she had given Mira a few minutes ago. "You were right. Errol is a sweetheart. And I could literally drown in that tub and go out a happy woman. I can't wait to have a night where I set up candles and soft music and . . . soak my body."

Murphy groans. "We don't have any tubs in our house, and it is a crying shame. I'm so jealous."

"Well, you're welcome to come by any time to use it." Vivian's eyes shift back to me. "What about you, Memphis? You a man who loves a good bath? You're also welcome to come by and . . . soak for a little while. You seem kind of tense."

I roll my eyes. "If you'll excuse me, I have some things to handle."

And before Vivian or Murphy can say anything else, I turn and book it through the dining room.

Past the kitchen, the hosts, and the crowd outside.

I don't stop walking until I've made it back to the house.

But then, once I'm there, I'm alone with my thoughts.

What a horrible place to be.

I've never met someone who has been able to crawl under my skin the way Vivian does.

Normally that's meant as an insult, but in this instance, I almost can't help but acknowledge that it's a compliment. What did she call it? A tendency to provoke?

The woman is . . . fucking stubborn. And maddening. And it makes me hard when she volleys back.

I'm a bossy guy. I know that. And most of my relationships in life revolve around work, so that means that when I tell people to do something, they do it.

And Vivian . . . does not.

She has no intention of giving me what I demand, yet it somehow feels like she's dangling everything I could *ever* want just inches away from where I'm standing.

It is a heady duality, and I hate how much I enjoy it.

Refusing to spend any more time tonight thinking about Vivian, I head toward my office. I need to finalize my selections for the temporary hand applications from the ones our HR manager sent my way.

On most nights, I help staff the restaurant. I fill in where it's needed—like last night at the bar, or last week when the kitchen needed extra hands and I stood at the pass to expedite orders.

Tonight, though, my presence isn't needed. Things are running smoothly, and I don't need to spend my night arguing with Vivian at the bar.

Even though that's exactly what I want to do.

When I stop in the kitchen for a snack before getting back to work, I find Micah, my father, my aunt Sarah, and our two full-time hands, Naomi and Edgar, at the table eating dinner.

"Memphis!" my aunt calls out to me, cheerfully waving me over. "Are you joining us?"

I pause for a second, considering the work waiting for me.

"It's been months since you've had dinner with us. We're having chicken chili."

I step all the way into the room, ultimately deciding that the applications can wait.

"It hasn't been *months*," I tell her, grabbing a bowl off the counter. "Maybe a few weeks."

Moving quickly, I dish out some food and take a seat at the table next to Edgar, then dive into my meal as conversation at the table swirls around me.

For as long as I can remember, we've had family dinner with the employees that work the land and live in the cabins on the other side of the property. The full-time staff has grown over the past twenty or so years, expanding from just the family and vineyard team to include people who do things like marketing, compliance, and customer service. But the vineyard crew has always been like extended family.

When I was a child, there were maybe fifteen people around this dinner table at any given time. My aunt and my grandmother always made enough to feed our family, the full-time crew, and the hands that took on longer stints of work during busier months.

During the two long months of harvest season, trays overflowing with food are laid out on the counter at every meal, and a line of temp hands stretches out the door. People know that they get treated well when they work for us, and it's a point of pride for our family. One we won't soon let go of.

"There's nothing so important that we can't all take time to be together for a meal at the end of the day." It was something my grandmother always said, and something my aunt has echoed a few times over the years.

The sentiment was actually what inspired the restaurant, the idea coming to me after a busy day when I was sitting at this very table. I figured that coming together for a meal might actually be something important enough that it could save the vineyard.

Ironic, then, that the very thing inspired by these dinners is also the responsibility that so regularly keeps me away from them.

I don't really come to family dinner anymore because I'm always at the restaurant in the evenings. I'm up with the sun, sitting at my desk or moving around the property, keeping on top of all the moving parts that keep this place functioning while simultaneously trying to figure out what we can cut or trim back to save extra here and there.

It would be nice if I could take a break and join everyone and revel in some of the camaraderie that makes the burden of this job feel less daunting. Unfortunately, that's not the reality of where we're at right now.

It's exhausting. And lonely.

But it has to be done.

"How're things going at the restaurant?"

The question jerks me back to the table, and I look to my aunt, finding her gaze on me, soft and open.

"Good," I answer. "They're going good. Numbers have been staying up from summer, which is great since most restaurants have a falloff during autumn for a little bit. The harvest is a big draw, so it's nice to see the impact it's having. We might actually increase the number of tours we offer each week through Thanksgiving."

She nods, a bright smile on her face. "That sounds wonderful. And how's it going for Murphy?"

I blink. "What do you mean?"

My aunt laughs. "I mean . . . how's your sister doing, leading the front of house? I ask her all the time, but I don't head over there too often, so I don't really know."

Sitting back in my chair, I cross my arms, thinking it over. "She's doing great, actually. The servers know the menus and do a great job of upselling the wines. The hosts are friendly and competent." I shrug. "She's amazing at things that are forward facing, so . . . it's been going really well."

Sarah beams. "I love hearing that." She reaches out and pats my hand lovingly. "Great job, Memphis." Then she turns and asks Naomi about her mother, the two of them falling into an easy conversation that reflects years of friendship.

One by one, the rest of the table gets up, having already been mostly finished with their meals before I joined them, until it's just me and Dad and Sarah left.

I glance at my dad briefly, then at my aunt. "Hey, can I get your opinion on something?" I ask her.

She nods. "Sure."

My father taps the table lightly. "I'll take that as my cue to head out. Have a good night."

Irritation floods me at the fact my dad is bowing out at the first sign of work-related talk, but I push it aside.

"What's up, honey?"

"I've been thinking about buying a printer and moving our labeling to an in-house process," I say, then launch into the details that I tried to share with my father this morning.

Unlike my dad, my aunt gives me her full attention, asking insightful questions and providing her feedback in pros and cons.

"It seems like you've already thought of everything," she says eventually. "My only real concern would be where you plan to actually set up this operation and how it will work in conjunction with the bottling."

I lean forward, resting my elbows on the table. "Well, the printing could happen anywhere. In the office building conference room. The warehouse. In my office, even. It's more about having the labels ready when the truck gets here."

When most people think of a winery, they assume that bottling happens on the property. But equipment for a bottling line is crazy expensive, and our winery isn't large enough to warrant owning machinery like that, especially when we only bottle a few days out of the year. So we do what a lot of medium-size wineries do since we're too small to own the equipment and too large to bottle by hand. We hire a mobile bottling line to set up shop.

We provide the wine, the bottles, and the labels, and they provide the machine and a few people to keep it running. The bottles get boxed up as they're pulled off the line, and the boxes get delivered to our warehouse or loaded straight onto trucks that head out for distribution.

It's a cost I've been trying to figure out how to eliminate, since it cuts so much from our profit right off the top, but until I can find a better option, it is what it is.

The labels, however, are another story. *That* is a cost I can minimize.

"If you know how it's all going to work, it sounds like you're making a great decision."

Something settles in my chest that I didn't realize was tight.

"You think so?"

She grins at me and pats my hands, something she did often over the years when I was a child and still does now, even though I'm definitely not a kid anymore. "If *you* believe it's the right decision, I'm on board. Because I believe in *you*."

When I slip back into my office later that night, I think it all over again. And again, and again. I run the numbers. Again. I make accommodations for things going wrong, for messing up labels, for issues with the printer we buy. I run it until I've gotten to a place where there is no doubt behind my decision.

Then I send off my final email to the sales rep I received the quote from, telling him I'm ready to move forward with the purchase.

But my conversation with Sarah is still a little thing flittering around in the back of my mind, even as I move on to the temp hand applications.

My aunt is a special woman, and I often look to her for advice. She's been around for most of my life, my dad and my siblings and I having moved back to the vineyard when I was seven or so. It was nice to have a mothering figure around during those days, when the world felt so dark and nothing was right.

As I've gotten older, I've been looking to her more and more in relation to business things. Unlike my father, who left the vineyard when he was in his late teens, wanting nothing to do with it, my aunt loved everything about the family business. She stayed and worked the land and helped my grandfather run things for years.

Until my mother passed away and my father returned, three children in tow.

Then, he took back his place as the eldest son and started working with my grandfather. My aunt took a back seat, spending a lot of her time, especially during those early days, helping my grandmother with the three of us. I mean, we were so young, and we'd lost our mother. Micah was barely a few weeks old, but Murphy was five and had all these big emotions and wanted constant attention.

They had their work cut out with us.

When I was a teenager, I started working the fields with my dad and grandfather. But it was my aunt who truly understood the business. So it makes sense—at least to me—that I look to her now. As I try everything I can to keep us above water.

Sometimes I wonder if *she* should have been the one in charge, if that would have made all the difference. Or whether this time of hardship was bound to hit us at some point, no matter what.

Chapter Six

VIVIAN

I stay in bed until almost noon on Sunday, even though I wake up at seven.

Fucking hangovers are the worst.

I love a bottle of wine as much as the next girl, but what I *don't* love is incessant phone calls from my ex. Which is what I dealt with last night after my tête-à-tête with Memphis at the restaurant bar. After the third call in thirty minutes, I decided that maybe waiting around for Murphy wasn't in the cards. I instead took a little trip to the liquor store and bought a bottle of tequila.

I didn't drink the whole thing—I mean, I'm still alive obviously— but I *did* play a foolish drinking game with myself that I would take a shot every time Theo called or texted.

A mistake, if ever one has been made.

After I finally stumble my way through putting clothes on and tucking my hair into a messy bun, I down a handful of ibuprofen, put on the biggest pair of sunglasses I own, and brave the outdoors. Thankfully, the worst of the summer weather seems to be in the rearview, and I'm greeted by a slightly overcast day, meaning I don't feel the need to shrink into the shadows like a vampire with every step.

Eventually, I make it to Rosewood Roasters. I order a flat white and take a seat on one of the big, comfy couches. I need to write today. My deadline is slowly creeping toward me. But when I take a seat, all I can manage is to close my eyes, hoping to will away my headache.

The sound of my phone beeping with an incoming text actually startles me, and I peek at it, hoping it's not another text from Theo. I'm not sure my liver can handle it.

I breathe out a sigh of relief when I see my screen.

Murphy: Hey, I have to head into SF with Wes tonight and prob won't be back for a few days. Some stuff's going on with his mom. You gonna be cool without me?

My brow furrows. I don't know a lot about Wes's mom, but from the few things Murphy has shared, it seems like she has some substance abuse issues that have caused drama at least a few times.

Me: No prob. I'll be totally fine. Hope everything's okay.

Murphy: She's . . . a lot. We'll see. Sorry I've been so busy since you got here!

Me: Not a big deal. I promise. And I basically showed up uninvited lol. Not expecting you to be available every minute.

Murphy: I know. But I've missed you and I don't want you to think I'm too busy to spend time with you.

I grin. Murphy's one of those sentimental types. The one who always wants you to know how important you are and who waxes poetic about your friendship.

I've never had a friend like her before. Most of the people I grew up with and socialize with in the industry are fairly vapid and self-absorbed.

Her energy is refreshing, even if our time together here has been limited.

Me: You're good. You love me. I love you. That'll still be true when you get back from SF.

Murphy: 😌

I set my phone down and close my eyes again. I hold my warm coffee cup between my hands in my lap. I sip it occasionally and let the lulling sounds of a coffee shop blur out the edges of my exhausted mind.

When another text comes through and I take a look, I grip my phone in frustration.

Theo: If I don't hear from you soon, I'm going to call your parents.

I push out of my seat and head outside, shoving my sunglasses back on my face and dialing Theo's number.

The idea that he's going to talk to my parents doesn't actually bother me. Our relationship has always been cold and fake, with both of them keeping me at arm's length, more interested in themselves than in their only daughter. So if Theo were to call them to say I disappeared, I'm sure their response would be neutral at best.

I'm more concerned that he doesn't seem to accept I don't want to talk to him. Ever.

He answers almost immediately.

"Well, if I'd known that was all it would take to get you to call me back, I would have threatened to call your family days ago."

"I don't care if you talk to my parents, Theo. I barely talk to them myself, so have at it. I'm done with these ridiculous text messages and incessant phone calls, so I'm letting you know that it's time to leave me alone."

"Come on, Vi. You're being ridiculous."

"That's what you keep saying." I stroll down the street, heading toward the Firehouse but without any real direction. "I personally don't think it's ridiculous to ignore someone's calls after catching them cheating *in my own fucking bed.*"

Theo sighs. "It didn't mean anything, okay? Besides, we hadn't had sex in months."

"Didn't *mean* anything? She's your ex. Of *course* it meant something. And the fact we hadn't slept together in months is irrelevant. Every couple goes through periods like that, and you know what helps? Time together. Date nights. *Not* sleeping with your ex."

"It was familiar, Vi. That's all. You know how I feel about you."

"Do I? Because I thought you loved me. I thought we were in a committed relationship. And clearly, I was wrong on both counts." I chuck my barely touched coffee into a trash can, needing the release of throwing something.

"Come on, baby. Come home. We can talk about this. You and me . . . We're meant to be together."

I roll my eyes. "I don't want to talk about it, Theo. 'You and me' were over the second you decided that it was okay to put your dick into someone else."

He groans. "Look, tell me where to meet you so we can talk, okay? Or at least tell me when you'll be home."

"I've gone on vacation for two weeks, Theo, so let it go. Your stuff is with the super. Just collect it and let's be done."

"Two weeks?"

"And please stop calling and texting me. I'm not going to pick up, and I'm not going to respond. We're over."

I hang up the phone, my heart pounding angrily in my chest.

Not just in my chest. I can feel it thumping everywhere. In my fingers and at my neck. In my knees, even.

I wasn't expecting to be so enraged after speaking with him. At hearing his voice.

And at the same time, I knew I would be.

I've spent years hearing that voice. Listening to the words that came out of that mouth. Laughing at the stories that rolled off that tongue.

Too bad it was forked in two.

Too bad it belonged to a snake.

Too fucking bad I didn't know it until after I'd already been bit.

Most of the day goes by in a blur, and I don't write a single word.

I don't even take notes.

After that messed-up phone call to Theo, I sat outside to people watch, but inspiration failed me.

Then I got lunch at The Carlisle—a chicken pesto panini that should have rocked my world but didn't because I was too distracted to appreciate it.

Finally, I went on a drive. That's what finally pulled me out of my funk.

When you're a kid growing up in LA, going on a drive means sitting in bumper-to-bumper traffic. So when I finally discovered the magic of road trips in areas where there wasn't a constant Carmageddon, I was hooked.

Road trips became my jam.

Today, it cleansed something as I listened to an angry playlist I found on Spotify. I rocked out with the music on blast, drove with the windows down, and sang at the top of my lungs. I didn't know half of the songs, many of them having been made popular when I was still in diapers. But the vibes were right, and I knew at least some of the lyrics. Like always, it fed something in my soul.

And even though I'm still plagued with questions—about my breakup, about the future, about the next chapter of my life—something that was sitting on my chest after I got off the phone has finally been purged.

Which is why I'm able to take a shower, do my hair and my makeup, and head to The Standard for a drink as the day comes to an end, with a promise to myself that I will *not* have another hangover tomorrow.

Murphy talked about this bar all the time back in LA, to the point that it feels familiar when I walk inside. There's nothing particularly special about it. There's a pinball machine, a pool table, and a dart board to the left, and a handful of booths and open tables to the right. A bar stretches along most of the back wall. It's the kind of town centerpiece that you see in TV shows and movies, and the perfect place to spend an evening.

I sidle up to the bar and take a seat, setting my clutch on the counter and returning the smile of the graying bartender.

"Would you like to see the beer and wine list? Or are you looking for something a little harder?"

I wince. "No liquor tonight. I'll take whatever's on tap that you recommend. Something local, maybe?"

He gives me a nod. "I got just the thing."

I turn on the swiveling stool to survey the room again, taking in the aging decor on the walls and the old glass lighting over the booths.

When I spot a familiar face, something unfamiliar flutters around in my stomach. I hope both that he looks my way and that he doesn't.

He's standing around the pool table, chatting with a few other guys, his expression easy and his posture relaxed.

When his coffee-colored eyes finally connect with mine, I see something I'm not expecting: a smile. It's small, but I see it all the same. It disappears almost immediately, though, masked with a look that reveals he's as uncertain about seeing me as I am about seeing him.

Memphis says something to one of the guys, then hangs his pool stick up on a rack before he crosses the room in my direction.

I should turn around and face the sweet old bartender, but I don't. Instead, I watch Memphis as he approaches, not even trying to hide the way my eyes scan him up and down.

He's wearing a long sleeve thermal and dark jeans that outline his physique. My memory jumps back to Memphis standing shirtless in the kitchen that first night, his broad shoulders and toned arms and chest on display. But he's as delicious fully clothed.

How inconsiderate.

"Enjoying the view?"

My eyes flick up to connect with his, then narrow as he comes to a stop before me.

"Hardly. Just trying to figure out why you won't leave me alone."

I spin in my chair so I'm facing the bar again, and Memphis leans against it to my left, dipping his body toward mine.

"I won't leave *you* alone. I live here. These are *my* stomping grounds. I seem to recall you showing up at my place of work *and* my home on several occasions . . ."

"Twice," I interrupt, holding up two fingers before giving the bartender a grateful smile as he sets the pale beer in front of me. "And I was invited."

"So if anyone is stalking anyone, it's the other way around," he continues as if I've said nothing.

"That's the narrative you keep putting out there, but from my point of view, I'm simply *existing* and you're crawling into my physical space like you can't get enough of me," I tease, bringing the beer to my lips and eyeing him over the rim. "The restaurant, the kitchen, the restaurant again, now here."

Memphis inches toward me, his face so close to mine as I take a sip. "You couldn't be more wrong."

"So that night in the kitchen was, what? You showing me your disinterest?" I roll my eyes. "Consider me convinced."

"I won't pretend that I wasn't interested. You're beautiful, there's no question, and any man would be stupid not to at least consider it."

I can't deny loving the compliment, but I immediately brush it to the side because I know there's a *but* coming just behind it.

"But I don't have time for what a girl like you would be looking for."

One eyebrow lifts. "Oh? And what is *a girl like me* looking for exactly? Please, inform the class."

"A beck-and-call boy," he says, smirking. "You look like a woman who is used to people catering to your every whim, men who follow you around like puppies. And I promise you, I am not that guy."

I lick my lips, chuckling under my breath.

"What's so funny?"

"Well, if anyone here is wrong tonight, Memphis, it's you. That's what's so funny."

"I'm not wrong."

"You couldn't *be* more wrong," I say, imitating his tone when he said the same words to me a few minutes go. "Besides, what I want probably isn't something you could give me anyways."

Something flashes behind his eyes.

Ah, so he's like every other man, easy to bait when you place a challenge in front of him.

"Oh yeah? And what's that?"

I lean the last bit in to him, so my lips are right by his ear. So I can whisper exactly what I want from him without risking someone hearing what I have to say.

"I want to be fucked, Memphis."

I hear his sudden intake of breath, a little thing, but noticeable nonetheless.

"I want someone to split me in half," I continue, pressing a finger into his chest, between his pecs, and tracing slowly downward. "I want to come so hard I black out."

I tilt back, putting a few inches of space between us, a thrill racing through me when I see how his eyes have clouded over. His lids are heavy, his mouth parted slightly. Part of me thinks if I were to press my hand between his legs right now, he'd be rock solid.

"So, like I said . . . I'm not so sure you're the right man for the job."

He watches me for a long moment, like something is warring inside him. Like maybe he's trying to decide if he wants to actually give in to this obvious attraction between us. It's easy to blow off something that happened in the kitchen in the middle of the night. Chalk it up to being in a weak mental state or not having the ability to resist temptation.

But there's something completely different about making an active decision to sleep with someone. There's no way to brush it off or place blame somewhere else.

Memphis seems like the type to confront his problems head-on. But for whatever reason, he keeps picking fights with me instead of accepting that he wants to get me naked.

When it comes to sex, I am definitely a head-on kind of gal. Exhibit A: my *I want to be fucked* speech. Though I'm also guilty of picking my own fights sometimes. I mean, I picked one with Memphis, didn't I?

"You want to be fucked, Vivian?" he says, his voice a low rumble. "Name the time and the place, and I'll be there."

I blink, mild shock flooding through me, followed by a wave of desire so strong that I can barely keep my enthusiasm to myself when I reply, "Right now, anywhere you want me."

He looks a little stunned, but it takes him less than a second to shift gears. Memphis tugs his wallet out, slaps a twenty on the counter, then takes me by the hand and leads me through The Standard. We storm past the bathrooms and what looks like a little office, before he pushes through a door into a dark room and tugs me in behind him.

"What are . . ."

But my words cut off when he shoves me up against the closed door and slams his mouth against mine.

Everything around us fades into nothing and I open for him, inviting him in, wanting nothing more than the taste of him on my tongue again.

And it tastes so good. Like beer and honey and something else that I recognize from the last time we kissed . . . something that is all Memphis.

It's an intoxicating combination, and only seconds pass before I feel drunk on him.

Bringing both hands up to his neck, I thread my fingers through the hair at the back of his head, I grip tightly and tilt his head how I want as I suck on his tongue and nibble on his lip.

But he pulls back, shaking my hands off him.

"You seem to think you're in control here," he says, keeping his voice quiet. "But if you want to be fucked, Vivian, then I'm in charge."

A shiver races through me, and then he's kissing me again. But this time, he's directing each movement. His mouth moves to my neck, his hands to my ass, and I let out a moan when I feel the thick rod between his legs pressed up against me.

Memphis licks and nibbles at my skin. My neck, over my clavicle, then down the deep V of my top. He tugs the stretchy material to the side, revealing the meaty flesh of my breast behind a bralette, zeroing in on my nipple and circling the nub with his tongue before sucking it into his mouth through the lace.

I squirm, the pulse between my legs growing as he lavishes me with his attention. First one breast, then the other. Over the material and then tugging that to the side as well so his tongue is directly on my skin.

It's been a long time since I've had this much focus on my breasts, and I grow wet as he continues, my lower lips surely glistening with desire.

"Do you know how hard it is not to stare at these?" he asks, his tongue flicking teasingly against one nipple.

"Probably as hard as it is for me not to ogle you in those stupidly tight polo shirts," I answer, whimpering as his teeth graze against me.

He pulls back and I mourn the loss of the contact. But only briefly, because his mouth is back on mine, his hands gripping at my hips and working at the button on my jeans.

I mirror his actions, my hands working at his fly with a desperation I wasn't expecting but can't seem to help.

The room is nearly pitch black, so even as my eyes adjust, it's hard to see much. But I don't need to see anything to know that the man in front of me is as desperate for this as I am. A fact that's only confirmed when my hand slips into his jeans and grips him over his boxers.

Memphis pauses, his hands rising and bracing on the door on either side of me, a groan coming from somewhere deep in his chest as I squeeze him.

"Is this for me?" I ask him, gently biting on his ear and loving the little breaths I can hear falling from his mouth.

His hips begin to shift, his dick thrusting gently against my hand. And when I slip my hand inside the cotton and grip his hot flesh, he whispers a quiet "Fuck" into my ear.

Everything after that seems to move in double time, each of us making quick work of ripping the other out of their clothing, barely enough to access what we want. In record time his pants are shoved down, the crinkle of a foil packet the only sound in the room apart from our heavy breaths as he wraps up.

My jeans and panties are at my feet a few seconds later, one leg freed and hitched up under his arm, opening me to him.

"God, you're so wet," he grits out as his thumb strokes me between my lower lips, confirming my earlier assessment that I'm fucking drenched.

He slides one finger inside me, then two, testing my readiness.

"I'm ready," I tell him. "Fuck, I'm so ready."

Memphis chuckles, then flicks his fingers. I whimper, feeling like he could resolve that ache deep inside me just like this, just at that little touch.

God, it's been so long, and I feel like I've been coiled so tight. I need this. So fucking bad.

Instead of letting him continue to tease me, I bat his hand away and grab his cock again. Memphis's laughter cuts off, and he inhales sharply as I guide him to my entrance.

"Fuck me," I tell him, rubbing his head in my wetness and then shifting my hips so that he begins to slip inside.

"Shit." It's the last thing he says before he's thrusting inside me in one smooth movement, all the way to the hilt, slamming against something deep inside that makes me cry out in the best kind of pleasure pain.

He pauses, though, and doesn't move his hips again. His hand comes up and covers my mouth, then he puts his forehead against mine.

"You need to be quiet," he says, smirking as he rotates his hips, his dick bumping against something delicious.

I whimper.

"Let me know if you can be quiet, Vivian," he growls, repeating both his words and his actions as his cock continues to nudge that same spot inside me.

I nod, desperate for him to keep moving.

"Good. Because there's a bar full of people fifteen feet away from this door. And it could be a big problem if they hear you screaming out my name."

Cocky shit.

But that's barely even a thought before he's pulling back and slamming in again, causing my entire body to throb with need.

Fuck.

Fuck fuck fuck.

Memphis thrusts a few more times before he pulls his hand away from my mouth, seemingly satisfied that I won't call out again.

And I manage to keep my cries to myself, but barely.

The way his cock spears into me, over and over again, hitting that spot inside me that hasn't been soothed in who the fuck knows how long . . . God, I can barely handle it.

My entire body is a live wire, and Memphis is the fuse.

He adjusts where he's holding up my leg, opening me wider, and I scramble to ground myself. My arms are wrapped around him and slipped up under his shirt, my fingers dragging along his damp skin, trying to find purchase.

"God, you feel amazing," he whispers, his mouth open and sucking against my neck. Then his head raises and his eyes drop to my breasts bouncing between us. "Pinch your nipples."

My hand moves immediately, following his direction. And when I pinch at one, and then the other, my pussy flutters around him.

He bites out a quiet curse as his movements stutter for a beat or two, but then he's grabbing my other leg and lifting that up as well, the entire weight of me now balanced on his arms and braced against the door.

I thread my hands into his hair again and yank his mouth back to mine, sucking at his tongue and moaning as quietly as I can until I can barely handle the tension coiling inside me.

"I'm close," I tell him. "Fuck, I'm so close."

His voice comes out in a rumble. "Rub your clit," he tells me. "I'll be right behind you."

I slip my hand between us and strum against my little nub, hardly needing to touch it before I splinter apart. Ecstasy ripples through me, starting where we're joined and then shooting outward, up my middle and out to my limbs, tingling in my fingers and toes and all along my scalp. All of it made more intense by the effort it takes to stay quiet and not scream out the way I want to.

I dig my fingernails into his shoulders, my head falling back and hitting the door behind me with a thump.

"I'm there," he says, and then his body jolts, the fluidity of his movements becoming jerky and uncontrolled as he follows me to bliss.

We stay there for a long moment, each of us panting loudly in the quiet room, our bodies still pressed together and slick with sweat.

I was wrong before about wanting to be split in two. That's not what I want.

This is what I want.

I didn't split in half.

I shattered into a million fucking pieces.

And it's never felt so amazing to be falling apart.

Chapter Seven

MEMPHIS

I pull out and lower Vivian's legs to the ground one at a time, bracing her as she wobbles slightly.

My arms and back are killing me, and I'm thankful for the brief reprieve the darkness provides so I can stretch my aching muscles for a second before I flip on the lights. Then I reach for the switch somewhere along the wall, squinting at the harsh brightness once I find it, my eyes unaccustomed to it after so long in the dark.

"You couldn't have waited until I put my clothes back on?" she asks teasingly.

I rake my eyes over her, taking in her very disheveled state—her jeans and panties on the floor around one ankle, one shoe missing, her top and bra tugged down, her breasts exposed, her mane of hair wild around her face where her mascara is smudged and her cheeks are flushed.

Fuck, it's sexy as hell looking at her and knowing I did that.

And I love it even more that she stands there with confidence, not caring in the slightest.

"Why would I want to wait?" I tease back. "The point was so I could see you naked with the lights on."

She rolls her eyes, but there's a hint of a smile there, and I don't miss the way her eyes flick up and down as I tug off the condom and tuck myself back into my pants.

"Easy to say when you're still mostly dressed."

I shrug, grabbing a tissue and chucking the condom in the trash. "Next time, I'll make sure I'm completely in the buff."

It's meant as a joke, but inwardly I cringe.

Next time?

Where did that come from?

This was a one-time thing, a release that we both needed.

There will be no next time. I barely had time for *this*.

But I don't like that thought, either.

Vivian redresses, hopefully oblivious to what's going on in my mind. Only a minute or two passes before we're both fully clothed again, looking not much worse for the wear.

"Where are we, exactly?" she asks, as she sits on the little couch and slips on her heeled boot.

"Just a break room. It doesn't get used a lot."

"And you know this . . . how?"

I grin but don't say anything, crossing my arms instead.

Vivian watches me with a playful expression. "Memphis! Have I been added to your break room notch count?"

I purse my lips and huff out a breath. "I am not touching *that* question with a ten-foot pole."

There have only been two other women I've brought back here over the years, but it feels like the kind of information that will get me in trouble, regardless of what the number is.

"Well, thanks for that." She's putting her hair up into a messy bun as she says it, and I can't help wishing she'd have left it down and wild so everyone would see just how mussed I made her. "You took the whole 'splitting me in half' thing seriously, and I commend the effort."

I blink twice, then can't help when I tumble into a bit of laughter, her casual attitude throwing me off guard.

"You are . . . ridiculous," I finally say. "And same to you. Thanks for the good time."

She giggles as she looks at her reflection in a mirror on the wall, swiping at her smudged mascara. Then she looks at me and smiles, and something inside my chest thuds. Hard.

I clear my throat, ignoring it, and turn to tug the door open. Both of us walk out into the hallway and back into the main bar.

My friends are still at the pool table, and I consider rejoining them for a brief second before deciding that it's probably time to head home.

"Do you need a ride?" I ask Vivian as we both make our way out the front door and on to Main Street. The late-summer air is damp and cool, and this late on a Sunday evening, nobody is really out in town anymore.

"Nah, I'm down at the Firehouse," she says, hitching her thumb down the street toward where the bed-and-breakfast sits at the very end.

"That's right. Well . . . Have a good night, then."

She surprises me, stepping forward and slipping her hand behind my neck. Then tugging me down and bringing our mouths together.

I don't hesitate. I let myself enjoy the kiss and the way it feels to slip my arms around her waist and pull her against my body.

It's easy. Natural.

Like breathing. Like blinking. Like falling asleep.

It's also too short, and when Vivian pulls back, her eyes slightly hooded like she could go for another round, I find myself wishing that she would invite me back to her hotel. Wishing that we were already in her room so we could roll over and go again in the middle of the night.

The realization is unwanted. I take a step away from her, turning my head to look up and down the street as something unfamiliar begins to bubble underneath my skin.

"Look, Vivian," I start, not even knowing exactly what I want to say, but still certain that I need to say . . . something.

"Wow. That was fast."

I tilt my head to the side in confusion, not sure I heard her correctly. "What?"

"It's been less than five minutes, and you're already breaking out the *this can't go anywhere* speech."

I'm a bit stunned, to be honest. Partially because I didn't realize I was so transparent, but also because I don't like that she was able to read me so easily.

"I feel like . . . I don't want what just happened to get back to Murphy," I finally say, my response clearly a cop-out. "I don't think she'd handle it well."

I'm even more surprised when Vivian laughs.

"*She* won't handle it well, or *you're* not handling it well?"

"Fine. I'm not handling it well. Happy?" I ask, my tone growing exasperated. "I don't want us scratching an itch and creating something more complicated when I really don't have the time for it. And you kissing me like that in the middle of the street is a recipe for 'more complicated.'"

"You don't have to worry about me wanting anything more from you than what you've given me," she replies. "I wanted to be fucked, and that's what you did. Thank you."

She says it almost casually, her little wallet thing tucked under her arm and her hands in her pockets. But I don't miss the little bit of hurt in her expression.

I grit my teeth and let out a long sigh.

"Are you sure you don't need a ride?" I ask, feeling even worse now about sending her walking down the street in the evening, alone. "I don't want you to feel like you can't ask."

She gives me a tight smile. "Memphis, in this moment, I wouldn't ask you for the time. Have a nice night."

Then she turns, striding off down the tree-lined street in the direction of the Firehouse.

My gaze drops to her ass as she goes. I bite out a curse at my own weakness before heading in the opposite direction, making for where my truck is parked closer to the highway.

I hop in and slam the door, turning the key and revving up the ignition.

But then I sit there for a few minutes, staring straight ahead, unseeing.

I'm sure I could have handled that better, but I . . . didn't know how. And telling her I didn't want things to be more complicated felt like the best choice.

It was honest, but also easier than explaining to her all the little things floating around in the back of my mind.

Of course I don't want Murphy to find out I slept with Vivian, but it's about so much more than just my sister hearing that I hooked up with someone she's friends with.

Vivian is her *best* friend. The confidante she's looked to for years. The person she has turned to when she felt like she didn't have anyone else. When she felt like she was alone. When she felt like *I* was the one letting her down.

Even though I might not be the most sensitive guy in the world, it's no secret that Murphy wants things between us to be better, for us to be closer. And I do, too.

And that's just the Murphy situation.

That doesn't even touch on the fact that I don't have any fucking time right now. Not when I have this much on my plate. When I'm already struggling to keep it all together.

But I can't explain something like that to Vivian.

Because who sits down with a one-night stand and says, *This can't happen again because my vineyard is on the brink of foreclosure?*

It sounds like bullshit. It sounds like the weirdest, most random excuse in the world.

Even though it's not.

Every single day, I spend every moment that I can trying to repair things. Trying to find the magic pill that will solve all our problems and bring the vineyard back to its former glory. Searching for every single opportunity to level things out.

I. Don't. Have. Time.

Not for anything that isn't directly related to work.

Not for anything personal.

Maybe that makes me an asshole.

But I'm okay with that.

So, even though I didn't *need* to handle things like that with Vivian, it's easier to cut things off at the knees. Make sure she knows nothing else between us can happen again.

No matter how desperately I might want it to.

And that's probably the most infuriating part of it all.

The following morning, my father and I drive the thirty minutes out to the Trager farm to pick up the produce order for this week's restaurant menu.

Normally, the farms that service our kitchen deliver directly to us on a rotating schedule. But the Tragers are having issues with their trucks this week, and so we agreed to do our own collection.

It's not ideal, since we have a lot going on. Harvest begins next week, but sometimes you have to reprioritize. And since the restaurant is bringing in the majority of our profit right now, stepping in to handle a delivery is one of those things that has to get done.

"You seen Keith recently?" I ask my dad as we pull out of the drive and head east.

My father and Keith Trager have been friends since they were kids. They might not get together regularly, but I know their friendship is important to my father. His daughter, Quinn, was best friends with

Murphy when they were growing up, and our families used to do a lot together.

Not so much over the past few years, though.

My dad shakes his head. "Not in a couple months, no. Not since . . . maybe since the restaurant opened."

"We should do something," I find myself suggesting. "With the Tragers, I mean. Invite them over for dinner at the house."

It's not an ideal time to add anything else to my schedule that will pull me away from work, but it still feels like the right call.

Dad gives me a friendly smile and pats my shoulder. "That sounds like a great idea, son."

We shoot the shit a little bit, discussing the likelihood that the Giants will make the playoffs—low—and the possibility that we'll get in a full harvest without a storm this year—high. Things between my dad and I can get a little tense, but we can still slip into casual conversation when the pressures of work take a back seat for a few minutes, even if it is a tad superficial.

Eventually, we pull down the long dirt road that leads to the Trager family's farm, coming to a stop outside their big white barn.

"Hey, guys," Keith calls down to us from the back of a refrigerated box truck parked outside the barn doors. He hops out, leaving a few other crew members to continue working as he crosses to us.

"Good to see you, Keith," I say, shaking his hand.

"Hey, bud," my dad says.

"Hey, Jackie." Keith embraces my dad briefly, the two slapping each other on the back before pulling away. "Sorry to make things difficult this week," he adds, thumbing in the direction of where I now realize the workers are unloading boxes of produce. "The truck won't stay cool once we start driving, so we're trying to do single runs at a time to avoid opening the doors and letting all the cool air out. Appreciate you coming out. We should have it all resolved by your next delivery."

I pat Keith on the back. "Hey, it's not a problem."

Dad and I tug on some gloves and head over to the stacks of cardboard crates filled with produce. We hoist them onto our shoulders two at a time and carry them over to the bed of the truck. It doesn't take very long with the help of Keith and his guys, and then we're closing the gate and climbing back into the cab.

"I hope things get sorted out soon," I call over to Keith as we wave goodbye. "Let us know if we can do anything."

"I 'preciate ya!" he calls back, giving a little wave. Then he taps the back of our truck, sending us off.

We're on the road for less than ten minutes when my dad speaks.

"I think their farm might be at risk of going under."

I look to him, taking in his tight expression. "Why? Did he say something to you?"

My dad shakes his head. "No. It's just a feeling. I know Keith, better than anyone. He seems . . . worried."

"But is there something that would make you think their *whole farm* might go under? I mean, that would be a huge deal. I can't imagine Keith wouldn't talk to you about it, right?"

"Keith's a kind man, but he's also a proud one," he eventually says, his gaze out the window. "And sometimes, you feel like there's only so much you can do."

He's quiet for a few minutes, and when he doesn't say anything else, I decide not to prod further.

Part of me wonders if my dad is thinking of his *own* pride more than Keith's. Even though we work together every day, that is not a conversation my father and I will probably ever have, especially when that pride is still a living, breathing thing.

At the end of last year, Dad lined up a buyer, planning to sell off the vineyard to some wealthy family that would probably see the operation as some weird pet project. I'd been shocked by the development and begged him to let me try to salvage things before he made a move. That's when I pitched him the idea of the restaurant, something that I'd only been ruminating on until there was a reason to throw it out there.

He relented, but with a time frame and a budget. He gave me a year and $50,000.

From ideation to construction to opening several months ago, it's been eight months. Thankfully, he hasn't brought up the idea of selling again, but I don't doubt it's somewhere in the back of his mind. It's an easy solution. One that allows him to pass the responsibility to someone else without having to face how he nearly ran the entire business into the ground.

Sure, the economy will always play a little bit of a role in success, but so does learning to adapt in an ever-changing market, or making smart choices when it comes to hiring and improving technology. Or even just knowing how to manage the finances and pay attention to the bottom dollar. All things my dad struggled with.

I'll never understand why he didn't ask for help. Why we all couldn't have worked on remedying things *together*, back before we were in such dire straits.

But I don't have the same type of bullish pride that my father has.

While my dad would rather turn a blind eye to his own mistakes and never admit how he failed, I'm able to very clearly address both.

I'm bossy, sure. That's a fault of mine.

But when push comes to shove, I'm more concerned with things being done right than with being right. I'm not so set in my ways that I'm unwilling to reach out for help. Or ask for advice. My sister might disagree, and I can admit it doesn't always come easily, but I've done plenty of both.

If my dad had kept things going the way he had been, our vineyard would have gone tits up less than three months after I took over the finances and operations.

Instead, I faced his poor management head-on, righting as many wrongs as I could in as little time as I could manage. I have plugged up every financial hemorrhage and cleaned up the budget. And I got the restaurant up and running by the skin of my teeth.

But not with the budget my dad gave me. That number wasn't even enough to hire a chef. So I took out a personal loan, deciding to go all in on saving the vineyard, even if I'll be paying off that debt until I'm in my eighties.

Leveraging myself was a big risk, but so far, it has proven worth it.

I still worry, though. I worry it's not enough. I worry that the decisions I've made weren't the right ones. That my choices about how to restructure things will bite me in the ass.

What I refuse to do, though, is lay down and die.

I refuse to let the legacy I've worked so hard for crumble when I've barely gotten my chance.

I will not let us sink, even if that means I spend every waking moment kicking under the surface so we stay afloat.

It takes about fifteen more minutes to get home, but then another thirty to unload the truck with Dad and Wes. I race back to the house and hop in the shower, then pop into the kitchen to make a quick lunch before I need to head over to the cellar.

I'm stepping in for Naomi for a few days, covering some of her daily winery tours while she and Edgar are getting the property fully prepped for the harvest. Normally, Micah is the tour backup, but they need his hands as well. When harvest season comes around, everyone becomes a jack-of-all-trades. It doesn't matter who's doing something as long as it's getting done.

It's been a few months since I've needed to do a tour, and I'm always on edge right before I have to do anything forward facing, so my attitude is already sour when Vivian walks into the kitchen, looking as radiant and breathtaking as she does every time I see her.

"Do we need to have another conversation about how you're stalking me?" I ask her, bracing my hands on the island.

She purses her lips, exasperation clear in her expression. "I'm here about last night. Can we talk in your office?"

"There's nothing we need to talk about, Vivian." I wipe my hands on a paper towel and chuck it in the trash. "I think we said enough, don't you?"

We also don't need to go anywhere more private, though I don't say that part out loud.

"Well, tough. I have something important to say, and you are going to stand there and listen to me say it."

I chuckle, shaking my head. The shit she says.

"Sorry. Can't right now." I glance at my watch. "Heading off to do a winery tour."

She opens her mouth but I speak again, cutting her off.

"And the harvest begins next week, so all of my free time is wrapped up in covering these tours, in case you're hoping to ambush me later." I grin at her. "Or tomorrow. You seem like the type."

At that she rolls her eyes, and as I stalk from the kitchen, I hear her call out from behind me.

"I'm definitely the type, Memphis! I'll be seeing you soon!"

I shake my head, unable to wipe the stupid smile off my face.

How is it that I can be so exasperated by her and so enamored with her at the same time?

The truth is that there is a part of me that wants to know what Vivian has to say. But that's only because a part of me hopes she'll bulldoze through my decision to keep her at arm's length. At ten-foot pole length. At football field length.

That we might end up hot and sweaty together again.

My neck goes hot at the memory of last night.

God, how it felt pumping inside her. The way her hands gripped my body, battling for control. Fuck, even just the tangle of our tongues.

If Vivian felt even half of what I did in that break room last night, I can only guess that's what it is she wants to talk to me about.

And I don't want to hear it.

Because it would be too easy to find myself giving in to that desire to be with her again.

Chapter Eight

Vivian

I shake my head and lean over the guitar I'm holding, erasing the notes at the end of the third staff, accidentally erasing the lines as well.

The fact that I came on this trip and didn't bring any music sheets is absolutely unbelievable. I can't remember the last time I went *anywhere* without a pad of staff paper, knowing that inspiration can come out of nowhere and in the least likely moments.

And inspiration has officially struck.

I woke in the middle of the night with a melody in my head and a chorus of lyrics, almost like I'd dreamed them into existence. I'd rolled out of bed and onto the floor, surely terrorizing the people in the room below mine, then ripped through my stuff before realizing I didn't have what I needed.

So I haphazardly created my own music sheet, which has proven very frustrating all fucking day.

At some point I'll need to visit the little music store next to the café and get some new staff paper, among other things. But apparently they're closed on Mondays.

Rude.

There's a kind of sizzle that happens at the base of my skull and along the back of my neck when I've truly tapped into a vein of creative genius. Those spidey-senses are tingling through my entire body, bringing something to life that I haven't felt in a long time.

It's been years since I've felt like this, and I would be an absolute fool not to recognize the possible connection to the sexual magic that happened between Memphis and me last night.

It was . . . transcendent.

And I can't ignore the muse when it arrives. Especially not when the future of my musical career rests on my ability to produce several more songs. Songs I need to record in . . . I glance at the date on my phone . . . exactly two weeks from today.

Which isn't enough time, if I'm honest.

But I can put my nose down when I need to, which is what I've been doing.

And I have the pieces of two songs swirling around each other in my mind, battling for attention.

The one that's winning right now is something I imagine to be my first single. I don't know why I think that when I've always assumed "Sharp Heart" would be. It's my favorite song I've ever written, an angsty piece I wrote in a fit of rage when the guy I was sleeping with at the time began to slowly cut me out of his life without telling me.

I truly believe it's the reason Humble Roads signed me in the first place.

But now, with this song beginning to tumble its way out of my head and onto the paper in front of me, I'm not so sure if "Sharp Heart" will be the showstopper I've always believed it is.

Now I wonder if maybe whatever this is that I'm working on might take its place.

A cool breeze ripples over my skin, but I don't stop to grab my sweater from the car. Instead, I push on. My notebook sits open in front of me, my phone on one page and my wallet on the other, holding them down against the tiny bit of wind that is rushing through the park.

I saw this spot on my way back into town from the vineyard, a beautiful little green space with a white gazebo and a bunch of picnic tables. It called to me, for whatever reason. So I pulled over and lugged my guitar out of the trunk, picked a sunny corner, and sat my ass in the grass.

And the music has flowed out of me ever since.

Which is also why I refuse to give up in my quest to talk to Memphis.

The man is infuriating. The idea that there is so much demand on his time that he can't talk to me for five minutes is just plain stupid.

The tour thing sounds like such a cop-out, too.

I adjust the tuning pegs slightly, laughing to myself.

God, I should sign up for one of his tours. Then he'd be obligated to talk to me.

My fingers slow as I think that over again, wondering if maybe . . .

I laugh.

It might be the most perfect idea ever.

I grab my phone and do a quick search for the Hawthorne Vines website, clicking around until I find information about the daily winery tours.

Blah, blah, blah, groups of ten once a day on weekdays and twice a day on weekends, blah, blah, blah, ends with a trip to the tasting room. Then I select "buy tickets."

Looks like the tour for tomorrow has two tickets available.

I smirk.

But then I see that Wednesday's tour has eight available.

Mischief rolls through me, and I don't even give myself time to think it all the way through before I'm checking out, eight tickets in my cart.

If there are a ton of people on the tour, he'll find a way to ignore me. I don't doubt that. It's in his nature to be as difficult as possible. And if I were to buy up all the tickets for, say . . . Friday, when all ten are still available, I'm sure he'd cancel the tour. The man loves nothing more than to storm out of a room.

But if there's one or two other people . . . I mean, there's no way he'd cancel on someone else, right? He'll *have* to give me his attention.

I double-check my email to make sure the confirmation has come through before I set my phone aside, feeling pleased and rather devious.

My muse is speaking to me, and I will let nothing get in my way to make sure it is heard.

◆ ◆ ◆

"Hey, Errol, how's your day going?"

He lifts his head, smiling at me as I stop at the desk where he's making notes in some kind of ledger.

"Hello, Miss Walsh. I'm doing well, thanks for asking. How about you?"

I lean on the counter and rest my chin in my hand. "Fantastic, actually."

"I'm so glad to hear that. Have you tried out the soaking tub yet?"

"Unfortunately not. But I'm hoping to, soon. I've been surprisingly busy since I got here. Which is actually what I was hoping to talk to you about."

Errol puts his pencil in his large black book and then closes it, setting it to the side.

"Is there some kind of community calendar? Or a place I can look up the events going on while I'm visiting? I want to fit in as much as I can while I'm here, and I might try to go to that . . . movie night thing."

"There is!" he says, placing a hand on his chest. "I apologize that I didn't give you the community hall's event calendar when you checked in. That was my mistake."

He turns and tugs a flyer out from a little shelf behind him.

"There's the movie night this weekend, and the Fall Festival next month. And there's also information about which vineyards have events coming up. Some of them do more than just wine tasting. Some of them host scavenger hunts or concerts. And then there's always the grape stomping, which is very popular."

I briefly eye the schedule, then tuck the flyer into my purse.

"Thank you so much, Errol. Time for me to take in what this community has to offer."

He grins. "Hey, before you head out, I wanted to tell you . . . I heard you singing to yourself this morning when you were walking through the lobby, and you have the most beautiful voice."

The genuine way he says it hits me square in the chest, and my hand raises to that spot to hold his compliment close.

"Oh my gosh, that is . . . the sweetest thing to say. Thank you so much."

"My wife had a voice like yours, one that makes people want to stop and listen, no matter what they're doing." His eyes grow wistful, briefly, the little wrinkles on his face growing more pronounced before his bright smile returns in full force. "Make sure you use it as often as you can. Everyone should hear it."

"Well . . . thank you. Seriously," I reply, my heart panging a little bit for him. "You've absolutely made my day."

"You have a great day, sweetheart."

The compliment from Errol is a welcome surprise in my day and a pleasant little thing in the forefront of my mind as I take a break to grab a quick lunch. But then I'm right back to work, tweaking my words and playing around with the notes on the bridge. I record my guitar melody on my phone and put in headphones so I don't disturb any of the other Firehouse guests as I work late into the evening.

On Tuesday, I hit the coffee shop again, enjoying the bit of consistency in my Rosewood routine. Then I finally take time to visit the music store, a little mom-and-pop place called Harmony and Vines. They sell local wines, of course, alongside hand-crafted instruments. I spend far too long perusing everything, ultimately leaving with a bag full of necessary goodies: an array of sheet music, a couple of colorful picks, and a shirt with the store name because I can't handle how cute it is and I'm a sucker for vintage tees.

Then I hit the road, driving slowly along the winding roads and rolling hills of Rosewood, stopping any time it feels right. My day is spent between random parks and lookouts, plucking at my guitar strings, working on the lyrics, and letting the muse speak to me.

There's something really settling about it. It takes me back to when I was in high school. I'd pull out my guitar during lunch and sit beneath a shady tree with my friends. It wasn't like I sat at lunch serenading everyone with my guitar every day. I've always been a social butterfly, and many of my days were spent laughing and talking and being a bubbly teenager. But there were other days when the mood would strike me, and I'd flutter my fingers along the strings, playing a melody I was still figuring out.

The creative process is filled with *figuring it out* moments, which is why it's normally so time consuming. I can think about a song over and over again, ad nauseum, and still not find the right words. And then bam, something will happen and I'll figure out how to say the exact right thing, wondering how I didn't see it before when it was right there the whole time.

On Wednesday, I arrive early to Hawthorne Vines, hoping to visit with Murphy at the restaurant for a little bit before my semiprivate tour of the property.

But when I get there, the hostess, Enid, says Murphy is still in San Francisco. She won't be back until the weekend. Surprising, considering she thought she'd only be gone for a night or two.

I take a seat at the bar and greet a bartender I haven't met before. I decide on a chardonnay before pulling out my phone and sending off a text to my friend.

Me: Everything okay? Enid said you're still in SF

Murphy has shared plenty with me about Wes, her sexy chef boyfriend who gives her the best O's she's ever had. But I haven't heard much about his mom, so I haven't a single clue what they're doing on this trip.

My phone buzzes with a reply as I'm taking my first sip of the crisp white wine.

Murphy: Yeah, the trip is just a lot different than I was expecting. I'll update you when I get back! But I promise, everything is okay. *smooch*

My shoulders settle a tad, the worry I felt when Enid said Murphy was still out of town beginning to dissipate. She's not the type to keep things to herself, so if something was wrong, she wouldn't hide it.

"How's that wine?"

I look up at the bartender, a handsome man maybe a few years older than me, with a thick beard and a genuine smile on his face.

"It's delicious, thanks," I reply. "I'm a chardonnay snob, and this is one of the best I've tried in quite a while."

He rests one hand on the countertop, the other on his hip. "The 2016 reflects the dry spell we had that year."

"Yeah," I say, lifting it to my nose. "It's got a toasty vibe."

"That's the oak barrels and a bit of vanilla." He chuckles. "Toasty vibe. I like that."

I laugh. "I call it like I see it."

"Cory," he says, sticking his hand out.

I set down my glass and place my hand in his. "Vivian. Nice to meet you, Cory."

"I've seen you here before. A couple of days ago. You visiting or new to the area?"

"Ah, visiting. Just in town for a few weeks for a little working vacay. Murphy told me Rosewood is the best place for an escape, and she was right."

Cory's head tilts to the side. "Oh, so you know the Hawthorne family?"

I swirl my wineglass. "I do. Murphy and I have been friends for a long time."

"You from LA, then?"

"Yup. Born and raised."

He laughs. "I didn't think anyone was actually *from* LA. I thought everyone moved there from somewhere else."

I laugh too, enjoying the truth in his words.

But before I can respond, a familiar figure steps behind the bar.

"Are we working, Cory? Or flirting?"

Memphis's question clearly flusters the bartender, but instead of giving Cory a chance to say anything, Memphis speaks again.

"The kitchen needs help with bringing out dishes."

It takes a second for Cory to understand he's being dismissed to go help somewhere else in the restaurant. Once he does, he tucks his bar rag into a back pocket and heads that way, barely glancing my way as he goes.

"It would be nice if I could talk to *any* of your bartenders without you sending them off to do something else like I'm some kind of leper."

"You know what *else* would be nice? If you weren't always trying to talk to my bartenders."

I smirk, leaning forward. "A little jealous? Because I promise you, I have no interest in Cory. There's only one man in this restaurant that I want to see naked."

His nostrils flare. "You already saw me naked," he grumbles, his voice dipping low.

"No, I *felt* you naked," I reply, my eyes trailing him up and down. "In the pitch black. And since I don't have infrared vision, I can guarantee you that I have not seen all I want to see." I pause. "Yet."

Memphis shakes his head, his lips upturned the tiniest bit. "You are incredibly stubborn."

"I prefer tenacious. Speaking of seeing you naked, I have a proposal for you."

He winces and glances at his watch in an overly dramatic fashion. "So sorry, but unfortunately I have somewhere to be, so . . ." Then he taps the bar top twice and heads off, just as Cory returns with a glass rack filled with freshly washed wineglasses.

"Thanks for the wine," I tell Cory, dropping cash on the bar as Memphis pushes through the back patio door and steps outside. "I'm sure I'll be seeing you again soon."

I haven't gotten a full tour of the property yet, since Murphy was supposed to take me around but then got pulled away to San Francisco. Thankfully, the instructions about where to meet for the tour were very simple and specific. All tours now leave from the restaurant patio.

Following Memphis's path, I step out onto the patio, grinning when I spot him. He's standing in a corner near a path that leads out into the vines, next to a small sign that reads VINEYARD TOURS. A cute young couple is with him, and he chats casually with them as he waits.

Then he sees me, and I know I don't imagine it when he seems to stand up a bit straighter.

Sometimes, I like to pretend that other people imagine me walking toward them in slow motion, and this is one of those moments.

I'm wearing a cute skirt, a short sleeve turtleneck, and a pair of boots that will be perfect for walking along the mulchy pathway through the vineyard. The outfit says "I want it to be autumn, but it's not cool enough yet." And I can see clearly in my mind's eye what Memphis sees as I stride toward him.

Tenacity.

"This the vineyard tour?" I ask, smiling at the three of them as I come to a stop.

"It is," Memphis answers, his eyes narrowed slightly even though a smile still sits on his face. "Unfortunately, the tour is fully booked today."

"Oh, I have a ticket. Let me just . . ." I look down at my phone and click into my email, then hold up my confirmation. "Here it is. My family isn't able to come, though. Which is such a bummer!"

"Your . . . family."

I nod. "Yeah, there was supposed to be eight of us. We reserved tickets and everything, but wires got crossed, and Uncle Bob ended up booking everyone spa treatments." I shake my head. "They're all over at some bougie place in Sonoma, but I didn't want to miss this tour, so I decided to still come."

"Uncle Bob, huh?" Memphis crosses his arms, a smirk playing at his lips. "Well, how fortunate for us that you've decided to . . . grace us with your presence."

I give him an obnoxious smile and tuck my phone back into my purse.

"I guess this is going to be our group, then," he continues, eyeing the other couple before returning his gaze to mine. "Let's go ahead and get started."

Chapter Nine

MEMPHIS

"We house our wine in a few different vats, depending on the kind of qualities we want a particular wine to have."

I turn, gesturing to the more than three hundred oak barrels stacked on top of each other in our wine cellar.

"Our most common are the oak barrels you see here. These are key in developing some of the more pungent flavors and aromas that winemakers discuss when they're sharing about their wines. You'll hear wines described as having hints of vanilla or cinnamon, hazelnut and tobacco, among other things. And all of that has to do with the type of wood that makes up the barrel, and how it was toasted during its manufacturing."

The couple on the tour—Max and Jolie—wander down one aisle scanning the oak barrels as I continue to share.

"We primarily use the barrels for our red wines, making up about seventy-five percent of the grapes we produce—merlot, cabernet sauvignon, and pinot noir. However, if you look to the other end of the cellar, you'll see we also have about fifteen stainless steel vats that we use for our whites—those are the chardonnay and pinot grigio."

I go on to explain the differences between the barrels and the steel vats, how many bottles of wine each can produce, and why we use different storage techniques for different varieties. It's my favorite part of the tour, and something I can recite in my sleep.

But I don't care how well you know something—having an attractive woman flirting with you while you're trying to provide information is incredibly distracting.

Vivian's not doing anything overtly outrageous as we take the tour. In fact, she seems genuinely interested in the information I'm providing. She has asked a few really insightful questions, too.

Doesn't mean I'm not hyperaware of her presence.

"Why are the stainless-steel vats so big and the barrels so much smaller?" Jolie asks.

"Great question. We want the red wine to be influenced by the barrels—grabbing those aromas and flavors I mentioned. And the more surface area a barrel has, the more liquid is touching that wood, resulting in either a faster absorption in a smaller amount of time, or a denser absorption over a longer amount of time."

Jolie nods, then turns and says something to Max.

I give them a few minutes to wander around, and as the couple turn down a new aisle, Vivian steps up to my side.

"I love winery tours," she says, gazing around the room. "Each winery does a lot of things exactly the same, but still, each vintage is completely unique."

I chuckle. "That's the magic and the downfall of winemaking. It's nearly impossible to create the same thing more than once even if you have almost identical circumstances. Because no matter what, *something* is always different. The weather, the soil, the new barrels . . ."

"Speaking of magic and creativity," she says, tucking her hands behind her and then bumping me with her shoulder. "I want to talk to you about something very important."

I purse my lips in a reluctant smile. "Vivian."

"Memphis."

"I don't have time for whatever is causing that mischief on your face."

She beams at me. "I certainly have no idea what you're talking about. I am the least mischievous person I know."

"I find that to be unlikely."

"Besides, you look like you have time right now." Then she turns, waving her hands around us. "In fact, it seems to me like you literally have nothing but time."

"There are other guests on this tour."

"Who have probably snuck off to go make out in a corner. Have you seen the two of them? Talk about handsy."

I cross my arms and pin her with a look.

Vivian likes to play, something I'm not accustomed to and something that definitely flips a switch I didn't know I had. It's not that she's funny, exactly. Except she is.

Or maybe it's just that she's fun.

That she doesn't take anything too seriously.

As much as I hate to admit it, almost everything in my life has been far too serious for far too long.

Maybe that's what draws me to her so much.

The fact that I smile around her more than I've smiled about anything in . . . god, in years, maybe.

"So what do you think? Five minutes? Maybe ten? And if you don't like what I have to say, I promise I won't bug you again." She lifts her hands and gives me the rock symbol, her pinkie and pointer finger raised up. "Scout's honor."

Letting out a long sigh, I decide to give in.

It's only five or ten minutes, like she said.

And realistically, I'll probably spend at least that much time thinking about what it is she would have said to me had I given her the few minutes she's asking for.

"Fine. Five minutes."

"Ten."

"Five."

"Nine."

I pin her with a look, and she pins me right back.

"Eight."

She beams at me, then sticks her hand out. "Deal."

I don't imagine the little thrill that runs through me when I take her hand in mine. I release her just the same to peer down a few aisles. I finally find Max and Jolie—I want to laugh—making out in a corner.

Returning to where I'd previously been standing, I call out to the room, my voice echoing against the concrete walls.

"All right, I think we're going to move on to the tasting room."

Thirty seconds later, the two of them walk out from the row where I'd found them, hand in hand.

"The barrels are so cool," Jolie says.

I glance at Vivian, unable to hide the smile on my face. "They definitely are."

"Enjoy dinner," I call out, giving Max and Jolie a wave as they head off along the pathway back to the restaurant. Then I mumble to myself, "If you even make it there."

Vivian snickers behind me.

She hit the nail on the head when she said the two of them were handsy. I can't say I'm not happy to see them go after watching Max grab Jolie's ass through the entire tasting portion of the tour.

"Thanks for the tour, M," she says as I close the door to the tasting room's patio and turn the lock. "Though I'll be honest, I'll never understand why your reds are where you put all your energy. Your whites are"—she kisses her fingers—"chef's kiss. Especially the chardonnay."

I tuck my hands in my pockets and lean back against the door. I cross one leg in front of the other, surprised by her opinion.

Mostly because . . . she's right.

"Historically, people have consumed far more red wine than white," I tell her, repeating what my dad always said when I brought up this topic in the past. "Our reds have always been the dominant vine, but I agree . . . our whites are better. They always have been."

"So . . . why don't you make more?"

I laugh, kicking off the door and crossing the room to where the tasting glasses are scattered on the counter in the corner.

"It's not that simple," I tell her, collecting each glass and placing it on a tray. "Whenever you plant a new vine, it takes several years before the crop will produce grapes. And that doesn't include all the work that goes into getting it established. Ripping out the old vines and setting new trellises. Then there's the soil analysis."

Vivian joins me at the counter, collecting the handful of glasses I can't fit on the tray and walking with me over to the sink.

"And on top of all the added expenses and years of work, the vines that are now gone aren't producing anything that can be sold in the meantime while you're waiting for the new vines to produce."

"So what you're saying is that it's far more complicated than just 'why don't you make more'?"

I chuckle softly. "It is." And then, before I can stop myself, I add, "And with how tenuous things are right now, we have to be really calculated about the risks we take."

Vivian tilts her head and glances at me, a crinkle in her brow.

I don't know why I said it, and I immediately backtrack.

"But anyway, that's all a bunch of vineyard business stuff that's boring as hell." I glance at my watch. "You have eight minutes. Starting now."

Her eyes fly wide. "What? Not fair! I'm not ready."

I cross my arms and lean a hip against the counter.

Vivian groans. "Okay, fine. Jeez, way to put me on the spot." She licks her lips and twists her fingers together in front of her chest. "How much has Murphy shared with you about me?"

"Not much," I reply. "Just that you were friends from LA. That you write music together sometimes."

"Well, I'm a singer. And a songwriter. But mostly a singer. And I was signed over the summer by a record label to create an album."

My eyebrows rise. "Really?"

She nods. "Yeah. And I'm supposed to go into the studio soon to record, but I'm still working on the last few songs, which has been"—she sighs—"a nightmare for more reasons than I'd like to share. When you spend years perfecting the music that gets you the recording contract, and they turn right around and want you to pump out more music . . . It can be really hard. And I haven't been inspired by much recently."

Then she reaches out with one foot and taps me on the shin.

"Until the other night at The Standard."

I blink a few times, feeling like she's saying . . . What is she saying?

"I don't even know how to explain it, Memphis, but my muse is back. My creative well has been refilled, and you had something to do with it. Sex with you, I mean."

At that, I bark out a laugh. "You're ridiculous."

"I'm not."

"So, what . . . my penis is your muse?"

Vivian laughs, and then we're both laughing. And I'm thankful that at least she realizes how laughable it sounds.

"I'm not joking around, okay?" She shrugs a shoulder. "We are . . . very obviously attracted to each other," she says, her hand waving back and forth between us. "And I want to propose a very casual, no strings attached, no expectations . . . fuck fest."

There's a beat of silence before we both burst into laughter again, the feeling of it like a dam breaking, something inside me that *needed* to laugh like this bursting forth.

"Why are we laughing?" she asks, her hands over her eyes and a smile stretched wide on her face, that beautiful giggle continuing to echo through the tasting room. "It's not supposed to be funny! It's supposed to be sexy!"

Which makes us cackle even harder.

Finally, our fits of laughter begin to subside, and we each take a moment to catch our breath. Vivian checks her makeup in the reflection of a plaque on the wall, wiping the mascara beneath her eyes.

"Okay, let's try this again," she says, spinning back around, her hands on her hips. "I am proposing a friends-with-benefits situation. But I guess we're more enemies than friends so . . . enemies-with-benefits. Bene-mies."

"We are not enemies," I assert, rolling my eyes. "We're just . . . easily incited."

"You mean we want to light each other on fire."

I chuckle again, though it fades quickly. "I mean, you set *me* ablaze."

Her mouth parts when I say it, and I realize that with those words, our laughable conversation has grown more serious.

I meant what I said. There's something about Vivian that sets me on fire in a way I'm not familiar with.

I'm not sure exactly what it is. Maybe it's the lighthearted, playful banter that keeps me on my toes. Maybe it's the explosive physical chemistry that has my skin tingling anytime she's near. Maybe it's a perfect cocktail of both.

But I would be a fool to deny that I'm more than eager to get naked with Vivian again. My mind is quickly making a convincing argument that I could afford to lose an hour of sleep here and there to find a way to make this proposal work.

"Okay, so, how do you envision this working?" I ask, crossing my arms and leaning back on the counter. "Because I'm not making excuses when I say I'm busy. Things are hellish right now, and the harvest starts next week, which is going to put even more demands on my time."

Her lips purse, her mouth twisting side to side as she thinks it over. "I'm not sure. All I know is that I want this to happen. In whatever shape or form it needs to for you to be on board."

I'm on board. I'm more than on board. There isn't anything else she needs to do in order to convince me.

"I want it to happen, too," I tell her, finally deciding to just . . . say it. To put it out there so I can't keep pretending it's not true.

Vivian beams at me, her eyes bright. "How about we . . . keep in contact," she offers, tucking her hair behind her ear. "If you have free time and you'd like me to come around. Or vice versa."

I mull it over. Playing it by ear is probably the only option that really meshes with the erratic nature of my schedule right now.

"I could do that."

"Great, well . . . I should give you my number, then?"

I nod, tugging my phone out, and Vivian does the same.

Once we've exchanged, I slip mine back into my pocket, only to feel it buzz almost immediately. And when I glance at it, surprise rolls through me.

Vivian: Busy tonight?

I smirk and look at Vivian only a few feet away.

"You're determined."

"I prefer tenacious."

Licking my lips, I think it over, knowing I need to get back to the restaurant to help, especially since Wes is on leave for a family thing and still in San Francisco.

"How about this," she says, seeing the obvious conflict behind my expression. "If you find that you have time tonight . . . no matter how late . . . stop by the Firehouse."

Vivian steps forward, her hand reaching out and hooking through one of the loops holding my belt. She tugs me toward her, bringing our bodies flush.

Then she bumps her nose gently against mine.

"Maybe we can have some more . . . ice cream."

She kisses my cheek and backs off, giving me a flirtatious little wave before walking out the door.

Desire skitters along under my skin, commanding that I call her back. That I make good on the picture I had that first night I met her of the two of us on the tasting room couch. That I make it so her cries of pleasure bouncing off the stone walls are a reality instead of an imagined sound in my mind.

But I tamp that desire back. I now have a very real opportunity to make it happen in the future.

Before, the idea of hooking up with Vivian was a lark. An improbable thing that I never would have made a plan for. Then, it became a one-time reality that I quickly wrote off.

Now, though, it's going to be a tease that lingers on the tip of my tongue, at the edge of my subconscious, barely within my grasp.

And knowing I can reach out and take it whenever I want—whenever *she* wants.

God, if that isn't a delicious sensation.

It's after midnight when I finally send the text.

Me: What would you say if I told you I'm parked outside?

After the tour and her flirtatious proposition earlier, I did exactly what I'd planned to do for the rest of the evening. I went to the restaurant and rotated between managing and busing tables, basically roving around and stepping in wherever it seemed like I could help. With Murphy and Wes gone, it was definitely needed.

No job on this vineyard is too small or too unimportant. My grandfather always said, "There's no such thing as a job that is beneath you." It's something that has guided me for years, especially during the times when it felt like my only contribution was too small to matter.

So when shit needs to get done—whether it's busing tables or laying mulch or suckering the vines—I'm always willing to get my hands dirty.

By the time we wrapped for the night, I was set on heading back to the house and crashing, my early day tomorrow an exhausting reality in the back of my mind. But as I stood in the shower, rinsing away the sweat from the day, I realized I wasn't as tired as I thought. Instead, I felt rejuvenated. Almost amped up.

It only took me ten minutes to shower, change, and hit the road.

Though it did take me a few extra minutes to muster up the courage to text her once I realized how late it was. If there was ever a text that said "this is a booty call," it was this text.

Ultimately, my desire for her won out.

Vivian: I'd say give me five minutes. Room 301

My pulse races at her response, and when I glance up to the third floor, I see a light flip on. It's definitely her, and I can only imagine what she's doing up there right now in the five minutes she requested before I come up.

Eventually I head inside and up the stairs, thankful that there isn't anyone at the front desk to spot me sneaking up to a room in the middle of the night.

When I knock, I hear the soft pad of her footsteps before the door opens.

Her hair is up in a messy bun at the top of her head, and she's wearing a pair of peach-colored silk boxers and a white tank top that is see-through enough for me to see her nipples.

She's sexy as hell. I shamelessly drink her in.

"Hey," she says, pulling the door wide and stepping back to invite me in. "I wasn't sure I'd hear from you."

"I wasn't sure if it would work out tonight," I answer honestly, crossing the threshold and walking a few feet into the room as Vivian closes the door behind me. "But then I pictured you here, wearing something not too different from that," I continue, gesturing to her top, "and I figured I could forgo a full night of sleep."

Vivian grins, and her expression turns teasing. "Well, thank you so much for your great sacrifice," she says, poking my stomach.

I want to laugh. I do. But that desire from earlier is thudding through me and doesn't leave room for much else.

So instead of giving into the usual playful banter, I grab the hand that's poking me and tug her forward. Her eyes widen in surprise, but then my mouth is on hers and she opens for me immediately, just as desperate for this to begin as I am.

I crowd her against the wall at her back, my hands on either side of her face as our tongues dip and slide against each other, my body pressed against hers.

She wraps her arms around my neck, her fingers digging into my hair as she nibbles on my lower lip.

"The bed this time," she says as I kiss my way down her neck. "I want to ride you."

If I wasn't already fully hard, I am now. I groan, rotating my hips and pressing my dick against her, desperate for her touch.

"What if *I* want to ride *you*?" I ask, imagining her on all fours with her ass in the air.

Vivian pulls back and gives me a seductive look. "We can make time for that, too."

"Fuck, the shit you say . . . ," I tell her, but then my mouth is on hers again, and I'm moving us across the room. Once at the bed, I give her a gentle push.

She drops down, her tits bouncing with the movement. I tug my shirt over my head in one fluid movement.

But when I reach for my fly, she sits up and bats my hands out of the way, taking over. She tugs my pants and boxers down, and my cock springs free, rock solid and ready to go.

"God, it's like unwrapping a Christmas present," she says, wrapping her hand around it and pressing the flat of her tongue against the underside and swiping from root to tip.

My head falls back, the wet heat of her mouth making pleasure coil tight inside me.

When I look down again, I find her watching me. She has a devious look behind her eyes, something filled with mischief, probably planning to tease me until I combust.

"Fuck, me," I whisper.

She lets out a seductive laugh.

"I plan to," she says, before taking me to the back of her throat.

Chapter Ten

Vivian

I close my eyes. I love the feel of his hands threading into my hair, guiding me as he thrusts gently into my mouth.

There are a handful of random things I'm *very* good at.

Playing "YMCA" on the harmonica.

Doing tricks with a yo-yo—thank you to that guy in the ill-fitting tuxedo who visited my middle school to put on a show back in the day.

And blow jobs.

I prefer a blow job over the other two, with the right man of course.

There is nothing more incredible than the power I feel when I'm on my knees. Especially in a moment like this one. I open my eyes, finding Memphis's eyes locked on what I'm doing, his lips parted, his pupils blown. There's a reverence on his face, like he can barely believe what's happening. Like he'd do absolutely anything to prolong the pleasure I'm giving to him.

I reach out and take his balls into the palm of one hand and wrap my other around the base of his dick, tugging on one and stroking the other.

His eyes close again, and he groans, his hip movements becoming more erratic as I change up my timing and tempo.

I revel in it.

In the way I make him lose that tightly wound control so quickly.

In how his hands keep moving, like he doesn't know exactly what to do with them.

In the deep, tortured noises falling from his mouth.

"You keep doing that, I'm gonna come," he says, pulling his dick from my mouth. "And I have other plans before I want that to happen."

That sounds promising.

He pulls me back up so I'm standing and slowly tugs off my top. He eyes my breasts for a long beat before he stoops and takes one nipple into his mouth, then the other. Then he squats and pulls down my shorts and panties in one motion, before guiding me back on the bed.

"Time to taste this pretty pussy," he growls, tugging my ass to the edge and settling between my legs, one resting on each shoulder.

His tongue slips through my folds, leaving no nerve untouched, before he spreads my lips with one hand, slides a finger inside me from the other, and then pulses his tongue against my clit.

Apparently, Memphis Hawthorne is *also* good at many things.

And while I can't name off something odd like yodeling or tap dancing, I can say with great conviction that Memphis *knows* how to go down on a woman.

I'm overwhelmed by sensation, by an almost immediate, desperate need to come.

But I can't, because Memphis has taken me straight to the edge of oblivion and then held me there.

"Memphis," I whimper, digging my fingers into the chestnut locks that fall a little messily around his head. "Oh my god, Memphis, I can't . . ."

He growls again, the noise vibrating through me, before stopping completely and standing tall above me.

I tug at my nipples, feeling empty and needy and almost frantic, as he tugs a condom from his wallet and slides it on.

Then he's there, hovering over me, his mouth back at mine and his cock gently pulsing at my entrance. His tongue spars with mine, and

I don't doubt at all that in this moment, he's teasing me. Drawing this out as long as possible.

Finally, *finally,* he slides inside me in one smooth movement, and both of us moan at the sensation.

"Jesus, being inside you . . . ," he says, though he trails off, his mouth dropping to my neck. He sucks and licks at the tender skin as he slowly fucks into me.

My hands slide along his back as he thrusts, gripping the expanse of warm skin, loving the feeling of his muscles bunching and shifting. I desperately want to touch him.

After a few moments, he pulls back and lifts one of my legs. His thrusts become faster and harder. His eyes flit back and forth between the place where our bodies are joined, my tits that are bouncing with the force, and my eyes that are surely clouded with lust.

Little flickers begin to flutter through my body from the place he's hitting inside me, over and over again, until that kindling finally catches, lighting me on fire from the inside out.

"I'm coming," I tell him, surprised at how quickly it has come over me, my pussy clamping down as my body goes rigid.

"Yeah, you are," he says, continuing to hammer into me. "And so am I." And then he cries out, his movements halting as he's racked with the same pleasure I'm coming down from.

A moment later, he collapses next to me on the bed, panting heavily, his eyes closed and a relaxed look on his face.

I love the little dimple in his cheek, the one that shows up when he smiles, and apparently when he comes.

"That was pretty spectacular," I say, twisting my legs together. The last faint flutters of my orgasm hum through my body. Then I pat him on the stomach, twice. "You did okay, too."

His head jerks to look in my direction, and then he chuckles and covers his face with his hands.

"The shit you say."

I giggle. "I give it an eight out of ten," I tell him, still panting. "Mostly because I told you I wanted to ride you and you commandeered the whole thing."

Memphis grins at me. "What is this? Yelp?" he says with a laugh, before his tone grows serious. "Impressed by the individualized attention to detail, even if I had to receive service after hours. Decent orgasm with a side of laughter. Four stars. I mean, what is that?"

I roll to my side as I cackle at his interpretation, wrapping my arms around my middle and turning my face into the bedding to muffle my laughter.

Thankfully, he's laughing, too. When I finally snag his gaze again, I see something there that's soft and friendly. So at odds with the normally obstinate, argumentative Memphis that I've interacted with so far.

"You are . . . unlike anyone I've ever met," he tells me, a bemused look on his face.

"I'm choosing to take that as a compliment," I reply.

Then I kiss him, thinking it'll be a prelude to a quick goodbye. But when I pull back, his hand cupping the back of my neck stops me. He tugs me back in for a kiss that is much deeper than I expected.

Eventually, it slows, and when I pull back this time I see something else on his face.

Surprise.

Then he's pushing out of the bed and standing, grabbing his jeans off the floor.

"I'm gonna head out."

I smile, knowing exactly where his head has gone. "Drive safe," I tell him, also standing from the bed. "I'm gonna hop in the shower, so . . . you can let yourself out, right?"

Memphis pauses as he's tugging his pants on, but then he nods. "Yeah."

"All right, well . . . Thanks. And if you want my honest review, it was a five-star night," I say, winking and then slipping into the bathroom. I quickly shut the door and turn on the water, giving it a chance to heat up.

I don't know what that was, at the end—how our casual banter became something more tender and sweet—but I can tell it unnerved Memphis. I figured the best thing I could do in that moment was make sure he knew I wasn't expecting anything from him.

He doesn't need to stay or give excuses for wanting to leave. We both know exactly what this is. A booty call. A no-strings fling. A chance for us to slake the lust that we seem to boil over with every time we're within a hundred yards of each other.

I'm not going to lie to myself and pretend like I don't feel really deep things when we're together.

I absolutely do.

I wouldn't be human if I didn't feel the very big, very powerful emotions that come along with being physically intimate. It's in our nature.

But those emotions belong in one place—on paper, translated into musical notes and lyrics, ultimately becoming songs that people can relate to. Once purged from my soul, my writing has helped me work through some of the biggest, craziest emotional ups and downs in my life.

I'm not interested in allowing any of the emotions that sex with Memphis inspires to take over my life. Or my mind. Or—god forbid—my heart.

I spend the next two days with my guitar glued to my hip, music sheets spread out in front of me, covered in notes and scribbles and arrows indicating changes and moved words or stanzas.

The creative muse is still speaking, and I have kept my mind open, ready to receive whatever comes my way.

But every creative process requires breaks, and I take one of those on Friday evening when I join Errol for some gelato and cinema at the last Summer Movie in the Park.

I had originally planned to ask Murphy, but she's still out of town. So when my sweet new friend asked if I was still planning to go, I knew immediately that Errol would be the perfect date.

"Thanks so much for coming with me," I tell him as we take a seat at one of the picnic benches next to two teenagers who look like they're on a first date. "I really wanted to come, but I was worried that it might be just for locals."

Errol swats at the air between us. "Nothing is only for locals. It's for the people who care enough to attend. But if you want to, you can consider me your ticket in."

I grin, then scoop another bite of raspberry gelato into my mouth. "Do you know what movie they're showing?"

He shakes his head. "No idea. I always assume it's something for kids."

I take in the children that are everywhere, then laugh. "I think you might be right."

"So tell me . . . What's a beautiful young woman like you doing traveling to wine country alone? I would have thought you'd have a hunky guy with you."

I wrinkle my nose. "There was a guy. But not anymore."

He hums softly. "Sounds like you might still be a little upset about it?"

"He cheated on me," I say, kind of blurting it out. "So, I'm upset about what happened, but I'm glad that it ended . . . if that makes sense."

Errol nods. "It does. So that's why you're on this trip alone? To get away?"

"Yeah. I mean, I'm working. But really, I wanted to leave it all behind and try to give myself a chance to breathe."

He gives me a sympathetic look and pats my hand. "I'm sorry, sweetheart."

I shrug. "It is what it is. He wasn't right for me, and I'm glad we didn't have to go any longer without me realizing it."

"I'm glad you're keeping positive."

"What about you?" I ask, turning my body around so I'm leaning back against the picnic table, my legs stretched out on the grass. "You have a lady love?"

He mentioned a wife and used past tense language, so I'm not surprised when his smile grows reflective.

"Oh, I had the greatest lady love," he says. "Norma was my best friend. That's how love's supposed to be. Someone you can tell your secrets to."

My lips tilt up, and I wish I knew what that was like. My parents were the only example of love I had growing up, and they shouldn't serve as an example to anyone. They only gave off the appearance of being in love when they were around other people, but at home, it was mostly silence, each of them seemingly lost in their own personal world.

Part of me considered for a brief time that maybe Theo and I would be different, though I couldn't have been more wrong. We ended up becoming younger versions of them, every interaction so exhausting that we simply avoided it as much as we could.

"She's been gone a few years now," he continues, drawing me back. His gaze grows distant. "It was her idea to refurbish the firehouse into an inn, and it took us several years to get it done right. She loved everything about it."

"Norma sounds like a smart woman. She had a job she loved and a husband she loved even more. I hope to be that lucky someday."

He hums and pats my hand again, his skin soft and warm. "You will, sweetheart. You will."

I can only hope he's right.

We chat for a bit longer, and Errol asks lots of questions about me being a singer. He's very excited for me when he hears about Humble Roads, Todd, and that I'm recording an album soon.

But once the movie begins, he tells me he needs to call it a night.

"I'm not the spry thing I once was," he jokes. "These old bones need to be getting into bed soon."

"I'll join you on the walk back."

I start to get up, but he waves in protest. "No, no, no. You stay and enjoy yourself. Who knows? Maybe you'll find a new hunky beau, huh?"

I laugh, giving Errol a wave as he walks slowly to the concrete path and then off in the direction of the Firehouse.

I leave the picnic table and head over to the food truck in the corner to grab a little bag of popcorn. Then I settle on the grassy area facing the screen that's hanging between the center posts of the gazebo.

The movie *is* a children's movie, though not one I'm familiar with. I only half watch it. Instead, my mind drifts to the last outdoor movie night I went to. With Theo.

We'd only been dating for a few months, and he took me on a date to a rooftop theater in downtown LA. They were showing *My Fair Lady*, which I *love*. And I remember thinking to myself that this guy really got me. That he understood my interest in theater and music and performance in general. It kind of cemented for me that I was into him, since it made me think he had more range than the kind of bro-ey dates we'd been on so far—sports bars and nightclubs and the like.

It was almost a year later that I found out he'd taken me there on accident. That, originally, we were supposed to get dinner at the sports bar in the same building, but that I'd been so excited about the movie, he'd kind of gone with it.

I hadn't been surprised when I found that out. It actually made a lot of sense. It clarified a few things for me that I was struggling to understand.

God, I wish I'd called things off sooner. Wish I'd taken the time to really reflect on how things were between us before I let them get so bad that they turned into the disaster they became.

I try to be a direct, honest person in my day-to-day life. But for whatever reason, when it came to Theo, I couldn't do it. I couldn't face what our relationship had become. We were roommates with a large number of overlapping friends who, occasionally, had mediocre, half-assed sex.

But neither of us really cared anymore. About our relationship. About the lives we had that barely involved each other.

So I guess, in the end, it makes sense that everything fell apart.

I stay for the whole movie, even though my thoughts are too busy for me to latch on to much of the story. After, I take a slow, meandering walk back to the Firehouse.

Only once I've kicked off my shoes and flopped onto the couch in the corner of my room do I realize I have a text.

Murphy: I'm back! Did you miss me?

I grin, replying immediately.

Me: Desperately. How was SF?

Murphy: Great, actually. Wes's mom decided to go to rehab, so we were there helping her get set up.

Me: Wow, that's a big deal, right?

I don't know anything about Wes's family, but anything to do with rehab has to mean someone's trying. Making the effort. And that's really all you can hope for.

Murphy: It is. I'll tell you more about it later, for sure.

Me: Awesome.

Murphy: But I wanted to invite you over for family dinner on Sunday. It's the night before the harvest begins and it'll be a lot of fun.

I consider it, wondering if it's a good idea.

Not because I don't want to see Murphy. Obviously, I want time with my friend. But because if it's family dinner, my assumption is that Memphis will be there.

And as much as I enjoy yanking Memphis's chain, now that we've hooked up a couple of times, it might be a little too much for me to constantly be in his space. Which is basically what I've been doing since I got here, even if it wasn't entirely intentional.

I smirk.

Except for the vineyard tour. That was intentional as fuck.

Me: Are you sure I won't be intruding?

Murphy: What? Definitely not. It'll be like, thirty people. We have a big dinner and we play games and it's this huge thing. You'll love it.

My eyes grow wide when I see how many people will be there. I know nothing about harvest time at a vineyard except that it's when all the grapes get picked. But I guess it makes sense that there will be more people to help with the job.

And if there are tons of people, it'll be easier to avoid Memphis.

Not that I want to.

I want nothing more than for us to fall into bed again.

Or fuck in a supply room closet.

Or maybe in the back of a car.

I don't actually care where it happens. I just know that it's the best sex I've ever had, and it's clearly having a positive influence on my music. So I'm not ready to give it up after two times.

So. It's settled once I text Murphy back. I'll go to the dinner. I'll mostly ignore Memphis to make sure he has plenty of space.

And then I'll proposition him for sex.

I smirk and roll my eyes at myself.

Perfect.

Chapter Eleven

MEMPHIS

Every year, the weeks leading up to the harvest are exhausting.

We are constantly monitoring the grapes and the weather to make sure we don't need to deviate from our schedule. We net most of the vines to eliminate possible pest issues. We service and clean all our equipment so there are no issues with contamination and no surprises when it's time to get started.

Then there's the staffing. Hiring all the temporary workers, making sure we have the right people with the right knowledge about pick bins and racking wands and destemmers and all the other equipment.

We are also one of the few vineyards that still houses and feeds our workers for the entire length of our harvest days—typically a two-month period, depending on how many people we hire. Three meals a day for fifteen people, plus the cost of renting the bunk trailer that we set up next to the cabins on the west part of the property—it's not a cheap investment.

But it's something we've always done, and while there are lots of *we've always done that* items that can be scrapped and replaced for something more effective, I truly do believe that we get some of the most kind, hardworking, exceptional people applying to work with us year after year because we treat them well.

There might be a day when we aren't able to afford it anymore, but that time is not now, and I plan to keep that as part of our process for as long as I can.

We typically launch the harvest at the beginning of September, and this year, we're right on schedule. The weather looks to be—at least for now—cooperating.

Which means tonight we're celebrating our annual Harvest-Eve—a small, casual dinner for the entire crew that is a thank-you-in-advance for all the work they're going to be putting in. They get fed, we play a silly game, and then everyone gets a good night of sleep before the first fourteen-hour day.

"Anything left that I can do to help you set up?" I ask Sarah, entering the kitchen for the first time today.

In years past, I've offered to help with the food and have caused more problems than I've solved. So it's an unspoken agreement between myself and my aunt that I relegate my efforts to setup and takedown when it comes to meals.

"Yes, baby, can you run out to your father's truck and grab the paper plates? I'm pretty sure he got them but might have left them in the cab or something."

I nod, grabbing Dad's keys off the hook and cutting through the house.

But when I jerk open the front door, Vivian is there, her hand poised to knock.

She smiles when she sees me, but it falls immediately when she sees my face.

"Everything okay?"

"What are you doing here?"

Vivian rolls her eyes. "Nice to see you, Vivian. Can I take your coat?" she says, deepening her voice, I'm assuming, to imitate me. "I don't know who taught you manners, but 'What are you doing here?' is not a polite way to greet guests. Especially when you've put your penis inside them."

My nostrils flare, but before I can say anything, Murphy barrels past me, wrapping Vivian in a big hug.

"I'm so glad you came! This is going to be so much fun." Murphy releases Vivian and then turns to me. "I invited Vi for Harvest-Eve. I think she's a shoo-in for biggest grape."

I purse my lips, but then I remember I'm supposed to be running an errand.

"Welcome," I say to Vivian, who winks at me as I walk past her out the door and toward my dad's truck.

"What do you mean by biggest grape?" I hear Vivian ask my sister before the front door closes.

I let out a sigh as I unlock the truck and tug open the back door. This is . . . inconvenient.

And exactly the thing I was worried about when I first agreed to Vivian's ludicrous but enticing proposal that we enjoy having casual sex with each other.

It's one thing to hook up with someone on occasion.

It's quite another to hook up with someone on occasion who also happens to be regularly coming over to my house and place of business, where our interactions are on full display for family and colleagues.

I grab the plates, shut the truck door, and go back inside, bracing myself for whatever is to come. I don't know how Vivian will act if I don't give her the attention she wants. If she'll be overly flirtatious or jealous or whatever.

When I was in my early twenties, I had a serious girlfriend. Lina lived in Napa, and at the time, I was commuting into town to take business courses at the community college, preparing myself for a future of running the vineyard.

It took a while to notice, but I started realizing that Lina was . . . controlling. She had issues with me talking to other women . . . like *any* women. Servers or bank attendants or even Naomi and the other women who work on our property threatened her, which was preposterous because I clearly need to interact with them on a regular basis.

Lina would drive to Rosewood, show up at the house out of the blue, and expect that I'd be able to drop everything to accommodate her. I usually tried to, but sometimes there was something important going on and she'd rail me about how I didn't give her enough attention or didn't care when she came to visit.

Eventually, it became too much, and I ended things.

So when it comes to Vivian, I don't know what to expect.

Though if I think back to that night in her hotel room, it's easy to see that she didn't really have any expectations. We had a wild ride, and then she thanked me and asked me to see myself out.

And gave me a five-star rating. Jesus, she's too much.

I laugh to myself as I enter the packed kitchen. The line of temp hands stretches out the back door. Seeing my aunt and Micah are helping dole out food and drinks, I put Vivian out of my mind and step in to help. Once we've worked through the line, Sarah, Micah, and I grab our own plates and join everyone for dinner on the patio.

I set my food down in an open spot next to Edgar, a few tables away from where Vivian and Murphy are sitting. I'm thankful, not for the first time, that my aunt Sarah knows how to make massive meals that are both filling and delicious.

The conversation around the table is light and easy. I take the opportunity to learn more about the newbies seated at my table and answer a few questions about what the next couple of months will look like.

"All right, everybody," I hear as we're all finishing up our meals, and I turn to look at my father, who is standing at the end of one table. "I recognize many of you from past years, but there are several brand-new faces. My name is Jack Hawthorne, and I'm part of the family that owns this vineyard."

Then he launches into his speech, the same one he gives every year. He talks about the legacy of this winery. The history of our Harvest-Eve dinner. And he thanks my aunt for cooking and the crew for the work they're going to be doing.

"Usually, I pass it off to my sister at this point so she can share a little about the game we like to play on Harvest-Eve. But before I do, I'd first like to bring my son up here for a second. Memphis, can you join me?"

I blink a few times in surprise, eyeing my dad over the crowd. Reluctantly, I push out of my chair, then cross over to where he is standing, sensing a bunch of eyes on me.

My dad slaps a hand on my shoulder, then continues speaking.

"What many of you might not know is that for the past few years, my son Memphis has been handling most of the vineyard business operations. He's been doing a great job, and I'd like to announce that I've decided it's time to officially designate him as the CEO of Hawthorne Vines."

Shock ripples through me.

"While I still plan to be around, helping out where I can, it's time to step aside and let Memphis's dedication and talent lead the way for the next generation of Hawthorne Vines."

There's a stretch of silence that follows my father's speech. I don't doubt it's because there are many who are as surprised as I am. But then I hear a few claps, before the entire group breaks into applause.

"Memphis, do you want to say anything?" My dad looks at me expectantly.

I lick my lips and chuckle awkwardly. I hate giving speeches, especially when I'm woefully unprepared. And blindsided.

"Well, thanks, Dad, for the vote of confidence. I don't have much to say tonight other than . . . I look forward to seeing where this harvest will take us. Thank you, everyone."

Then I give everyone a small smile and look to my aunt Sarah, who is standing off to the side.

"Sarah?"

As I return to my seat, she launches into her speech, surely sharing information about what meals will look like for the next two months and what her role is at the vineyard.

I assume that's what she's saying because I don't really hear her.

What the fuck was that?

An announcement like that on the night before the harvest?

Especially when we hadn't discussed it at all.

And what does he mean by designating me as CEO? Does that mean he's signing everything over? Or giving me a title? What role is he planning to have?

My eyes connect with Micah's over the heads of our workers.

What does this mean for my brother? He works this land constantly, and though he might not be the business-minded type I am, he's just as passionate about the vineyard. I've always known it was my father's intention to pass the business down to me—his eldest son—as has been the generational tradition since my great-great grandfather back in the early 1900s.

But it's one thing to know it in theory, and another to look your brother in the eyes—the one who busts his ass, laboring, day in and day out—knowing that he's seen as . . . nothing more than an employee.

Something about it doesn't feel right.

I doubt Murphy will care at all. But Micah . . .

He nods at me, his expression soft, before looking away, out to the rows of vines stretched out before us and the muted light in the sky, the sun having already dipped behind the mountains in the distance.

Something wells up inside me. Something that's a mixture of sadness and irritation and confusion. And guilt.

But I do my best to tuck it away. Set it aside for now.

There is plenty of time for me to address . . . whatever this is. For me to make sure that whatever next steps are taken, they're the right ones.

Right now, though, there's work to do.

Twenty minutes later, everyone has finished eating, and we've cleared away all the plates, trash, and tables. The part-time and full-time crew stand at the base of the steps that lead down from the back patio, on the path that leads around and through the vineyard.

My attention snags on a flash of copper-colored hair. Vivian is chatting easily with Murphy and Naomi. She throws her head back and laughs, and I don't miss the many eyes that turn her way, probably observing her in the same way I am.

Part of me is a little surprised that she hasn't come to talk with me at all. I had assumed she'd try to slip by me in the kitchen or sit across from me at a table. But she's been wrapped up in her conversations, completely ignorant of the fact that I've been struggling to keep my eyes off her.

It almost makes me laugh.

There I was, worried she was going to be too demanding or desperate for my attention, and she hasn't looked at me once.

I don't know if I should think it's funny or be offended.

Maybe a little of both.

But then her eyes connect with mine, like she knew exactly where I was standing, and she winks my way before returning her focus to Naomi.

Just like that, I realize how much I want her attention on me.

"What's that look for?"

I turn to look at my dad, who has stepped up to my side. "Huh?"

"That look? Haven't seen a smile like that from you in I can't remember how long."

I wipe my face clean. "I'm not smiling."

My dad turns and looks out to the right where Vivian stands off to the side. I don't miss the way his brows furrow when he spots her.

"Isn't that . . ." He trails off, his eyes flicking back to mine.

I don't doubt he's remembering Vivian from the kitchen last weekend. It might have been the middle of the night, but I doubt anyone who has ever met her has failed to remember her.

She's that kind of unforgettable.

"Is the redhead talking to your sister and Naomi the same one . . ."

"I'd really like you to not ask that question," I say, interrupting him before he can get the entire thing out. "Because I'd really like to not have to answer it."

He studies me for a long moment, then pats me on the back. "All right, son. Good luck with that."

We stand in silence for a moment longer before my aunt puts two fingers to her lips and whistles, calling everyone's attention.

"All right, everyone. On the night before the harvest, we play a little game we call Quest for the Best. Everyone is randomly assigned to a vine, and then you're given five minutes to search the entirety of your vine for the single grape you think is the best."

As much as it pains me to admit it, I love this game. It's one of the few childish, silly things I allow myself to do anymore, and it's always a good time. It's also just good team building to have everyone laughing and running through the vines in a way that's low pressure and a bit of fun.

"I judge the final selections based on weight, color, and taste, and the winner gets a crate of wine from last year's harvest. Jorge has been the winner for the past two years, so I'm excited to see if someone is able to emerge from our newbies and set a new bar." She pauses and gives everyone a sheepish look. "I have *grape expectations* of you all this year."

A bunch of groans emerge from the group, plus a handful of laughs.

"Can I get some more wine with that cheese?" Murphy calls out.

"Oh hush," my aunt says, waving a hand at my sister. "Now, if everyone can please grab a Popsicle stick from Edgar, it'll have your vine number, and then we'll head out so you can get lined up."

It only takes a few minutes for all of us to select a stick, and then we're walking out along the path until we get to the end of the vines.

"What's your number?" Vivian asks, bumping into my shoulder and holding up her stick, which has the number twelve on it.

I grin at her and show her mine. Thirteen.

She grimaces. "Oh, bummer. That's an unlucky number."

"I don't believe in superstitious nonsense like that."

Vivian smirks, then stops at the end of her vine. I continue, stopping about ten feet away at the end of mine. "Neither do I, but I'm very competitive, so I'll take whatever advantage I can get, even the paranormal kind."

Murphy jogs past us both. "Good luck, Vi!" she calls out, not stopping. "Suck it, Memphis!" she adds with a laugh, continuing on to her vine at the far end of the path.

I shake my head, my smile coming easy and my chest light.

Lighter than I was expecting, considering the heaviness of my earlier reaction to my father's announcement. But I can be very good at compartmentalizing, and right now, I don't want to waste my mental energy on my father when I could be focused on having this little bit of fun instead.

Especially with Vivian a few feet away.

"Meet me in the tasting room tonight," I say, the words escaping my mouth before the idea has fully formed in my mind.

Her eyes narrow, and for a second, I worry that she's upset with me. That I've been too forward. That I've somehow asked wrong, or waited too long before suggesting we get together again.

But then she speaks.

"Don't try to throw me off my game, here, Memphis," she says, pretending to roll up nonexistent sleeves, then crouching low. "My mental focus is going to stay entirely on finding the grapiest grape. Keep your ideas about sexy shenanigans to yourself."

"You're a nut," I tell her, smiling wide.

She dips her chin and gives me a look filled with mischief. "Always."

"I'm going to count down from ten, and then you'll have five minutes," my aunt says into a bullhorn. "There will be a one-minute warning, and a countdown for the final ten seconds, at which time everyone must have returned to the end of your vine. Are we ready?"

There are a bunch of cheers, and then she begins counting down.

I take a few steps so I'm standing behind Vivian, my chest to her back. "Make sure, while you're looking for that grape, that you're imagining the orgasm I'm going to give you later," I say, my voice low, just for her. "I'll certainly be imagining the one you're going to give me."

She growls at me—actually growls. But then the alarm sounds from the bullhorn, and she's off, racing down her lane, leaving me in the dust.

I laugh, then take off running down my own row, my eyes scanning the bunches hanging on the vines to my left.

The air around me is filled with laughter and people calling out to each other. I know a handful of people will mostly snoop a little bit and pluck a random grape, while others will take it really seriously. The game itself is a little absurd. The idea that anyone can really find the best grape from thousands in five minutes an impossibility.

But people who work with grapes on a regular basis tend to know some of the secrets that make it easier to identify an area of the vine that has a higher likelihood of producing a big, swollen grape. And having either tagged along with or worked alongside my father and grandfather for twenty-four of my thirty-one years, I'd say I know a few of those secrets.

After a minute or two, I zero in on a handful of bunches, tucked up into the vine at the very top, about two hundred feet from the end of the row.

"I think I found the winner!" I call out, grinning when a handful of retorts come flying back.

"Yeah, right, Memphis!"

"Try again! Mine is way better."

"How do we know you didn't come out here weeks ago to scout your favorite grape?"

That last one was Vivian, and I turn back, peering through the vine to where she's searching.

"Trying to throw me under the bus?" I ask.

She laughs. "Hey, I call it like I see it."

I shake my head and turn around, returning my attention to my bunches to decide which grape to pluck.

The one-minute warning echoes out from the bullhorn just as I make my decision, plucking a fat purple grape from its home. Then I head down to the end of my row and wait for the final countdown.

"Lemme see yours."

I close my fist gently around my grape, hiding it from Vivian.

"Oh, come on. You're no fun."

Chuckling, I hold my closed fist out. "I'll show you mine if you show me yours."

Vivian giggles. "You're a child."

"Rarely. But you bring it out of me."

Something soft crosses her face, and she holds her hand out, her grape resting in her palm. It's a pretty good one, especially considering Vivian isn't a wine worker. I open my fist as well, showing her the one I selected.

She stares at both of them, side by side, then peers up at me with an embarrassed expression. "I can't see any difference."

"Yours is a little bit bigger than mine," I begin. "So you have that going for you. But yours is a little bit lighter, which means it didn't get as much sun and might not have as much sugar."

"You can see a difference in the colors?" she asks, bringing her grape closer to mine, still staring at them. "They literally look exactly the same."

I shrug. "Part of the wine game, I guess."

She closes her fist around hers again, just as the alarm sounds. "Well, I'm still pretty confident. You're going down, Hawthorne."

We all make our way back to the house, where Sarah sits at a table with a scale and a notepad. Then we rotate in front of her, one by one. She inspects each grape, then weighs it, before putting it in her mouth. It's a time-consuming process, and we alleviate the waiting game by passing out small plates of chocolate cake that were prepared earlier.

Finally, after far too long, she stands, grinning at us all.

"There were three contenders for the winning grape. Jorge. Micah. And Vivian."

I hear Vivian gasp. Then she bumps me with her hip. "Told you."

"But when taking all the information, I've decided that the winner is . . . Jorge. Congrats, for the third year in a row."

The crowd cheers, and Jorge waves at everyone with his plastic fork, his mouth filled with cake.

"Thank you, everyone. You're free for the evening. We'll see you all at two o'clock."

Vivian turns to me, a disgusted look on her face. "Two? As in . . . a.m.?"

I nod. "We harvest during cooler hours. Two to six. There's other work that happens during daylight hours, but the actual cutting of the vines and wheeling bins of grapes through the vineyards . . . That's done in the dark."

"God, you couldn't pay me enough to work those hours. I go to bed at two," she offers, laughing.

"Yeah, I'm not a morning person, either. Thankfully, I've been able to avoid being part of the early-morning crew."

She raises an eyebrow. "So . . . you don't need to go to bed? To get a good night of sleep?"

"I don't," I tell her, glancing at my watch. "I have a few hours at least before I should call it for the night."

And several things that I need to get done in those few hours. But I don't say that. Because the part of me that wants to meet Vivian at the tasting room and finally . . . finally . . . hear the sound of her voice echoing off the stone walls is too tempting to resist.

"I'm gonna say bye to Murphy," she tells me, stepping closer and dropping her voice, "and I'll meet you in about thirty minutes."

I lick my lips, something electric racing through me.

For the first time in who knows how long, I'm putting my own needs and wants first.

And it feels fucking great.

Chapter Twelve

Vivian

If I thought being underneath Memphis was a thrill, I can safely say that riding him is even better.

My hands are twisted in his, and he braces me above him where he lies back on the couch, his cock deep inside me as I bounce up and down.

"Fuck, you're so deep," I tell him, struggling to continue, my body shaking every time he hits that spot when I take him all the way in.

I release his hands and then place mine on his chest, gyrating my hips in a way that gives my clit some extra attention. But Memphis regains control, gripping my hips and raising me up before yanking me back down again.

I cry out, the sound of my voice echoing loudly around us.

"Shit," he groans, slamming me down again and again and again.

My voice grows hoarse. I'm nearly to tears, the pleasure overwhelming in the best of ways.

And then that familiar white heat races down my spine before it explodes outward, my mouth dropping open and my eyes slamming shut as I fall apart.

"Look at me," Memphis says.

I force my eyes open again. He thrusts two more times, his eyes locked on mine, before he groans with his own release.

My muscles shake from the exertion. Collapsing on top of him, I try to catch my breath.

"Jesus Christ," he says, his hands against my back. "You're going to kill me."

I giggle. "What a way to go, though, huh?"

We lie there for a few minutes, and I close my eyes, breathing in the scent of him. Sweat and sex and a hint of that cologne he wears, though I can't tell what it is. Something toasty and delicious.

My body is light in a way it hasn't been in weeks. Months, even. A kind of bliss that, sure, can be attributed to the orgasm I just had. But it's more than that.

There's been a restlessness in my bones for a long time. This feeling that the very core of who I am—this ballbuster, playful, silly Vivian—is wrong. Wrong for existing, wrong for playing, wrong for being exactly who she is.

Toward the end, Theo made me feel that way. Like my very existence was a nuisance. Like I needed to be less of me in order to deserve his love.

And when you're faced with that, day in and day out, you start to wonder . . . *Am* I too much? *Should* I change? *Do* I deserve to be loved just like I am?

But lying here, in Memphis's arms, I'm so at peace.

Because the person Memphis knows is nuts. She's crazy and sassy and wild and unapologetically herself.

And he still wants her.

Me.

He still wants me.

And it feels so fucking good to be falling . . .

I freeze, my eyes flying wide when I realize what I almost thought.

Almost.

Almost.

I didn't think it.

But I almost thought it.

Fuck.

Fuck, fuck, fuck.

That is not supposed to happen.

I sit up quickly, pushing off Memphis, very careful not to look him in the eye.

Because to be honest, I don't know what he's going to see there.

"Well, thank you for the ride," I joke, keeping my voice light and jovial as I grab my clothes off the floor and begin to put them back on.

Memphis pushes off the couch and slips his boxers back on. He grabs the blanket he laid down on the couch and wads it into a ball.

"You okay?"

I lick my lips, then turn and give him the most genuine smile I can muster.

"Yeah, why?"

He shrugs. "Just checking." He pauses. "Wanna make sure I wasn't too rough."

My shoulders fall, and I shake my head. "Not at all."

I make quick work of putting my clothes back on, and I'm fully ready to go as Memphis is tugging on his jeans.

"I'm gonna head out." I aim my thumb toward the door. "See you later?"

He gives me another assessing look before nodding. "Yeah. Have a good night, Vivian."

I give him a little wave and then turn, heading out through the door, into the cooling evening air.

My feet move me quickly along the path that leads back through the vineyard to the Hawthorne house, and my car still parked out front. I almost trip a few times in my haste, but I don't think about how fast I'm moving. I just go.

It almost feels like I'm running.

And who knows?

Maybe I am.

◆ ◆ ◆

I'm sitting in the coffee shop waiting for Murphy, earbuds in, a recording of the melody I've been working on playing in my ears, when Theo drops down into the seat across from me.

I audibly gasp, shock ricocheting through my body at his sudden presence in Rosewood. In front of me. Smiling and casual as if him being here is the most normal, natural thing in the world.

"What the fuck are you doing here?" I whisper, pulling out one earbud.

"You wouldn't come talk to me. So I'm here. Trying to talk to you."

The look on his face is fucking smug. I want to slap that smile off, yank him out of that chair, and send him packing.

Theo has always presented himself like he's charming, like he's the great guy any mother would want dating their daughter.

And he ticks all the boxes at first glance. He's classically handsome, with thick dark hair and bright eyes. Confident and well dressed. Successful at his job.

It took me far too long to realize that he's actually a selfish, egotistical asshat.

And that smile is nothing more than a mask that covers up the truth of who is underneath.

"News flash. When someone says they don't want to talk to you, and then they fly to another place to get away from you, and you show up uninvited, that's called stalking."

And not the good kind. Not like what Memphis and I have joked about a few times since I've been here.

No. This is the unwanted kind.

The kind that goes completely against my wishes.

And possibly a few laws.

"How the hell did you even know where I was?"

He sighs and holds up his phone like I'm an idiot. "You didn't turn your tracking off," he says.

As if that's a normal response.

"Jesus, Vi. You act like me being here is some crazy thing." He reaches out and puts his hand on mine. "You know you're gonna forgive me. I'm here to grovel, okay? So just . . . tell me I'm a prick or whatever and I'll apologize and then we can go home."

"Oh my gosh. Theo?"

The sound of Murphy's voice draws my attention, and I find her standing a few feet away, an awkward smile on her face.

With Memphis at her side, an unreadable expression on his.

"Hey, Murphy!" Theo says, letting go of my hand and standing. He gives a big smile before tugging her into a hug.

"Hi, Theo," she says, watching me with wide eyes over his shoulder, patting his back before stepping away. "What are you doing here?"

"Came to visit Vivian. But it's great to see you. It's been a while."

Murphy nods, that same strange look on her face as she glances at me, then up to Memphis.

"Well . . . that's great," she says, before her voice dips slightly and she adds, "I think."

Murphy turns then, gesturing to the man standing behind her, his expression like stone.

"Theo, this is my brother Memphis."

I know what's about to happen before it does, and for whatever reason, I'm helpless to stop it.

Theo gives Memphis that same not-so-charming smile and extends his hand. Memphis takes a beat or two, but eventually he mirrors the behavior, reaching his hand out as well. The two shake briefly.

"And Memphis, this is Theo," Murphy continues.

"Vivian's boyfriend," Theo adds.

I see the flare of surprise in Memphis's eyes, and I'm on my feet immediately.

"*Not* my boyfriend," I grit out, finally finding my voice. "My *ex*-boyfriend, who came here even though I said I didn't want to talk to him."

Memphis's eyes flick between us, assessing the situation, his jaw going tight.

"Oh, uhm . . ." Murphy lets out an uncomfortable laugh.

"Come on, Vivian. These people don't need to know that we're in a rough patch, okay?" Theo turns to me and steps closer. "I told you, I'm here to grovel, right?"

"I don't need you to grovel, and we are *not* in a rough patch," I declare, my voice strong and unwavering. "This relationship is over, and I told you that already. So . . . go home. I'm not fucking around."

Theo puts his hands on his hips. "Vivian, this is getting ridiculous."

"I think she communicated how she feels, and pretty clearly," Memphis interjects. "So . . . how about you give her some space."

His tone is light, but I can see on his face that he's not asking. He's telling.

But Theo is a shithead who doesn't know when to call it quits.

"Look, bud. I get it . . . the whole chivalrous guy thing . . . but this really isn't any of your business."

Memphis takes a step forward, so he's standing right at my side, his eyes like ice as he stares my ex down.

"It actually *is* my business." His voice is tight, brooking no argument. "So, like I said, maybe it's time to back up."

Theo stares at him for a second, then looks at me, a cold smile creeping onto his face. Then he points at Memphis.

"You really started fucking some wine country bumpkin?" he says, his voice callous.

"It doesn't matter what I'm doing or who," I answer, my eyes narrowed. "We aren't dating anymore."

Theo ignores me again and puts his hand on my arm, his grip tightening as what little patience he has left begins to fray at the edges. "Jesus, Vivian, just fucking . . ."

But his sentence cuts off as Memphis grips him on the back of his neck and yanks one of his arms behind him.

"It would be great if you'd learn to listen," he growls at Theo, then drags him out the door.

Embarrassment rolls through me as I see how many people are looking our way, and I wonder how much they saw. How much they heard.

"He's such an asshole."

I hear what Murphy says, but I'm busy watching Memphis and Theo outside, a couple of feet from each other. Theo shouts something. Memphis stares him down and says something quietly. Then Theo finally turns and flips me the bird through the window before storming off down the street.

I shouldn't be surprised that he wouldn't listen to me when I said we were done. That he wouldn't let my answer be enough to leave me alone. I've seen it before, the way he can't seem to let things go when he doesn't get his way. Just another example of the stupid things I've ignored about Theo that are now so glaringly obvious.

Memphis comes back into the coffee shop, his eyes still wild, looking like he could light the world on fire. But he takes one look at my face and something settles.

"You all right?" he asks me, his tone gruff but caring.

I nod but don't say anything, my throat tight.

He licks his lips and turns to Murphy. "I need to take a walk." Then, before she can even respond, he turns and storms out of Rosewood Roasters. Back on the street, he heads away from where Theo went.

Letting out a long breath, I drop down into my seat. An emotional swell builds in my chest as I begin collecting my things.

"Can we hang out another day?" I say, the reality of dealing with Theo making me want to go back to the hotel and crawl into bed. "I'm really not in the mood . . ."

"You don't have to explain anything. I'll call you later, okay?"

I sling my bag over my shoulder, but Murphy doesn't let me slip away. She wraps her arms around me and gives me another big hug.

"I love you."

"You, too," I tell her, before hightailing it out of the coffee shop.

The tears begin to fall only seconds after I've pushed outside. I bat them away, hating how they streak down my cheeks and onto my neck.

I rarely cry. Mostly because I don't think there are that many things in my life that have been cry-worthy. But also because I'm usually one to laugh away my discomfort instead. This, though . . . this was a completely different monster.

Maybe it's foolish of me to cry right now, when I haven't really cried yet. Over any of it. Not the cheating, or the end of our relationship, or purging everything of his from our home.

But him showing up here was a violation that was somehow worse than the cheating.

Being in Rosewood has been . . . such a balm on my soul. A true opportunity for me to take a break from the real world and the real problems going on in my life. And him being here felt like a baseball bat to the back of the head.

A reminder of everything I'm trying to escape.

Him being here shoved my face back into the mess I was trying to avoid thinking about, and what little peace I'd begun to feel is now rattled.

I glance both ways and then walk quickly across the street, the Firehouse coming into view in the distance.

It makes perfect sense, though. That Theo would come here to try and make things work out the way he wants them to, putting his own desires and preferences ahead of mine.

It's always been that way.

And it's just more proof that being with him was a mistake.

One I'm more than happy to be moving on from.

"Vivian!"

I stop at the sound of Memphis's voice calling out to me. I wipe away the tears as best I can as he jogs over. He comes to a stop in front of me a little ways away from the Firehouse.

"Hey. Are you all right?"

"You already asked me that."

"Yeah, but I was angry when I asked before," he says, giving me a tight smile. "And now I'm asking for real."

A few fresh tears roll out from my eyes. "It might not seem like it, because I'm crying, but I'm actually a lot better now than I was before."

His head tilts to the side as his eyes flick across my face.

"I knew I did the right thing, ending my relationship with Theo. We weren't meant for each other. But sometimes you just need . . . something to confirm it for you. You know?" I shake my head, surprised at the honesty as it rolls out of me. "Him showing up here? Acting like that? That might have actually been exactly what I needed."

Memphis's hands flex at his sides. "Can I walk you back to the Firehouse?"

Something warms in my chest at his words. We can literally see the inn from where we're standing, so it's completely unnecessary. It's not hard to see that Memphis, Mr. I'm-Busy-All-The-Fucking-Time, is going out of his way.

"I appreciate that, but actually, I think I'm gonna go on a drive," I tell him. "Sometimes driving and music help me clear my head."

Memphis watches me for a long moment before he speaks again. And when he does, he surprises me.

"So then . . . let's go for a drive."

Thirty minutes later, we're sitting in the bed of Memphis's truck, our backs against the cab with our legs stretched out in front of us, overlooking a beautiful valley.

We haven't said much since we hit the road, the two of us simply enjoying the quiet and the breeze and cooling weather outside as we drove.

But now that we're sitting here, I can feel Memphis's attention on me. I don't doubt he wants me to share what the deal is with Theo. I'd definitely want answers if I was in his shoes—if I was sleeping with someone who suddenly had some woman coming to town claiming to be his girlfriend.

But once I start sharing, I'll have to face some facts about myself, that I haven't necessarily been ready to address.

Not everyone is ready to look themselves in the mirror and accept all the things they see. I'm not sure whether it's that I'm finally ready, or whether it's the ease I feel around Memphis . . . regardless, now feels like the right time to finally come to terms with the reality of my relationship with Theo.

"We were dating for three years. And he cheated on me."

I can see him in my peripheral, looking my way. He doesn't say anything, but I know he's paying attention.

"It might not seem like the most catastrophic thing in the world. People get cheated on every day." I lean my head back against the cab and close my eyes, trying to enjoy the sun on my face as it breaks out from behind a cloud. "But it upset me so much because I wasn't surprised. And knowing that . . . knowing that I'd stayed with someone for that long when I knew in my bones what he was capable of . . ." I trail off.

It's embarrassing.

I see women in the media all the time, or people I'm friends with in real life, and I wonder why they would ever stay with a someone who treats them so poorly. Someone who treats them like they're disposable.

But it's not so cut-and-dried.

"When you start to build a life with someone, even if you're just dating, there are so many things that become intertwined," I tell him. "Routines and friends and housing. Not to mention the emotional investment, the years of being there and putting up with things and seeing little hints at progress. It's like you can't help but hope."

Tugging my legs to my chest, I wrap my arms around them and then put my face in my knees.

"Of course you had hope," he says, his voice warm and comforting.

I turn my head to the side, and his soft eyes meet mine.

"When things are hard, all you really have is *hope*."

I sigh, tucking my face away again, and finally decide to say the real truth. "It's just . . . so embarrassing."

Memphis reaches out and rests a hand on my back, rubbing in calming circles.

"You have nothing to be embarrassed about. It sounds like you gave your partner the benefit of the doubt until he confirmed who he was."

We sit like that for a long moment, Memphis's hand continuing those comforting circles on my back, me with my chin in my knees staring straight ahead, my mind a mess. Thinking over the little things that I've been avoiding since I've been in town.

All the ways he showed me exactly who he was, and how I rationalized each one.

How highly critical he was of everyone we knew, even the people he supposedly cared about, which should have been enough for me to know he was probably just as callous about me when I wasn't around.

The sneaky, underhanded way he approached things.

His inability to deal when he didn't get his way.

The concerns I had about how flirtatious he was with other women.

In the beginning, I didn't say much because I felt like I was still getting to know him. And then the longer that time went on, the more I tried to excuse the things I didn't like by highlighting the things I did. The parts of him that made him the guy I accepted a first date with.

But eventually, those things became negatives as well.

Today is a direct example of the fact he doesn't know how to listen when someone gives him an answer he doesn't like. In the early days, I said he was tenacious, like me.

In truth, he's just a child who didn't know how to accept when things didn't go his way.

"I can't believe he actually came here," I say, shaking my head. "That he tracked my phone and flew here after I'd already told him we were done."

Memphis is silent, his jaw flexing as he stares out in the distance.

"I'm sorry he came," I say.

His head turns to me quickly, his eyes widening. "You have nothing to apologize for."

"You looked . . . upset, though. Before."

Memphis rubs his hand over the stubble on his face, then chuckles.

"I'll be honest, I was surprised when he said he was your boyfriend. But I believed you the minute you said he wasn't. Most of my anger had to do with the way he talked to you."

I feel a little bit of disappointment at that, but I try to tamp it down.

I shouldn't feel anything but relief at Memphis's explanation for why he reacted so strongly to Theo. Especially considering my own visceral reaction to how I felt yesterday in the tasting room.

I should be glad he wasn't jealous.

I should be happy that he was defending me out of common decency.

I should be thankful that his reaction wasn't a revelation that his feelings for me are rooted deeper than he originally planned for.

I should be all those things.

Too bad I'm not.

Chapter Thirteen

MEMPHIS

It's been less than twenty-four hours since my drive with Vivian, and she's been on my mind ever since. Her hair blowing in the breeze as we drove back to the Firehouse with the windows down, the soft way she smiled at me as we pulled up out front, the raspy sound of her voice when she thanked me for taking her on a drive.

A part of me wondered when I'd finally be able to fully focus on work again. But now that my father is standing in front of me, my time with Vivian has firmly taken a back seat in my mind.

"You wanted to talk?" he asks, taking a seat on the opposite side of my desk.

"Yeah. Thanks for coming by," I reply, leaning back in my chair.

It's like I've called him in to talk to the principal . . . and I'm the principal. An odd feeling as a son looking to speak with his father, but it is what it is.

"Look, I wanted to talk to you about the announcement at Harvest-Eve."

He shrugs. "What about it?"

"I appreciate what you were trying to do by giving me a vote of confidence and sharing it with everyone, but . . . don't you think it's something we should have talked about first?" My tone makes it clear that we absolutely should have talked about it first. "I mean, you dropped that bomb on everyone right before one of the busiest times of the year."

My dad shakes his head. "It's not dropping a bomb, Memphis. Everyone knew this was coming."

"I didn't know," I reply, frustration growing at his indifference to something that, to me, is a big deal. "You've been handing things over to me, but I had no idea this was coming my way so soon. Did you ever think to talk to me about it first? Make sure I felt prepared? Maybe ask me if this is what I wanted?"

The surprise on his face is enough for me to know that he never considered any of those things.

"I assumed that, with everything moving the way it has been, that you understood this was the ultimate goal. To pass everything over to you."

"But you always assume things, Dad. You never take the time to ask the questions that will get the real answers." I push out of my chair and walk to the window, looking outside at the vines that stretch into the distance. "Of course I want to be part of this vineyard's future. I've been working toward that my entire life. Obviously, I knew things were moving in that direction. But that doesn't mean I'm ready."

"You're ready, Memphis."

"I'm not!" I spin around, my hands on my hips as my frustration boils over. "I'm not ready for it to all be on my shoulders when I'm buckling beneath the weight as it is. And the fact you can't manage to fucking sit down with me and talk about anything is infuriating. I don't want you to dump everything at my feet."

"Well, sometimes that's how it happens, Memphis," my dad says, standing suddenly, his voice raising as well. "Not everything gets to be a picture-perfect ceremonial passing of the torch, and sometimes, you just have to handle the shit that's shoveled your way. You think it was easy for *me*? To step into that role when *my* dad died? At least I'm still here to talk to you about things if you need me. I had *nobody*."

"Bullshit I have you to talk to," I shout back. "Any time I try to bring anything your way, you look like you want to sprint from the room. And sometimes you do. Trust me when I say that I'm just as alone in this as you were. And it's that much more horrifying because you are *right there*, and you could help if you wanted to. But you don't. Because you don't care. You don't give a flying fuck about this vineyard, and you never have."

"You have no idea what things were like for me. What they've *been* like for me. Or the kinds of sacrifices I've had to make. So until you can say you've given up everything in your life for this place, keep your goddamn opinions to yourself."

He turns and nearly runs into Micah, who is standing wide-eyed at the threshold.

My brother and I stand there, silent, while our father storms down the hall. A slam of the front door echoes through the house.

"What was that?" Micah asks, glancing back over his shoulder in the direction Dad went. "I don't think I've ever seen him like that in my entire life."

I sigh, dropping back into my chair and resting my face in my hands.

That was Dad, finally having a fucking breakdown.

But I don't say that.

"He'll be fine," I say, running my fingers through my hair. "Once he gets over himself," I add with a grumble.

Micah takes a seat in the spot Dad just vacated, but he doesn't say anything for a few minutes, which I appreciate.

He's good like that, knowing when to give people time.

"What can I do for you, Micah?" I ask him eventually, once I've finally taken that wild conversation and tucked it safely away to deal with later.

He eyes me warily, but I shake my head.

My brother clears his throat, and then he sits up a little bit straighter in his chair.

"In the past I always brought this stuff up to Dad, but . . . now that he's announced you're in charge, I figure I should come to you. I'd like to recommend that Naomi get promoted."

I blink a few times, my confusion likely evident on my face. "What do you mean?"

Micah chuckles. "I'm sure you know what a promotion is, Memphis."

I grin sheepishly, then sit up in my chair. "I do, but we don't really have a hierarchy here for the vineyard crew. You know that. So there isn't really anywhere for Naomi to be promoted *to*."

He takes a deep breath. "That's the other thing I was hoping to talk to you about."

Leaning forward, he slips a folder onto my desk. I open it and do a quick scan through the materials—an organizational chart, a sheet of position descriptions, and a proposal for salary changes.

My eyes flick back up to his.

"You want to restructure?"

He nods, but he doesn't say anything else. Just sits quietly while I review everything he's brought to me.

It's a completely different organizational model that redistributes a lot of the responsibilities. But it's clear that Micah has put a lot of work into this.

"All right," I say, leaning back in my chair and motioning to my brother. "Tell me your thoughts."

Micah looks surprised for a second, but then he launches into a proposal. One where everyone is given a lot more independence and where individual skills are utilized in a much more intentional way.

It would be a huge change from the way we've always done things, mostly because it separates all the vineyard operations into three departments—hospitality, vineyard management, and business operations. Literally . . . a complete restructure.

"What do you think?" he asks, once he's finished explaining it all to me.

"I think . . . that you are really fucking smart, Micah," I tell him, spinning the organizational chart around to look at it again. "How long did this take you to come up with?"

He shrugs, though he looks pleased at my assessment. "I've been playing around with it for a couple of years."

"Why didn't you say anything before?"

"I did."

I furrow my brow.

"But this wasn't the kind of thing Dad wanted to talk about. You know how he is. He wanted to do things the way he'd been taught, even if those methods don't work anymore."

I grunt my acknowledgment.

"And I haven't taken any business classes like you, but it felt like something I could see so clearly and could make a big difference from an internal perspective."

"You *do* see it clearly. Now I'm wondering why I couldn't."

But Micah shakes his head. "You're busting your ass trying to keep our doors open, right?" he says, surprising me. "Sometimes when you're looking at something too closely, you aren't able to take a step back and see the bigger picture. If you only ever see things in black and white, you can miss the gray." He shrugs again. "I don't doubt you would have seen something like this if there weren't so many other things on your plate."

I'm not sure what to say, exactly, so I don't say anything. Instead, I return my attention to the documents in front of me.

"Let me sleep on this for a few days," I ultimately tell him. "But I like this, Micah. I really like it."

He stands, that unassuming smile on his face. "Hey, no pressure. And if you decide against it, you know, I support you. I know you're doing what you think is best."

Then he gives me a wave and takes off, the sound of his boots echoing on the tile down the hall until they fade away.

I have to admit, I'm shocked by that conversation. Not because I didn't think my brother was capable of bringing that kind of business savvy to the table, but because I've never seen him do it.

Though I guess that's not surprising, either.

If you're working in an environment that doesn't reward innovation, doesn't value change and improvement, and is only focused on "how it's always been done," there isn't really room for conversations like the one we just had.

It further highlights to me a fact I've known for a while now.

We are overworking our staff but underutilizing their skills.

And if we don't figure out a way to get better about both of those things, this vineyard won't stand a chance.

The frustration from my argument with Dad earlier simmers in the back of my mind all day. Eventually, I seek out my aunt, approaching her after dinner to see if she has a few minutes to chat.

"I'll handle cleanup tonight," Micah offers. "You two take off."

"I'm not going to turn that down," my aunt replies with a laugh, and then the two of us step off the patio and begin a stroll into the vineyard.

We used to do this when I was a kid, wander around and race up and down the pathways. Murphy and I always had a ton of energy, and when we first moved here after my mom died, Sarah would take us on nightly walks to help us get out our zoomies.

Sometimes my grandmother joined us, but mostly it was just Sarah, pushing a stroller with Micah tucked inside.

So any time my aunt and I have a long conversation, it feels natural to walk out along the paths that weave through the vines.

"Did you ever think you'd be the one to take over the vineyard?" I ask, once we've gotten a few minutes away from the house. "That grandpa would have given it to you, instead of Dad?"

She tucks her hands into her pockets. "There was a time when I hoped he would," she answers. "But I knew he was old world, and passing down a business to your son is what he'd always planned to do."

"For a while it wasn't an option for it to go to Dad, though, right? Because he wasn't here."

After my dad graduated from high school, he left the family behind and moved away with my mom—his high school sweetheart. Together they created a new life in San Francisco away from the responsibilities of the vineyard and small-town Rosewood. Based on everything I've ever heard, that's what he always wanted. To leave. To find something different.

But when I was seven and my mom died, he returned and slipped back into the role he'd left behind. The one he never wanted.

Sarah exhales heavily. "Yeah, and during that time, all those years your dad was away, *my* dad refused to discuss the future of the vineyard. Just . . . adamantly refused. Would redirect the conversation if your grandmother or I brought it up at all."

"I guess Dad gets his stubborn attitude honestly, huh?"

She laughs. "That he does."

"And if I asked you if you wanted to be in charge of the vineyard *now*?"

We come to a stop where the path splits, and Sarah looks at me warily.

"If I said I'd pass over the reins to you, instead of having them come to me . . . If I said you should have always been the one in charge, what would you say?"

I've thought this over a few times in the past months, but it's been an ever-present, looming idea in the back of my mind since my father made his announcement a few days ago. How much easier it would be to not have to deal with it. To pass the responsibility over to someone who will do it right.

I know Sarah would do it right. She loves this work. She loves everything about Hawthorne Vines. And she has a smart, level mind.

And I don't doubt that my grandfather should have looked to Sarah as the next person to oversee the business. As much as I loved him, and as smart as he could be, he was blinded by the same thing that blinds my father: pride, and the mentality of "that's how it's always been done."

Sarah has acquiesced to that in the past, because the men around her have dictated it that way. But I see the excitement she has when we decide to do something new, when change is around the corner.

So it wouldn't be far-fetched to believe that she could be a great leader for this company. For our family. For the next generation of Hawthorne Vines.

"Oh, sweetie," she says, reaching out and squeezing me gently on the shoulder, a mixture of appreciation and sadness in her eyes. "I love you for that. I do. But those days are behind me."

I shake my head. "That's not true."

"It is, Memphis. I'm nearing sixty, honey. And even though I have a lot of life left in these bones, the days of me running a business are long gone."

My shoulders fall, the disappointment of her words hitting me.

She loops her arm into mine and gives me a tug, getting us to continue walking where the path veers to the right.

"There was a time when I would have jumped at that kind of offer. When I would have had all the energy and optimism that you need when you're taking over and leading a company in a new direction. But now, it's your turn. You and Micah and Murphy. It's a chance for you to champion this vineyard and see what you can do with it."

Sarah rests her head against my shoulder as we walk, and I don't doubt for a second the motherly affection she has for me.

"But I keep feeling like I'm doing the wrong things," I finally tell her, the fear I've been holding on to finally tipping over the top and spilling out. "What if I run this place into the ground?"

"I've been watching you handle the problems you've faced, and I don't doubt for a second that you're making the right choices." She stops us. "And you wanna know why I think that?"

I blink at her, waiting for her next words like a little kid, desperate for her approval.

"Because you're smart, Memphis. You're smart, and you're intentional, and you're doing what you think is best, and that is all we can ever do."

I think over my conversation with my aunt late into the evening, reconciling what she said with the things I know to be true.

Even though part of me regrets that she feels it's past her time to head the company, her answer also settled something in my soul. For years, I've wondered about how she feels when it comes to the family business and what role she has played in its longevity. And while I'm sad that there was a time when she wanted that opportunity and didn't take it, there is a pride inside me knowing that she believes in me and what I can do.

But not just me.

Me and Micah and Murphy.

When I was a kid, sitting on the ATV and following Dad and Grandpa around the vineyard, I felt like part of a team. Like we were all in it together.

The more I think about what the future holds for us, the more I'm starting to think that mentality is the right mindset to have.

The reason I'm this stressed and exhausted and overworked is because I'm trying to do it all alone. I'm trying to carry the burden alone, when the better choice—the smarter choice—is for us to take on whatever comes next together.

The phone rings three times before she picks up, and when she does, an unfamiliar warmth spreads through my chest.

"Well, hello, Mr. Bartender."

I smile like an idiot, glad she can't see me on the other end of the line.

"Hey. Wanted to check in. See how you're doing."

She hums, and even though there's nothing sexual about it, the sound still zips through me, pulsing between my legs.

"I'm doing really good, actually. I've been working on my music, which is the best kind of therapy. And I'm going to Napa with Murphy on Thursday for a little pampering."

"And Theo? He hasn't given you any more problems?"

Vivian chuckles. "No. A certain someone scared him out of town and right back onto a same-day flight."

"Good. I'm glad he took what I said seriously."

"What exactly did you say to him to get him to listen to you?"

I smirk. "I might have told him that I have a lot of machinery and a huge property where nobody would find his body."

She gasps. "You did not!" Then she bursts into laughter.

"It might have been a little much, but it felt right at the time."

She continues to laugh for a long beat, and I lean back in my desk chair, enjoying the way the sound ripples through me.

"Thank you for that. I really needed a laugh today." She pauses. "How about you? How've you been?"

Exhausted. Mentally drained. Overworked.

But I don't want that to be the direction of our conversation, so I focus on something else entirely.

"The harvest is going well. The team seems to be gelling, and we're staying on schedule, which is pretty great during the first few days. There can be a steep learning curve for the newbies."

"Does the harvest feel different now that you're the head honcho? Or is it pretty much the same?"

At that, I can't help the sigh that leaks from my mouth.

"*Oooh*, that awesome, huh?" she says, laughing lightly. "Did I poke at a sore subject?"

"A little bit, but it's not a bad thing," I answer. "It's just . . . my dad didn't tell me that he was going to make that announcement. It was kind of out of left field. I'm not sure I'm ready to handle the weight of the entire vineyard on my shoulders."

Vivian's quiet on the other end, and I shake my head, regretting my choice to be honest. I should have kept my mouth shut and said things were going well.

"That sounds like a tough position to be in," she finally says, her voice soft and serious. "Have you said that to your dad?"

I snort. "Do *you* confront your parents about things that upset you?"

"God, no," she answers. "But my parents are Hollywood nepo babies who live behind a fake persona with everyone, including each other. That's all I knew growing up. So the idea that they would be open to having a *real* conversation about something that bothered me would have been wishful thinking."

Vivian's response surprises me. A few of the things she's said to me since we first met have made it seem like she comes from money, but I never would have guessed she had ties to Hollywood. Not that I know much about it.

"Sounds rough," I offer, wanting to know more, while at the same time not wanting to pry.

"In some ways, it was. Like the fact that they never came to any of my performances growing up because they were always *so busy*," she says, drawing out the last two words with all the sarcasm she can muster. I can practically see her rolling her eyes. "But I had a lot of freedom. And I think that's what helped me figure out who I am. Otherwise, I would have just been shrouded in their version of what life is supposed to look like."

I nod even though she can't see me.

"Sorry, didn't mean to info dump," she says, laughing lightly. "What I *meant* to say is that my parents don't care about how I feel. I'm just wondering if your dad might respond differently. If you talked to him."

"I *did* say something. This morning, actually. It didn't go well."

She makes a humming noise again. "Not everyone is ready to be confronted with the truth behind the mistakes they've made."

I let out a humorless chuckle. "Ain't that the truth."

"I'm sorry you're dealing with that. I hope you know that his reaction is more about him and how he feels than it is about you. Murphy had plenty to say on that subject before she moved home, but after she moved back, she made it clear that as infuriating as he could be, her big brother was a great guy."

My lips turn up at the sentiment. "You've known this whole time what a great guy I am, and you *still* gave me grief when we first met?"

She laughs. "I'm a loyal guard dog, okay? And Murphy's my girl."

"Yeah, I'm just giving you a hard time." I sigh, sitting up in my chair, knowing I need to get back to the paperwork in front of me. "Well, I'm glad you're doing all right."

"Thanks for calling to check in."

I wish her a good night, we say our goodbyes, and I finally hang up the phone.

I don't know what I was expecting when I called Vivian, but something in my chest is lighter now that we've talked.

It's unfamiliar, this ever-present, subconscious desire to check in with her. To connect. To see how she is and what she's doing.

Somehow, despite all my best efforts, Vivian Walsh is continuing to burrow her way into my life and under my skin.

And I can't help but wonder how hollow it will feel when she's gone.

Chapter Fourteen

Vivian

Even after the complete disaster that was Theo showing up in Rosewood unannounced and unwelcome, I'm still spending long days writing music. My muse is still speaking to me. My time here so far has proven that my emotions—about both Memphis *and* Theo—need to be put onto the page.

I finish one of the songs I was working on. I still need to figure out a bridge for the second, and I'm feeling inspired enough to start a third.

Sure, there's always the possibility that none of these will be what my manager or my label is looking for. But something inside me says they're going to love what I have.

What's coming out of me right now is raw. And painful. Like I'm bleeding onto the pages in a way I didn't know I could.

And that's saying something.

The songs aren't *about* Memphis, exactly. Or even about the sex.

They're about the kind of feelings that being with him evokes within me.

The one in front of me now that I'm tentatively calling "Safe for my Soul". . . It's slow, acoustic, heartbreak on the page. About desperately seeking a place to be yourself. About never feeling right.

I've known Memphis for a very short time. There's no way I see him as that safe place. But that feeling of safety . . . of knowing that I don't have to temper myself with him the way I've had to with men in the past . . . that I could sit next to him in the back of that truck and share the truth about what I'm going through . . . It's definitely an inspiration for the words I have on the page, for the melody and tempo of the song.

It reminds me of him.

It probably always will.

I work on that song at an almost frantic pace, the words pouring out of me to create a splashy mess on the page, the melody a clear and true thing in my mind, as if it's a song that already exists.

So when Todd calls, I don't ignore him.

"How's the writing coming?"

"Actually, it's going really fucking good."

He laughs. "You know? I think that's the first time you've ever told me it was going well and I really believed you."

"Good thing I'm a singer and not an actress, huh?"

"I'll say. Now . . . tell me about what you're working on."

It's surprisingly easy to explain my new songs to Todd, and I even play him a little bit over the phone. He seems into it, which is always a good thing, and encourages me to keep going.

"I booked you a flight for Sunday morning. Studio Monday, eleven a.m., all right?"

"Oh," I say, realizing that's only a few days away. "Yeah, sounds good."

Todd says goodbye, and we hang up. I'm left . . . unsettled.

Flying home Sunday morning means only three more days in Rosewood.

Which, admittedly, puts me at barely over two weeks.

That *should* be plenty of time.

Plenty of time to get out of town. To take a break from the rat race. To recharge and calm my soul. To write all the words and find inspiration.

And I did do all those things.

But I'm not done.

Even if I'm not entirely sure why.

"Are you sleeping with my brother?"

The question makes me practically levitate out of my skin. When my eyes connect with the woman who is currently doing my pedicure, I give her an uncomfortable smile. Then I turn to look at Murphy, who is sitting in the chair next to me, sipping a boba tea.

On the other side of her, also watching me with wide eyes, is Murphy's childhood friend Quinn, who she reconnected with when she moved back home.

To say I'm mortified at all the eyes currently on me is an understatement.

We're in Napa at a little boutique spa, enjoying some self-care in the form of some very necessary manis and pedis. But the relaxation I was feeling moments ago has officially fled the coop.

"What did you just say?" I ask, buying myself a second to consider her question.

And how I want to answer it.

Murphy raises an eyebrow and doesn't repeat herself. Instead she stares at me, giving me a chance to gather the courage to tell her that, yes, in fact, I *am* allowing her brother to put his penis inside me.

Though I don't phrase it that way.

"We've . . . been intimate," I finally say, my eyes flicking to the blonde at my feet again, though this time she is looking studiously at where she's painting on a deep peach color. "Yes."

Murphy makes a face. "Gross."

"But it's not serious, I promise."

It feels wrong the minute I say it, like I'm some kid in high school lying about how much she likes a boy because she doesn't want her friends to know.

But I don't take it back.

Murph furrows her brow, a bemused look on her face. "In what world does it make it *better* if you're not serious?"

"In a world where you would have to listen to sordid details about how big his penis is or how good the orgasms are. If it's just a few bangs on vacation, I mean . . . you don't have to deal with any long-term repercussions."

Quinn laughs, and I can't help but join her, especially at the mortification on Murphy's face.

"Did you really have to say all of that? Really?"

I shrug. "Just trying to paint a picture."

"Please don't. I don't ever want a picture like that hanging anywhere in the house of my mind. Please." She takes a long sip of her boba before she points the straw at me. "But also what you said surprisingly makes sense."

I smile and adjust the button on the chair, closing my eyes and letting the massage against my lower back really work out those tense muscles.

"If you need to get under my brother to get over Theo, consider this my blessing."

I burst into laughter. "I cannot believe you said that."

She wrinkles her nose. "Me, either. It's seriously so gross."

"Theo's the ex?" Quinn asks.

"He is. The *cheating* ex. So I can very much confirm that I'm not trying to *get over Theo*. I am already all the way over him."

"Thanks to Memphis's penis."

Quinn and I laugh again, giving each other air high-fives as Murphy covers her face with both hands.

I instantly liked Quinn when I met her. She's a lot quieter than I am, but she is such an optimist and loves to laugh. I've always considered that to be a great quality in a friend.

"Speaking of penises, Quinn . . . Have you thought any more about finding your own postrelationship sexcapade?"

I gasp and lean forward, excited for the change in conversation and a huge fan of sexplorations.

But Quinn's looking at Murphy with narrowed eyes. "I'm not ready yet."

Murphy turns to look at me. "I've been trying to talk Quinn into meeting single men because she's . . ."

"She's right here," Quinn interjects, pointing to herself. "And she's not ready."

My eyes flick back and forth between the two of them, knowing there's plenty more to be said that Quinn doesn't want to talk about.

As much as I would love nothing more than to hear about Quinn's dating mishaps, I also can tell when someone doesn't want the attention on them.

So, after the woman painting my toes finishes and tells me to sit for a few minutes to let them dry, I reluctantly redirect the conversation back to Memphis.

"Hey, Murphy, how did you find out? About Memphis and me. I mean, he didn't, like . . . tell you, did he?"

"Oh no. Thank god, no." Murphy shakes her head almost violently, her attention returning to me. "I don't want to *ever* talk with Memphis about anything sex-related. We very briefly edged around the topic when I was first hooking up with Wes, and it was so awkward."

I nod, thankful. Not because I want Memphis to keep secrets from his sister, but because telling her feels like something we should have decided on together.

"The night of the Harvest-Eve dinner, you said bye, but then I saw you walking out to your car, like, two hours later."

I roll my eyes at my own stupidity.

"And Memphis walked in, like, five minutes after that, so . . ." She shrugs. "I'm not a sleuth, I promise you. You guys are . . . really not good at hiding it."

"I don't know what you're talking about. I'm like a ninja." I narrow my eyes. "A ninja assassin."

"Make a joke about murdering my brother's dick and *I'll* turn into an assassin."

We burst into laughter as all of us climb out of our chairs.

"Thanks for inviting me, ladies," Quinn says once we've left the spa and settled in at a little sandwich and salad place a few doors down. "The past few months have been exhausting, and I really needed this."

"Quinn just had a baby," Murphy offers, beaming.

My mouth drops and my eyes widen. "Oh my gosh, congratulations!"

Suddenly, Quinn's protests that she's not ready to find a new relationship are cast in a new light. She has a whole other human to consider now.

"Thanks. Willow is thirteen weeks tomorrow."

I blink. "I don't know what that means."

Quinn laughs. "She's a little over three months." Then she tugs out her phone and shows me a picture of a sweet little brunette with big, beautiful eyes.

"She looks so much like you."

Quinn smiles and scrolls through a few more photos, and I ooh and aah as she does. Then the server arrives to take our order, and we all scramble to pick something, having not taken any time to look at the menu.

"I've been thinking about it," Murphy says, once the server has left to go grab ice waters, "and I would like to suggest . . . again . . . that you try that open mic night tomorrow at The Standard."

"That's right. Murphy's been bragging about you nonstop since she moved back. I'd love to hear you play."

"I'd be happy to play for you," I tell Quinn, before pinning Murphy with an unamused look. "But I'm not playing at an open mic night."

"Look, what Todd doesn't know won't kill him. Besides, you said you've been writing a lot, and this will give you a chance to test out your music before you go into the studio, right?"

It's one of those frustrating things about signing with a label. To some degree, they own you. There are stipulations on what clearances you need from which people before you can perform, how large or small the venue size can be, and whether or not it can be recorded.

So even though it's *just* an open mic night at a bar in the middle of nowhere, it's still probably a bad idea.

I've thought plenty about it, though.

Performing is like serotonin straight to my veins. It's been a few months since I signed with Humble Roads, which means it's also been a few months since the last time I got up in front of an unfamiliar crowd, nothing but me and my guitar.

And this new stuff I'm working on . . . I'm nervous about taking it to Todd and his boss, Jonas, because it feels like me, but different. Me on a different level.

I don't know how they're going to respond.

So, yeah. The idea of this super tiny, no big deal, open mic night at The Standard has been buzzing around in the back of my mind.

And if I'm honest with myself, I haven't ruled it out completely.

At least not yet.

"I'll think about it," I tell her, hoping that will assuage her from continuing to pester me about it. "But I make no promises."

When I spot Errol with a book in the little library inside the Firehouse, I veer his way, plopping down on the armchair opposite where he's sitting.

He startles a little bit before he smiles.

"Hey there, sweetie. Having a good day?"

"Yeah. Had myself a girls' day out in Napa with friends. Massages and pedicures and lunch."

Slipping one foot out of my sandal, I lift it slightly so he can see the new polish.

"That is quite the color."

I laugh. "I figure it's a little bit wild and a little bit sweet."

"Sounds like you," he offers, slipping a bookmark into his book and setting it down on the table next to him, giving me his full attention.

"Ha! You don't know me well enough to say if I'm sweet."

He grins at me. "Something tells me that you are, even if you don't always like to give off that impression."

A pleasant thread of surprise laces its way through me at his words, ones that make me think he has a fairly good picture of who I am, even though we've only had a few interactions.

I tuck my hair behind one ear. "Look, Errol. If you're going to keep giving me these lovely compliments, I'm going to have to start paying you."

Errol chuckles, shaking his head. "If I remember correctly, you're checking out soon, right? What fun things are you going to do with your last days in town?"

I blow out a breath, the reminder that I've only got two more full days in Rosewood a sad reality I'm not so sure I'm ready to face.

I booked my room at the Firehouse for two weeks, figuring it was a good starting point and not sure how long I was planning to stay. Now that my time in town is coming to an end, I'm starting to wish I didn't need to go so soon.

But even as I think it, I'm sure it's unrealistic to assume I could have stayed longer. I have a life to get back to. Studio time to get to. Responsibilities. And a cat that is probably not missing me at all.

"I'm not sure yet, but I'll probably go hang out with my friend tomorrow at her family's vineyard. You know the Hawthorne family?"

"I do."

"Murphy and I are besties, so . . . probably gonna head over there and bug her a little bit. Maybe go on a drive." I shrug. "I might perform at the open mic night tomorrow."

Errol's eyes light up. "I love open mic night."

"Really?"

He nods. "My wife used to play the keyboard and sing, and she'd sign up to perform every so often. It's been a long time since I've been to one."

I try to imagine cutie pie Errol at The Standard, sitting in his little sweater vests with an Arnold Palmer, and suddenly I want it more than anything.

"If I decide to perform, will you be my date?" I ask him.

He claps his hands together, joy alighting on his face.

"I'd love nothing more."

Chapter Fifteen

MEMPHIS

I frown as the text pops up on my phone.

Vivian: Busy tonight. Sorry!

Setting my phone aside, I get back to work, reviewing the report from yesterday's harvest and comparing it to the same day from the past few years. The first week of the harvest's yield has always been a strong indicator of what we can expect from our crop. Typically, it's about comparing the percentage of grapes that have been cut from the vine to the weight of how many grapes are considered underripe, diseased, or damaged.

Things are looking promising as I compile the handwritten notes from the staff and enter them into my database.

But instead of reveling in those good numbers and what they might mean for this batch of wine, I'm still focused on Vivian's text.

Obviously, she doesn't need to be available just because I've asked her to be. She made it clear that she's working on this trip, and I'm definitely a person who understands prioritizing work.

But I can't hide the disappointment of learning she has other plans.

I was lying in bed last night, my fist between my legs, stroking to the memory of that night at the Firehouse. When I'd gotten to taste the sweetness between her thighs. And as I'd come into my palm, I thought . . . What the hell am I doing?

Vivian and I were pretty clear that we were both open to sporadic fun, and while I hadn't wanted to push it with the drama from her ex coming to town, I also had a feeling that she'd be down if I reached out. Which is why her response is so surprising.

Sighing, I scrub my hand over the hair that's been growing thicker on my face for the past few days. Then I get back to reviewing my reports, putting Vivian and hooking up tonight completely out of my head.

Eventually, I call it for the day on administrative work and head over to the restaurant to do the winery tour. It wasn't my intention to continue handling these for Naomi, but when I talked to her about it last weekend, it was clear that her schedule was overflowing.

"I'm surprised you're here," Murphy says as she collects a handful of menus.

My brow furrows. "Why?"

She shrugs. "I figured you might . . . I don't know . . . be at The Standard or something."

When I still look confused, because I rarely ever have time to go out for drinks anymore, my sister rolls her eyes.

"I know you and Vivian are hooking up, okay? You don't have to play stupid."

Then she tucks her menus into her hip and opens the door, calling out for *Charlotte, party of four.*

I couldn't be more surprised than if she whacked me over the head with a bat. When did Murphy and Vivian have this conversation? And why am I only now finding out about it?

She takes her sweet time, walking the group of twentysomething women to their table and chatting with them for a few minutes before returning to the host stand.

"I'm not playing stupid. I didn't . . . realize you knew."

"Next time you want to sneak around, maybe make sure you're actually being sneaky," she says, laughing as she pulls out another handful of menus.

"What does that have to do with The Standard, though?" I ask, glancing at my watch, confirming I still have a few minutes before I need to head outside.

Murphy tilts her head and assesses me. "Vivian's playing the open mic night tonight. Did she not tell you?"

I shake my head.

My sister doesn't wait around for me to say anything else. Instead, she walks past me and opens the door, calling out the next group. *Williams, party of three.*

I shouldn't be surprised that Vivian didn't tell me she's performing. We were both clear that our intention was to have fun with each other. For it to be all about sexy time, nothing personal.

So then why am I bothered that she didn't tell me?

It's not like we've ever really talked about her music before, apart from when she briefly shared that she was inspired by being here in Rosewood. Inspired by me.

Maybe that's what it is.

Maybe it's that a part of me thinks I should be invited to observe the creative genius that's been even somewhat influenced by me, as selfish or self-centered as that might sound. Though I can't imagine that I've really made much of a difference.

Or maybe it's that Vivian and I share a connection, and I'm surprised she didn't think to tell me.

"You should go."

I turn to Murphy, who has returned from seating the Williams party.

"I can't go. I'm working."

She rolls her eyes. "Do the tour and *then* go. This place is a well-oiled machine." Then she pats me on the shoulder. "I've got this. Don't stress."

Murphy leaves the host stand behind and heads off to collect a tray of food from the pass, making it clear that I'm not needed.

I glance around, taking in the serving staff moving through the room with smiles on their faces, then the bartenders at the wine bar interacting with customers. And if I go push the kitchen door open, I'll see Wes and his crew in there, in complete control, creating the exceptional dishes from our seasonal menu.

Once outside, I step over to the sign in the corner that lets guests know where to gather for the winery tour and greet the people who signed up for this evening. I introduce myself and give everyone an overview of what they should expect, then lead them off the patio and down the path.

What Murphy said doesn't get tucked away somewhere in the recesses of my mind, though. It's at the forefront all throughout the tour. From the vines, to the warehouse, to the wine cellar and the tasting room, I'm thinking about the implications of what my sister said.

That I should go watch Vivian perform—I've already decided I want to go.

But also the idea that the restaurant is a functioning machine.

That the people we've hired to manage things are doing exactly what they're supposed to be doing—managing things, keeping everything moving, and handling the business.

And that includes my sister.

When I finish the tour, I step back inside the restaurant off the back patio. Murphy moves through the room, a smile on her face as she chats with her tables and interacts with her host staff. She pokes her nose into the kitchen to check in on whatever it is that she's staying on top of.

My chest puffs up, a sense of pride beginning to build. But not because of anything I've done. Just because of who my sister is.

I was worried about Murphy being involved with the restaurant when she first moved back to Rosewood, and that was foolish of me.

And now that I know better, it's time to stop being such a fool.

"I'm gonna take off," I say to Murphy where she's standing at the kitchen pass, as I tuck my hands into my pockets. "Heading to The Standard."

She smirks at me. "When I asked Vivian about you two, she was very 'it's not serious, don't worry' with me. But part of me thinks maybe she's wrong."

I lick my lips and shake my head, a protest forming on my lips.

"And I have to admit, you two didn't make sense to me at first, you know? She's such a big personality and so fun and vibrant all the time and you're . . . you."

Pursing my lips, I level a glare at my sister.

She laughs. "I just mean that you're more uptight and regulated. Structured. You are an Excel spreadsheet, and she is a watercolor painting."

"Wow. I sound so fascinating."

"Memphis, will you listen?" she says, exasperated. "I meant that it didn't seem right at first, but the more I thought about it, the more it seems like maybe you guys could actually be perfect for each other."

"Thank you for that raving endorsement. How so?"

I shouldn't ask what she means, because truthfully it doesn't matter. I don't have time for a relationship and Vivian is leaving at some point—at least I'm assuming she is—probably soon. So again, it shouldn't matter.

Yet, I want to hear what my sister's opinion is more than anything.

"Think about it. You're an Excel spreadsheet, and she's a watercolor painting."

I roll my eyes. "You already said that."

She shrugs a shoulder. "Yeah. But if I explain it to you, where's the fun in that?" Then she turns a tray on the pass and hoists it onto one shoulder. "Have fun tonight!"

When I get to The Standard, I'm not surprised by the size of the crowd. This place is busy on most weekends, but has always managed a packed house on the open mic nights. It's been a long time since I've been to one, but at least that's what I remember from back in the day during the few times I came to watch Murphy sing.

I don't see Vivian, though. There's a man playing the saxophone on the stage where I thought I might see her.

Maybe she changed her mind?

I make my way up to the bar and grab one of the few open stools.

"Hey, Memphis, what'll you have tonight?"

"Hey, Gabe. Just a pale ale on tap would be great."

He sets a coaster in front of me. "Coming right up."

I didn't think through what I'd say or do tonight when it comes to Vivian and her performance. Maybe she didn't want to see me, and my presence will be unwelcome. Or maybe she'll be surprised and thrilled that I'm here and want me to go back to her hotel room with her.

I can't lie, I'm hoping for the latter. But I'd settle for her being happy that I'm here.

A surprising realization.

When Gabe brings my beer, I take a long sip before setting it on the coaster and looking around again.

"Thank you so much, Frank, for that beautiful performance of Kenny G's 'Forever in Love.'"

I look up to the stage, spotting Gabe's wife, Gigi, holding a microphone and smiling at Frank as he packs up his saxophone.

"All right, everyone. We had a last-minute signup from a very talented singer and songwriter. I've been told by our favorite hotel manager, Errol, that she is going to take the world by storm, and we should expect to see her name in lights very soon."

I spot Vivian emerging from the hallway that leads to the break room, her guitar already slung around her shoulder.

"Welcome to the stage, Vivian Walsh."

Gigi puts the microphone in the stand and then exits the small stage, giving Vivian's arm a squeeze as they pass each other by.

And then Vivian is there, up in front, a wide smile on her face as she greets the crowd giving her friendly applause.

"Hey, everyone, I'm Vivian." She strums her guitar once. "I'm in town visiting. I've been here for the past couple weeks on a little working vacation, writing music and enjoying the very delicious wines from Hawthorne Vines."

There are a few cheers, and then she strums the guitar a couple of times.

"Tonight, I'm hoping to play you all a new song I finished a few days ago. It's called 'Sweet Escape,' and I hope you like it."

Vivian clears her throat, and then she begins to play.

Almost instantly, I'm drawn in. Not only by the folky melody, which is catchy and bright, but also by Vivian.

It's apparent almost immediately that she belongs on a stage.

That she is the type of performer who has the ability to draw people in in a way that is almost supernatural.

A quick glance around the room, and I see that everyone has stopped talking. All eyes and ears seem focused on the beautiful starlet at the front of the room.

And then, she starts to sing.

It's a song about belonging, with lyrics about long drives through the hills and rows of vines. About laughter late into the night. Sweet nothings and soft sighs.

The longer she sings, the more I'm drawn in. Drawn forward. Like I could literally be tugged off my stool and over to where she stands.

Her guitar strumming and her voice echoing in the bar bring me back to our night in the tasting room, to the sound of her voice bouncing off the stone walls, but in a way that strikes an emotional chord in my chest. Like the sound of her voice is a physical thing that has made its way through my center and wrapped itself around whatever it is that makes up my soul.

And when she's finished, after she sings out the long, throaty last note, there's a lull in the room for only a brief second before the entire place erupts in cheers.

I don't, though. I sit there in stunned silence, knowing I just witnessed something incredible. Something beautiful. Something I wouldn't be able to describe to anyone who wasn't here.

Vivian smiles and waves at everyone and then says thank you into the microphone before Gigi hops up next to her, absolutely beaming.

"I'm sure I'm not the only person in this room who wants to offer a heartfelt thank you for that incredible performance," she says, looking at Vivian. Then she turns to the crowd. "Let's give Ms. Walsh one more round of applause, shall we?"

Her red hair bounces around her as she grins and takes the few steps down from the stage.

I watch as she embraces Errol Barker, the two of them enjoying a bit of conversation before he pats her on the shoulder and then heads for the door.

Her face brightens as she's approached by Quinn Trager, her daughter, Willow, in one of those chest wrap things pressed to Quinn's front. They talk for a few minutes, and I wait, giving her the space to greet her adoring fans.

When Quinn says goodbye, Vivian scans the crowd, her eyes briefly passing me before flying back to mine.

I raise my glass to her, and she holds up a hand with a single finger.

Eventually, after she's talked with a handful of people, she slips in between me and the person on the stool next to mine, tucking her body into the space between my legs.

"What are you doing here?" she asks, lifting my half-drunk beer from the coaster and taking a sip.

I shrug. "Someone might have mentioned you were performing, and I figured it might be a good idea to hear what kind of slanderous things you're spouting about your muse and his penis."

"You should be grateful that I decided not to sing my other song, wholly inspired by you. It's called 'The Man with the Tiny Grapes.'"

Chuckling, I lean closer, speaking low in her ear.

"You know how big my grapes are. They fit perfectly in your hands."

Vivian pulls back, her eyes flashing. "You dirty bird." She pokes me in the stomach, then picks up my beer and takes another sip, smacking her lips together dramatically when she's done.

"So when you said you were busy tonight, it was this?" I ask, tucking my fingers into the loops in her jeans.

"Yeah. It's been forever since I've performed. I wanted to test out some of my new music."

"I thought maybe you were officially tired of me."

Vivian smiles. "You fishing for compliments?"

"Always."

"Well, Mr. Bartender," she says, before leaning in to me and bringing her lips to my ear. "I love the way your cock feels inside me, so if you don't have plans tonight, consider this my official invitation back to the Firehouse."

I swallow thickly, lust racing through my veins, my dick beginning to throb between my legs.

"For once, it would be great if you could compliment my outfit," I reply as I slip off the stool and take her hand in mine. "Or my personality. You know? Some people think I have a great laugh."

"They must not know you well."

The smile on my face is fucking massive as we cut across the bar and she grabs her guitar case. Then we step out onto Main Street, into the cool night air.

We continue to tease each other as we walk down the road, and she makes me carry her guitar case up to the third floor, shaking her ass at me the entire way.

When we finally get to her room, she walks backward away from me, stripping off her jacket and her top. Teasing me. Drawing me forward like she's still on that damn stage.

"I'm in the mood for a bath," she tells me, her hands reaching behind her and unclipping her bra. "Wanna join me?"

Her bra falls to her feet, and I step forward to take her breasts in my hands, my thumbs stroking across her nipples. I revel in the way her head falls back and her mouth opens slightly.

"Do I get to fuck you in this bath?" I ask her, dipping down and sucking one nipple into my mouth.

She whimpers, and my cock grows harder.

"You can fuck me anywhere."

I growl, releasing her and pushing myself back. "If you don't go start that bath right this second, it'll never happen."

Vivian laughs and then turns, stepping into the bathroom. A second later I hear the water running. She pokes her head out. "I'll call you in when it's ready," is all she says before she closes the door.

Chapter Sixteen

Vivian

When the water is nice and hot and the bubbles are bubbling and the candles are lit, I strip off the rest of my clothes and crawl into the bath. Then I call out to Memphis.

I'm a little nervous, knowing that he's going to come in here and see how I've set everything up. It's a little more romantic than the *let's just fuck* vibes we've had in the past. And maybe that was a mistake.

But part of me couldn't help myself. A slow, steamy, candlelit night in this dreamy tub was too much of a magical idea to pass up. And sharing it with Memphis, a man who is somehow slowly stripping me of all my defenses, makes it all the better.

He opens the door, and when he spots me already in the water, his tongue peeks out and strokes against his top lip.

"This might be the hottest thing I've ever seen," he tells me, slipping off his boxers and stepping into the soaking tub on the opposite end, his legs stretching out on either side of my hips.

"I've been here for two weeks and haven't used this thing, can you believe it?" I shake my head. "It was the entire reason I booked this room, too."

"Well, you're using it now, right?" he offers.

I crawl up on my knees and inch toward him. "Barely fitting it in, though. I'll need to use it again tomorrow before I leave to make sure I get good use out of it."

Memphis's body freezes. "You're leaving tomorrow?"

I shake my head. "Sunday morning. I have to be in the studio on Monday."

I'm not ready to go.

Not ready to leave Rosewood.

Not ready to leave this bit of fun with Memphis behind.

It feels like more than fun, a little voice whispers in the back of my mind.

But I push that thought aside.

Instead of allowing my mind to dip into the well of sadness that my time in Rosewood is ending, I wrap my arms around him. My breasts, covered in bubbles, press deliciously against his chest.

His hands grip my hips, his fingers stroking my skin under the water, his eyes never leaving mine.

When I lean down to kiss him, something begins to well up in my chest. Something I'm not expecting. Something that makes me think that last weekend in the tasting room wasn't just a one-off night where I was too emotional.

Maybe it's truly Memphis who makes me feel this way.

Like everything is so big and so important and so meaningful, even though I don't know that we have the history to warrant those emotions.

I try to push those thoughts away and instead focus on what I know to be true.

What I can taste: Memphis's tongue as it strokes against mine.

What I can hear: the sweet sound of his groans as I settle myself over him.

What I can feel: his cock as it presses inside me, one delicious inch at a time.

"Fuck, I'm not wearing a condom," he says, once he's fully sheathed within my walls.

I shake my head. "I'm on the pill. I've been tested, and everything was negative."

His eyes lock with mine. "Me, too."

"Good, because I'm not sure anything could make me stop right now."

Memphis grips the back of my neck and he pulls my face closer to his. "Me neither." Then his mouth collides with mine.

I begin to move, up and down, melting into that delicious, amazing bliss. He hits that spot inside me, forcing me to continue moving even though my muscles are already beginning to tire. He grabs my ass under the water, and then he begins to thrust as well, each of us doing our part to slam our bodies together.

It's amazing, and the water in the tub sloshes around us, splashing up and over the edge of the porcelain in a way that I'm sure I'll regret later when I have to clean it up.

But for now, it's everything.

It's a visual representation of the way I feel inside right now.

Of the turmoil in my soul as he continues to fuck into me.

God, I've never felt like this.

Never known a pleasure like this.

Haven't ever felt so whole and so broken at the same time.

Something about the way he watches me tells me that things aren't as simple as they were that first time.

Or even the second.

Somewhere along the way, between the playful barbs and the sassy comebacks and the intimacy of the best sex of my life, this thing with Memphis became . . . more.

And as we tumble into ecstasy together, staring into each other's eyes, I can't help but wonder what comes next.

After we finish in the tub and catch our breath, I stand to get out. But Memphis grabs my hand and pulls me back down, turning my body so I'm tucked into his chest, snuggled against him between his legs.

We talk about my singing career, about how I got started and what I did while I was trying to find a manager and a label. I tell him about moving out of my parents' house in Brentwood Park when I was nine-teen and getting a condo in Santa Monica. About the various waitress-ing and nightclub jobs that stretched over nearly a decade as I did open mic nights and took any singing gig I could.

I tell him about Todd and Humble Roads and the music I'm work-ing on.

And I've never felt so heard.

The way Memphis asks questions, how he manages to zero in on the small things that matter about what I have to say.

I don't want to do him the disservice of comparing him to Theo, because literally *anyone* listens better than my ex.

But just this conversation, right here, this casual nothing-burger conversation about the shitty jobs I took before I finally made it . . . It's proof that men like Memphis are in a completely different league than men like Theo.

Men like Theo are interested in listening to themselves talk. They focus on their own interests and expect everyone around them to cater to that. It was a constant point of frustration between us, and one of the most frequent reasons we fought. Because he never fucking listened to anything I had to say. I never understood why he could remember so much about so much, yet so little about the things that mattered to me.

It's because he literally didn't care about those things, so he didn't want to hear about it.

But men like Memphis . . .

There is nothing sexier than a man who listens when you have something to say. Who asks questions that show he's paying attention.

Even back when we were just lobbing semifrustrated, semiflirta-tious comments back and forth at each other at the restaurant or The

Standard or anywhere else, it was still so apparent that he was listening to me. His callback is incredible.

I've never truly realized how much I love being the focus of his attention.

So when he asks me to come to the vineyard as he's tugging his pants back on, it's an easy yes. I might be leaving on Sunday, but that doesn't mean I can't enjoy the time I have left.

"Come to the vineyard tomorrow," he says. "It's harvest, so things are really busy, but that means there's a lot for you to do. You can ride the ATV around and see the whole property—maybe even tag along with the staff and cut bunches."

I tug an oversize sleep shirt on, then take a seat on the bed, something occurring to me.

"And what will you be doing all day?"

He laughs. "I've got a lot of work to do, so I'll be in my office for most of the day, which is far less interesting."

I'm surprisingly disappointed by that, but it makes sense. Memphis has made it clear from the very beginning that he's under a lot of stress with work, so it would be silly for me to assume that he'd be able to play hooky.

"All right, well, thanks for the invite. I'll try to come around maybe . . . ten-ish?"

Memphis smirks. "Sounds good."

Then he slips an arm around my waist and tugs me forward, his mouth dropping to mine in a delicious kiss that is equal parts sensual and surprising.

Sensual, because it's Memphis, and the way his tongue tangles with mine makes my toes curl.

Surprising, because this is the same man who seemed concerned about the easiness of our kiss on the street after the first time we had sex. As if it was okay within the confines of active intercourse, but not when it's a sweet moment with nothing but the kiss in mind.

I get it. Kissing while we're fucking, that's a battle. A competition for dominance, each of us desperate to squeeze every drop of pleasure out of each other that we can.

This right here, this gentle, tender kiss . . . It's intimate in a different way. Its purpose is affection. Warmth. It communicates a desire for closeness that is more than just getting in and getting off.

I can't help but lean into it. Revel in it.

In him and the magic of his arms around me.

When he pulls back, his eyes search mine for a long moment before he releases me. "I'll see you tomorrow."

And when he leaves, I crawl immediately into bed and turn out the light.

Because if it's dark and I'm tucked away, I don't have to face the truth.

◆ ◆ ◆

Riding around on the ATV with Micah is a lot more fun than I thought it would be. I've never been a girl who likes roller coasters or thrill seeking of any kind, but as Micah comes to the top of a hill and then our speed accelerates as we go down, curving along the path around the vineyard, I think I finally understand the appeal.

I'm sure any true theme park lover would roll their eyes at me comparing an ATV going thirty miles an hour with a roller coaster, but hey, it's the best I can do.

We started near the house, first doing a circle of the entire property. I don't know why, but I never realized how large the vineyard is. Even though Memphis talked about it being eighty acres during our tour last week, I think conceptualizing how large that is in real life wasn't something I was capable of without this drive around. And the vineyard tour only covers the northeastern part, which makes everything seem really close.

Once he'd given me a full lay of the land, Micah showed me the employee cabins—where Naomi, Edgar, and Wes live, and where the temporary hands' bunks are set up—along with the equipment sheds and the areas of the property where some of the oldest vines are being dug up and the ground tilled and resoiled.

Now, we're driving through the middle of the vines, returning to the warehouse after touring where the crew is hard at work de-netting the rows that are going to be harvested.

"So, what do you think?" Micah asks, glancing over at me with a sweet expression once we've come to a stop. "You impressed?"

I laugh. "Of course, I'm impressed. This place is amazing."

He smiles. "Glad to hear that. When Memphis told me to give you the VIP tour, in the middle of the harvest no less, I figured it was pretty important that you be good and dazzled by the end."

Something sentimental rolls through me.

I warm knowing that, even though Memphis isn't driving me around the vineyard himself, he still made sure it was a special experience.

"I have to drop off some reports back at the house, so if you give me a few minutes to grab them from inside, I can walk with you over there if you want?"

"That would be great."

Micah heads inside the warehouse, and I turn, looking out over the vines and the beauty of the scene before me.

Rosewood is a special place. I felt it when I first got here.

But this vineyard is its own brand of extraordinary.

And maybe that's me being biased because it belongs to the family of one of my closest friends. Or because the man I'm sleeping with lives, sleeps, and breathes this land.

Both of those are true, but I think it's more than that.

I think it's just one of those places that resonates with a creative soul.

I know the hard work that goes into cultivating something, working it over until it becomes that perfect creation that you've envisioned.

Meredith Wild & Jillian Liota

And I understand the sense of accomplishment once that creation becomes a reality.

I don't doubt that the Hawthornes feel that way every season, once they've gotten through the harvest and are able to revel in the work they've accomplished.

"All right, ready?"

I turn, spotting Micah holding a manila folder and a notebook, and I nod.

"So, what's the deal with Memphis?" I ask as we begin a moseying walk down the path that leads back to the main house.

"You're gonna have to be more specific with your question," he says, laughing. "There are many layers to my brother. I need to know which one you're looking to reveal."

"Okay . . . What makes him happy?"

Micah stops, and I stop, too. He looks at me with a curious expression, but then he shakes his head and starts walking again.

"To be honest? I'm not really sure. For a long time, I would have told you that working the vineyard makes him happy. He loves this place." Micah pauses his description of Memphis for a beat, seeming to be looking for the right words. "But now, I'm not so sure."

"Does he do anything other than work? Because he talks about this place like it's the only thing he does with his time."

"Not really. He tell you anything about what's been going on?"

I shake my head.

"I won't get too deep into it, but Memphis is basically fighting to keep our doors open right now."

My head jerks back in surprise. "What?"

"I don't think he realizes how much I know, but the truth is that my grandfather was a great owner, but my dad wasn't really into it, so when things fell to him, he struggled. And now Memphis is dealing with the fallout."

Sadness ripples through me.

No wonder he's been so adamant about needing to be at work.

174

He's desperate to keep this place running. And it's more than just his own livelihood at stake. It's the livelihood of his entire family.

The conversation we had about him being worried to take over the responsibilities and the weight of the vineyard . . . now I understand it with a clarity that I didn't have before.

"I'm sorry you guys are facing all of that," I finally say.

Micah gives me a soft look. "We'll make it through," he tells me, a quiet confidence in his tone. "My brother has his faults just as much as the next guy, but when he cares about something, there's no lengths he won't go to. He's the most hardworking person I know, and if there's a way to sort things—which I don't doubt there is—he'll find a way."

We're silent for a few minutes, the only sounds the mulch crunching beneath our feet and the gentle hum of machines in the distance.

Then Micah speaks again.

"I'll give you this much, though. You asked what makes him happy? I've seen him smile more in the past two weeks than I've seen in the past two years." He shrugs. "Take from that what you will."

A little part of me thrills at Micah's words.

When we finally get to the house, Micah leads me inside and down a long hallway. Tucked away in a corner is a large office where Memphis is seated behind a big wooden desk, his eyes narrowed as he stares at something on his computer screen.

"Got the reports from yesterday," Micah says, crossing the room and dropping the folder on the desk in front of Memphis. "I think you'll be pleased."

Memphis's head turns, his eyes connecting with mine. He doesn't smile, but I can tell he's glad to see me all the same.

"Thanks. And thanks for taking the time to give Vivian the tour," he says.

"Enjoyed our chat," Micah tells me. "Hope the rest of your day is great."

Then he gives me a wave and strides out of the room.

Memphis clicks around on his computer a few times. Then I see his screen go dark, and he shifts slightly in his chair so he's facing me, his elbows on the desk.

"How was the tour?"

I beam, coming up behind one of the high-backed armchairs and folding my arms against the top. "Amazing. This place is so cool. Micah drove me all over the place on the ATV so I finally got, like, a really good picture of everything."

"Good. I'm glad you had fun."

Looking around the room, I take in the wall of shelves opposite where Memphis sits, filled with dozens of three-ring binders in a variety of colors, stacks of paperwork, equipment manuals, and plenty of books on vineyard management and wine chemistry.

"So this is where you spend your days, huh?" I ask. "I thought there was an office building by the warehouse. How come you don't work over there?"

"This is where my grandfather worked, and my father as well," he says, shrugging. "I personally like that I get a little distance from everyone here."

I giggle. "Sounds like a you thing," I say, taking a closer look at a few photos on the wall.

There is one of Memphis, his dad, and an older gentleman—his grandfather, maybe?—with rows of vines stretched out behind them, smiles on their faces. There's another of an older couple standing in front of a warehouse that looks a lot smaller than the one on the property today. And then there's a picture that looks like it's from forever ago of a couple and a baby standing in the middle of a dirt field.

"That's my great-great-grandfather and grandmother, holding my great-grandfather, on the day they bought the property," Memphis offers when he catches me staring at the last photo. "I always used to ask my dad why they looked so unhappy on a day that was supposed to be so wonderful."

I laugh. "They do look kind of irritated."

"Apparently it was the thing back then. Photos took a long time to take, so people didn't smile."

"It's wild to think about how long this land has been in your family. It doesn't feel like we live in a world where people work in the family business anymore. Are you glad it's being passed to you? Does it make you happy?"

He leans back in his chair, and it makes me think he's really trying to decide how to answer that question honestly.

"Apart from all the stress, I am," he finally says, his eyes focused on the corner as he continues to think it over. "It's not always a happy job, but really, that's any job, right? You're not going to be happy one hundred percent of the time. But I am definitely glad it has been passed to me, and I'm hopeful for what's to come."

I grin. "You sound like you're giving an inspirational speech to your staff."

Memphis laughs. "I'm serious."

"I don't doubt that you're serious," I reply. "But does it make you happy? What you do, working here, every day. Do you love it?"

I'm prodding too much. I know it.

But Micah was pretty clear that he's not sure if Memphis is happy. And for whatever reason, it's important to me that he is. Really and truly, and not just for show.

"I hope I am again one day," he replies, his expression filled with chagrin.

It's stunningly honest, and I don't press further.

Chapter Seventeen

MEMPHIS

Vivian hangs out in my office for a little bit, looking through my things. She settles into one of my armchairs with a book about vineyards for a while, flipping through it slowly and occasionally asking questions.

I'm shocked by how much I like it.

I've never imagined what it would be like to have someone hang out in my office while I'm working. My first assumption is that it would be distracting.

And it is, a little bit.

But I find that the longer she's there, the more I enjoy it.

The little sounds she makes when she's read something interesting.

The way she reveals how her mind works when she asks a question.

And I find that in the lulls of her silence, I'm waiting for her to speak again, eager to hear what else she has to say.

"Do you want to go get lunch?"

Her head pops up in surprise.

Hell, I'm surprised the words came out of my mouth as well.

"Yeah, that sounds great," she replies, a smile stretched wide across her face. "Right now?"

"Yeah, I'm hungry and I figured . . . you have to sit and eat at the restaurant before you leave town, right?"

As soon as I say it out loud, I wish it weren't true. But I ignore the tightness in my chest at the fact that she's leaving tomorrow.

Tomorrow.

Jesus.

Vivian drops her legs from where she'd been sitting sideways in the armchair and returns her book to the bookshelf while I save and close out the things I'm working on.

The restaurant is in full swing for a Saturday lunch service when we arrive.

Murphy's eyes widen when we walk in together.

"Hawthorne, party of two," I say, keeping my face as serious as possible.

My sister laughs and grabs two menus. "Like I'm going to add you to the waitlist." She looks to Enid. "Take them to table nine, please."

Enid smiles and motions for us to follow her through the restaurant and over to a two-top situated against the wall of windows looking out to the back patio and the vineyard.

"Your server will be right over," she says before going back to the front.

As Vivian peruses the menu, I'm hyperaware of her. I zero in on the little details, trying to absorb everything about her before she goes, like the graceful way she rests her chin on the back of her hand, how she adjusts her hair by bringing it forward over one shoulder.

It's unfamiliar, yet I can't help it.

"Murphy said this whole restaurant was your idea," Vivian says, finally looking up at me with a smile. "That you thought of every detail. It's a very impressive space."

I bob my head, pride swelling in my chest, both at the way my sister has been talking about the restaurant and at Vivian's perception of it.

Even if Murphy complained about me quite a bit to Vivian over the years, at least there was some balance to it, right?

"Thank you. It was definitely a very complicated thing to get going."

"What made you decide to open a restaurant in the first place?"

I blow out a breath. "I was looking for a way to bring in more business, something other than just selling wine. The price point of a wine bottle can only sustain so much growth, so if we wanted to be more profitable, we needed to look at different ways to do so."

"Seems like it would be a massive ordeal to open this place, right? I mean"—her head tilts back and she looks at the building—"it's gorgeous, and you've clearly made top-notch choices with . . . everything."

The server arrives then, cutting off our conversation. But when I see it's Harper, I can't help but laugh inside. According to Murphy, she's great at her job, except for when I'm around. My sister says it's because I'm intimidating.

"Hello, Mr. Hawthorne," she says, giving me a tight smile. "Can I get either of you something to drink?"

"Chardonnay?" I ask Vivian.

She smiles and nods.

"A bottle of last year's chardonnay, please."

Harper nods and then scurries away, not telling us about the specials or asking if we'd like to order any appetizers, and I can't help but chuckle.

"She looked terrified. What did you do to her?" Vivian asks, one eyebrow raised.

I shake my head, smiling. "Nothing! I didn't do anything. She's easily flustered by handsome men, would be my best guess."

Vivian barks out a laugh. "You know, I always figured you were a guy who couldn't fit his ego through a doorway, and you've finally confirmed it for me."

Lunch goes pretty smoothly after that. Harper manages to take our orders without having a meltdown. Vivian and I talk about the vineyard and what it was like for me, growing up in a small town and then taking over the family business.

It's easy. Natural.

Like everything is with Vivian.

But she's leaving tomorrow.

The thought has stayed ever present in the back of my mind throughout the day, and remains at the forefront as I pay the check and we finish off our last glasses of wine.

I can barely admit it to myself, but the truth is right there, plain as day.

I don't want her to leave.

I don't want these two weeks to be the only thing we get.

Not that she could stay.

That would be unrealistic.

And I am a realist over everything else.

But maybe . . . this doesn't have to be the end.

Not yet, anyway.

I wait off to the side while Vivian and Murphy chat for a few minutes, and then the two of us leave the restaurant and meander back to the house.

"So, what are you going to get up to for the rest of the day?" I ask as we come to a stop next to Vivian's rental parked in our driveway, stalling for time.

She shrugs. "I need to pack, but . . . I'm not really sure what else. Probably practice one of my new songs. Or something."

"The one about my massive, oversize grapes?" I tease, trying to keep the tone light even through the twinge of sadness.

Vivian pokes my stomach. "Obviously."

I lick my lips, trying to think of anything else to say. Wondering what I *should* say.

She can't just leave, right? I mean, not that abruptly.

I swallow hard. "Is this goodbye, then?"

"I'm supposed to come by to have breakfast with Murphy in the morning," she offers.

"You could stay here tonight, instead of the hotel."

I say it before I've thought it all the way through, and part of me is embarrassed at how vulnerable it makes me feel. Like I'm begging her to stay, somehow.

Vivian tucks a strand of her hair behind her ear, looking out toward the highway.

"Wouldn't that be weird? Me staying overnight?"

When she asks, something settles in my chest.

Because she's asking a question that's making herself vulnerable, too.

"It doesn't have to be. You're leaving tomorrow, right?" I shrug. "And if you feel weird because of Murphy, well . . . She stays out at Wes's cabin most nights anyway."

She nibbles on her lip for a second, thinking it over.

"All right, I'll stay."

I don't realize how much I want her to say yes until she does. That's when my mind races into overdrive, sorting through the things I need to get done and the things that can wait until tomorrow.

"Go pack up and do whatever you need to," I tell her. "And then come back whenever works for you. You can practice literally anywhere on the vineyard or in the house. And then tomorrow, you'll have breakfast with Murphy before you go."

Her lips tilt up at the side, her eyes searching mine.

We're walking into murky water, here. I can feel it.

But it also feels right. For whatever reason.

"Okay. I'll be back in a couple of hours."

I tug her forward and bring my lips to hers, kissing her like I've wanted to since she first showed up this morning.

The truth is that I don't know how many more times I'll get to do that. So I need to take advantage of it while I still can.

I bust my ass while she's gone, trying to get through as much work as I can.

I update reports. I review our data. I make notes on the paperwork Micah left me with my own ideas about how the restructure might work, mostly leaving it as he's laid it out, but with a few adjustments.

But my ear is always listening for a knock at the door or a text to let me know that she's on her way.

So when I head to the kitchen to grab a quick dinner and spot Vivian out at one of the tables on the patio, chatting with my aunt Sarah and some of the temporary hands, I can't help the surprise that ripples through me.

Or the little bit of hurt that she didn't tell me she was here.

I step through the patio doors, prepared to give her a hard time, but then her eyes connect with mine. And the smile she gives me is nothing short of magical. It stomps out that modicum of irritability. I take my plate and drop into a seat at the end of her table.

She gives me a grin, but then she returns her attention to my aunt, who is telling her a story about one of Murphy's earliest performances, a talent show back in junior high where she sang some pop song with her friend Quinn.

"It had choreography and everything, and she was such a little performer, even back then."

"Murphy is incredibly talented," Vivian offers, her elbows on the table and her water cup dangling loosely in her hands. "She's going to be getting songwriting credits on several of the songs on my album."

"Oh, how nice. She mentioned before that she loves writing music with you. Did you guys work on anything together while you were in town?"

"Unfortunately, no. It didn't work out. But my writing style is pretty independent, so I don't know that we would have done more than sit with our guitars in our laps and just talked, you know?"

"Well, I'm sorry we didn't get more time to chat while you were in town. But I hope you enjoyed your time in Rosewood, and safe travels, sweetie."

Vivian smiles. "Thanks, Sarah. It was great meeting you."

My aunt pushes back from her chair and leaves us, probably to check on the food on the island and clean up.

"I really like her."

I smile. "She's pretty great."

Vivian leans back in her chair and crosses her arms, the plastic of the folding chair creaking with her movements. "How's work coming along?"

"Good. I've gotten a lot done." My curiosity gets the better of me, and I can't keep my question to myself. "How come you didn't let me know when you got here?"

She shrugs. "Your work is important to you, and I figured I was more than capable of entertaining myself until you had a free minute or two."

My lips tilt up at the sides at her understanding of the responsibility I have toward my work.

"I was thinking I might go on a little walk around the vineyard and then sit out here with my guitar and work on some of my music. As long as it won't be distracting."

Everything about Vivian is distracting, in all the best ways.

"That sounds like a great idea. I've got a few more things to finish up, and then I'll come meet you out here when I'm done?"

"That sounds great."

I take my empty plate inside, give my aunt a thank-you kiss on the side of her head, and dip back into my office.

But standing at the threshold, looking into the room, I'm immobile.

My computer is still bright, an open spreadsheet on the screen. An unread compliance report needing my attention sits on the desk. And I don't doubt there are at least a dozen emails that have remained unread for most of the day that I should be responding to.

Yet . . . I can't think of a single thing that absolutely has to be completed right this minute or the vineyard will shut down tomorrow.

So instead of crossing the room and rounding my desk to get back to work, I flip the light off and return to the patio.

Vivian is standing at the edge, pulling her hair into a messy bun at the top of her head as she looks out at the property. When I come to a stop next to her, she does a double take when she sees me.

"Mind if I join you on that walk?"

A smile stretches wide on her face. "I'd love that."

We wander for over an hour, a slow mosey through the vines and all the way across to the other edge of the property, easy conversation flowing between us the entire time. And on the way back, when her feet start to hurt from her poor choice of shoes, I carry her to the house piggyback style, not even trying to pretend I don't love having her arms wrapped around me and her body pressed close to mine.

After we get back to the house, she gets out her guitar and we sit on the now empty porch. She idly strums melodies that sound brand new and familiar at the same time. It's the first time I can remember in months—years maybe—sitting outside and enjoying the sunset as it dips behind the rolling hills in the distance.

"Are you looking forward to getting back to LA?"

Vivian takes longer than I'm expecting to respond, to the point that I wonder if she didn't hear me. She continues to gently strum her strings and look off to the side.

But when she does answer, I'm more than surprised at what she says.

"No, actually. I'm not."

"Why?"

She rolls her neck around, then leans her head back against the house, her fingers on the guitar coming to a stop.

"I mean, I *should* be excited to get back. I'm recording an album this week. I've been dreaming about this since I was old enough to hold a tune." She shakes her head. "But a lot has changed since I left. And when I go back, I'm gonna have to face it."

My brow furrows as I consider what she's just said.

"You mean Theo?"

Vivian sighs. "Theo, yeah. But also me. It's like . . . I've changed, somehow," she says, her voice wistful and almost unsure. "And maybe it's about Theo. But also, maybe it's not."

"Do you want to talk about it?" I'm not sure if that's the right question, but I want to be someone she *can* talk to.

She looks at me for a long moment, considering. But then she shakes her head. "I appreciate it, but let's just enjoy the evening," she says, giving me a regretful smile, before her fingers begin to move again.

I can't begrudge her for not sharing. She's leaving tomorrow. Should she really be pouring her heart out to some guy? And why fill what little time we have left with conversation about things that are hard or emotional or frustrating?

But in the same breath, I can't help the little bit of disappointment that she doesn't want to confide in me. That she doesn't want to share whatever it is that's causing this bit of melancholy when she thinks about going back to LA. We've talked about some pretty important things, and I'd like to think I'm someone she can confide in.

Even if I am *some guy*.

I let it go, deciding that for now, the two of us need to just enjoy our final moments together. As horrible as that sounds.

Our conversation takes on a lighter tone after that. Vivian sets her guitar aside and pulls out her phone, taking a few pictures of the sunset and the vines stretched out before us. We stay out on the patio enjoying each other's company until long after the very last hues from the sun have disappeared and the sky is truly dark.

Then we go inside and back to my room.

"Bathroom's right there if you want to change or brush your teeth or whatever," I tell her, leaning back against the door and watching her casually study my belongings.

I wonder what she's noticing. What picture she's getting of me that she didn't have before. I try to follow her gaze to assess what it is that she's seeing and how she's seeing it.

The queen bed with simple dark-blue sheets and comforter. The solid wood nightstand and matching dresser that I've had since I was in high school. The bookshelf in the corner with pictures from high school and books I've wanted to read but haven't made the time to do so.

Suddenly, I'm concerned that my life might seem too small. Too basic. Too unimportant for a woman like her, who has the world at her fingertips.

Not that there's anything I can do to change any of that.

Not that I'd necessarily even want to change it.

But I want it to be enough, all the same.

"I'm just gonna go make sure the house is locked up. I'll be back," I tell her, slipping into the hallway and giving myself a bit of a distraction.

Vivian doesn't seem like a judgmental person, by any measure. But it isn't hard to see that she lives a more affluent life than I do, and probably has a different idea about what a thirty-one-year-old man's bedroom should look like.

Everything has always been tight around here, even back when we were kids and the vineyard was doing well. My grandmother did a great job making this house warm and welcoming all the way up until she passed away when I was in my early twenties, but our clothes and our furniture were thrifted. Our food was bought in bulk. Our family never went on vacation.

The things that make up this home and the life I've lived are humble and unassuming and probably a lot less luxurious than Vivian is accustomed to. So even though she might not notice or care, I'm suddenly a lot more self-conscious about it all than I expected.

The house is quiet as I flip off the lights and make sure all the doors are latched. Most everyone retires to bed after dinner to get in some sleep before the two a.m. harvest time. When I slip back into my bedroom, the light underneath the closed door to the bathroom and the sound of running water is plenty for me to know that Vivian's getting ready for bed.

I strip down to my boxers and climb into bed, and just a few minutes later, Vivian slips out of the bathroom.

Her hair is up in a messy bun, exposing her long neck. She's wearing an oversize shirt that falls off one shoulder.

And, god, she's gorgeous.

She leans up against the doorjamb, and with the expression on her face, I don't doubt for a second that she knows exactly how sexy she looks right now.

"I'm ready for bed," she tells me, her voice a husky thing, filled with flirtatious energy, before she rounds to the other side and crawls in.

I flip the light switch and plunge us into darkness, just the moon outside casting a bit of glow across the room. Then I turn, each of us lying with our heads on our pillows, watching each other.

I reach out, tuck some of her loose hair behind her ear and stroke down her cheek, along her jawline.

Then I lean forward, pressing my lips against hers. Soft and gentle and searching.

She parts for me immediately, and our tongues stroke against each other, our bodies shifting closer until my arm is wrapped around her and we're pressed together from nose to toes.

It's electrifying, being connected to her, and then my hands begin to rove and touch. When I realize she's not wearing a stitch underneath that shirt, it takes everything inside me not to rush, not to move at a breakneck pace. To keep us moving slowly, savoring every moment. Breathing in every delicious scent.

I try to touch her everywhere, wanting to caress every inch of her body.

I lick and suck at her neck, pinch at the sweet berries of her nipples, press my face between her breasts. I kiss slowly down her middle until I'm settled between her thighs, spreading open her lips and stroking my tongue through her folds, dripping with her arousal.

And fuck, do I take . . . my . . . time.

My cock is like stone where it presses into the mattress as I eat at her. I gyrate my hips, desperate for relief but unwilling to move any faster than I absolutely have to.

By the time I slide my fingers inside her, searching for that spot that I know drives her mad, she's a shaking, whimpering mess. Her hands are fisted in my hair as she tries to control my movements. But I am an immovable force. I continue to circle her clit as my fingers massage inside her.

Finally, I relent, my mouth closing around exactly where she wants me. I flick at her little nub over and over again until she splinters apart, her face pressed to a pillow to muffle her pleasure.

I crawl up her body, kissing her damp skin as I go, until my nose bumps hers and my cock rests at her entrance.

"There is nothing like the way you taste," I whisper, then kiss her, our tongues tangling in a lazy duet.

I suck at her neck and begin shallow thrusts, testing her readiness.

She reaches down and grabs my ass. Her knees bend and her legs wrap around me, opening herself to me completely. Her head falls back, her mouth open as I push all the way in.

"And nothing like being inside you," I say, her wet heat clamping down around me, an almost unearthly thing.

"Memphis, please," she whispers, her fingers gripping at my back.

I pull out and thrust back in, gritting my teeth and already struggling not to tip over any second. But I hold off. I hold off as long as I possibly can, returning to my leisurely pace, stroking in and out of her in a way that keeps us both right on the edge, right on the cusp, for as long as I can manage.

When that control breaks, I hook one hand underneath her knee, opening her wide to fuck into her, slam into her, our bodies colliding and slapping together over and over again until if feels like my soul cracks wide, a chasm splitting me in half and everything inside me pouring out. Vivian's inner walls grip me with a pressure that's almost unbearable as she follows me over.

Her forehead glistens, damp with sweat. Her sweet mouth falls open in her delirium.

We are like cats in heat as we come down, each of us exhausted but desperate for each other's touch. We kiss for long minutes. Our hands still gently roving and touching each other, almost like our hands are the reassurance that we're still here. That we still exist. That we're okay.

Or maybe that's just me.

I'm not sure.

All I *do* know is that when Vivian eventually drifts off to sleep, I stay awake for a long time, watching her in the dark, wondering how I'll ever let her go.

Chapter Eighteen

VIVIAN

I wake long before my alarm, even if my body is still exhausted from last night's activities.

Memphis is asleep and snoring quietly beside me. I can't help but smile and shift so I'm completely on my side, my eyes tracking over his handsome face and taking in all the little things I haven't noticed before.

His facial hair has grown a bit more pronounced—I felt it between my thighs last night as he went to town. The handful of freckles around the edge of his hairline. How long his lashes are, pressed against his cheeks.

Last night was . . .

I can't even put into words what it was. How it made me feel.

God, what it made me feel . . .

Even before last night, sex with Memphis was the best I'd ever had. But until last night, I've never considered that sex itself could be life-changing. I've never been so centered as the focus of a man's attention. Not ever have I felt so completely worshipped and adored and treasured. So revered.

So precious.

The bar has been raised to a level I didn't know existed. Memphis makes me feel things that I probably shouldn't with a man I've known for such a short time.

And it's not just the sex, even though some of how we flirt and spar and talk certainly plays a part in making the sex so good.

Micah wasn't joking when he said that when Memphis cares about something, it gets all his attention. Memphis has an attention to detail like no one else.

I've felt it in how he talks to me, how he listens to me, the questions he asks, the attention he pays to me when we're intimate.

It's intoxicating.

Too intoxicating. I'm a pot on heat, and I'm at risk of boiling over.

This entire vacation was supposed to be a chance for me to get away from the very complicated, very emotional parts of my life. An opportunity to have some fun and let go of the realities I face back home.

Yet somehow, this thing with Memphis is becoming one of those complications.

I turn onto my back and stare up at the ceiling, knowing that's not entirely true.

Memphis isn't a complication.

But this thing between us does come with complications.

Added emotions and challenges.

I mean, I'm leaving today. In hours.

I'm supposed to go home. Back to LA. Back to my real life and my big dreams and everything I've wanted for my future.

So how do my feelings for Memphis fit into that?

Should they? Should they fit into my future?

Or should I be able to leave this fun fling behind and move on with my life?

Even that prospect makes something roll over in my stomach and heat begin to collect around my neck.

I *don't* want to leave Memphis behind.

I *don't* want this thing between us to be over.

But in the same breath, I do.

Because something tells me that falling for Memphis Hawthorne just might break me.

If I thought what happened with Theo was too much to handle, I can only imagine what heartbreak with Memphis might do to me.

How it might wreck me in ways I can't even comprehend right now.

Not to mention the complications it could cause with my friendship with Murphy.

It's infinitely safer to avoid these emotions altogether.

No matter how hard it might be to leave him—leave this—behind.

"You're really going to leave without saying goodbye?"

I curse under my breath and freeze a second before loading my guitar case into the trunk of my rental.

I wish I had been faster gathering my belongings as I snuck around Memphis's room earlier. I'd hoped to sneak out without waking him. But clearly, Murphy was right when she said I'm not very stealthy.

I drop the trunk closed then turn, looking at Memphis where he stands a few feet away on the cold concrete of the Hawthorne driveway. His hands are on his hips. He's wearing a T-shirt and a loose pair of basketball shorts.

And looking far more hurt than I'd anticipated.

"I figured it might be easier for everyone if I left early," I say, crossing my arms. It's the only thing I can think of, having not prepared anything to say.

"Easier for who?"

He steps closer, resting his hand on the back of the car, pinning me with a look that makes my chest ache. His eyes search mine, and I get the sensation that he's looking for something, though I'm not sure what.

"Where are you going?"

"I'm leaving, Memphis. It's time to go home."

"You're not leaving. You're running."

My head jerks back. "What the hell would I be running from?"

He waves a hand in the space between where we stand.

"From this. From us."

It's too much . . . way too much. Whatever's developed between us is too big, and I'm not ready.

"What *us*, Memphis?" I stare him down. "This is a vacation fling. Some fun sexy times that are supposed to be nothing more than fun and sexy." I blink rapidly, trying to convince him while trying to convince myself, too. "That's all."

"You don't believe that," he says, his eyes searching mine. "If this was a bunch of fun sex and nothing more, it would be easy to wake up and fuck again and then have breakfast and leave for the airport. Right? Wouldn't that be easy?"

I shove my hands into my sweatshirt pockets, my fingers bunching and releasing over and over. I stare back at Memphis with my head high and my chin out. I don't want to hear what he has to say. Because I'm terrified that he's right. That he can see right through me.

Memphis takes another step forward, his hands coming to rest on my shoulders before sliding down and squeezing gently at my biceps.

Our gazes tangle again, and I get that same sense that he's searching for meaning.

"You . . . make me feel something." He shakes his head. "Something I didn't know I could feel. Something too early to name. But what I can honestly tell you is that I'm not ready for whatever this is between us to end. Not yet."

A shiver races down my spine at his honesty, at the raw and vulnerable way his eyes look into mine.

"And maybe I said the wrong thing before, when I first came outside." His hands come up and frame my face. "So let me try again. Please don't leave without saying goodbye."

Memphis leans down, bringing his face within inches of mine. Our noses bump, and I press up onto my toes, unable to refuse the invitation to touch him again.

The kiss is gentle and sweet and reverent, and my body warms despite the cool fall morning.

It had taken all my mental strength to push myself out of bed earlier, to quietly tiptoe around Memphis's room, collecting my things and then slipping out, to get on the road to the airport hours before I need to go.

I'd made up my mind. I needed to leave, and leave immediately.

And now, standing here, wrapped in his arms as this slow, lazy kiss rolls through me, the little wall that protects my heart continues to crack. And I'm even more convinced that I'm making the right choice.

I pull back, take a step away from him, and cover my mouth with my hand. As if I can hold his kiss there forever, save it for later when I need it most.

He watches me, uncertainty in his expression, and I know that I have to convince him that me leaving is the best thing.

For both of us.

For what we want out of the future.

The plans we each have.

Because if I can't convince him, if I can't convince *myself*, I don't know if either of us will be able to let go.

"What kind of life do you picture for us, huh?" I ask him. "My entire life is in LA. My career is in LA. Everything that matters to me is in LA."

He takes a step back, looking away from me briefly, and I don't doubt that what I said has wounded him. But I don't relent.

"I'm *just* on the cusp of living my dream, Memphis. I am right there, about to reach out and take everything I've wanted. Everything I've worked for. Am I supposed to give that up? Come here. Live in this town while you work sixteen-hour days? Play open mic nights?"

My words are like tar on my tongue, sticky and hot and poisonous. But I keep going, wanting to drive my point home.

"Or are you going to be the one who does it? Are you going to quit the vineyard, come to LA, and live the city life? Follow me around while I'm on tour?"

Memphis's fists clench at his sides. "You know I can't do that."

"I *do* know that. And what's more, I would never ask you to. Just like you wouldn't ask me to give up my dreams, either."

I lick my lips and let out a sigh, watching as his heart breaks, and feeling mine do the same.

"You might not be ready for it to end, but that doesn't mean it's not over."

My words hit him like a physical thing, and I watch as it rolls through his body. Every cell in my body screams at me to go to him. To wrap my arms around his chest and place my ear over where I know I'll hear his heart thumping that steady rhythm.

But I can't.

There's no path where this works. No reality where we are anything more than a bit of fun distraction.

And I can imagine nothing more devastating than giving something between us a shot, only to watch the good, kind, caring parts of us begin to fall apart.

Just like with Theo.

Just like with my parents.

Just like every other relationship that has inevitably crumbled and come to an end, or fallen by the wayside.

It's safer to tuck this time away as a memory. Let it be a good time and nothing more.

Too much of my heart would be at stake with this man. And that's the exact reason I need to leave.

"Goodbye, Memphis."

My words are quiet, but I know he hears them.

Then I do exactly what I told myself I needed to do. I leave.

I get in my car, and I drive away.

Memphis stands there watching me, his figure growing smaller in the rearview as I take the dusty drive out to the highway.

And that's when the first tears begin to fall.

The flight is easy, and I'm home before I know it, pushing open the door to my tenth-floor condo with a sigh, far more exhausted than I should be.

Something inside me is . . . empty.

My cat, Roger, greets me at the door. I pluck him up and snuggle him close, despite his protests. I pick up the little note on the entry table from my neighbor Mary, telling me he's been fed already.

"Missed you, Rodge," I whisper, squeezing him tight for a minute before dropping him back to the tile floor.

I tug my bag and suitcase inside and kick the door closed behind me. The open room feels as empty as I do.

I put Theo's things in storage before I left town, and it still feels strange. Like that time after Christmas, when all the decorations are taken down and the living room suddenly seems stark and lifeless.

When I cross over to the bedroom, I find that it's the same. The king-size bed frame sits empty in the middle of the room, the bedding and mattress having also been removed during the purge.

It's a good thing. I know that.

But it's also sad. I'm sad.

So instead of unpacking, I grab a glass of wine and retreat to my balcony. I take a deep breath of the salty sea air and settle into a chair.

I want to do nothing. I want to be no one. I just want to sit here and listen to the ocean and drink my weight in wine.

But that's unrealistic, so after a few sips, I pick up my phone and call Todd.

"Hey, your travel home go okay?"

"It did."

"Good. You ready for tomorrow?"

"I guess."

Todd laughs. "Yeesh. Don't sound so excited. It's only your dream coming true."

I chuckle a little bit, knowing he's right. "Sorry, I think I'm tired. And nervous."

"I'm sure you are. It's always intimidating to go into the studio for the first time. But remember, you aren't expected to come in with all your shit perfectly put together. Life has thrown you for a loop recently. Lean into that pain. Use it to create some really amazing music. And I mean, based on the stuff you sent me, it seems like that's what you've already done."

The truth is, sure, I'm still upset over Theo and the bullshit he put me through. But most of what I'm dealing with right now is not about the man I was in a relationship with for three years.

It's about Memphis. The man I've known for two weeks.

And that's something I don't really know how to explain.

Nor do I want to try.

"I'm sure it'll go great," I say, trying to put some enthusiasm in my tone.

Todd laughs. "Look, take some time tonight, review your music, feel the feels. And then bring that in tomorrow. I promise you, it'll be worth it."

We get off the phone, and I give myself until the end of my glass of wine to sit outside and stew. To ponder the unfairness of it all. Then I make a promise to go over every single song that we've been considering for the album.

My emotions are fragile as I strum the guitar, trying to infuse the right emotions into the right moments. And I do what Todd suggests. I let myself feel the feels.

When I pull open the door for the music studio in Century City where I'm scheduled to lay down my first track on Monday morning, I'm still emotional and still nervous, but more in control.

The nerves are unfamiliar. I can stand up on a stage and sing my heart out. I can lead presentations, talk in front of groups, go live on social media . . . I mean, anything, really.

But this is different.

I've never gone into a real, honest-to-goodness studio. So after I worked through my songs, I lay in bed late into the night reading through *what to expect the first time you have studio time* posts online, and I felt like I'd be prepared.

But the nerves are still here.

And I'm realizing it has more to do with the actual music I'm hoping to record than it is about the studio time itself. Todd really liked the snippets I sent to him, but it's hard to know how the songs will land with a manager or label when it comes time to lay down the tracks.

Todd is sitting on the couch in the recording room when I get there, and his boss, Jonas, is at the soundboard next to Richie, the producer who will be working on all the tech stuff that doesn't make sense to me.

"I hear you've been writing some pretty incredible stuff," Jonas says, leaning up against the soundboard, his arms crossed. "I'm looking forward to hearing it."

"I shared a few of your recordings with Jonas," Todd interjects. "Had to make sure he knew that you were really up to something special on your trip."

"I'm really, really happy with what came out of this trip, and I think it will be well worth it," I say to both of them.

Jonas nods but doesn't look entirely convinced, though I think as the head of A & R, it's his job to be skeptical until he hears proof that the music is worth the hype. Todd, on the other hand, looks like a proud father, which helps alleviate some of the pressure.

I get out my guitar and start strumming, warming up and humming the melody as Richie messes with the soundboard.

"You know what?" Todd says, rubbing thoughtfully at his chin. "We talked about recording 'Sharp Heart' today, but why don't you play one of the new tracks. I have a really good feeling about this new stuff. Jonas, I'd like you to hear at least one full song before we get started. What was the one you sent to me?"

"'Sweet Escape,'" I tell him, my fingers fluttering across the strings.

It's the one song I didn't practice last night, of course. My emotions felt too raw to relive my performance at The Standard, so I'd skipped over it.

They still feel that way now. But as I begin the opening chords, the melody flows out of me. It's almost effortless, the way my fingers move. The way my memory recalls the lyrics and how my voice rolls over the tune.

Easy. Natural.

The welling of emotion in my chest that I felt as I wrote it, with each change I made until everything was perfect.

And by the time I finish, I'm on the verge of tears, singing about finding something special, finding belonging, in a place I hadn't expected.

I finally look at Todd when I'm done, and a thrill races through me at the smile on his face. Jonas sits with his arms crossed, one eyebrow lifted high on his forehead.

"Well, fuck. I don't know where you've been for the past few weeks, but you are free to head back any time if it's going to bring us something like that."

At Jonas's reaction, Todd claps and says something to Richie, and then we're moving, all of us, getting me set up with the mics behind the glass.

There are only two things on my mind.

Holy shit, it's really happening.

And, surprisingly . . .

How much I wish I could share this with Memphis.

Chapter Nineteen

MEMPHIS

When I pull on the door to enter the restaurant, it doesn't budge. I peer through the tinted glass, taking in the fact that the lights are off and the chairs are upside down, resting on the tops of tables.

Which is when I realize . . . we're not open on Mondays.

I stand outside, my hands on my hips, unsure of what to do. The autumn sun warms my cool skin.

I've been losing myself in work over the past two weeks, waking at oh-dark-thirty each morning and joining the harvest crew to cut bunches of grapes. It's physically demanding, and the manual labor is a great stand-in for the workouts I've been struggling to fit into my routine. The work also keeps me just on the edge of fatigue and doesn't allow my mind to wander too much.

An appreciated exhaustion, because I know exactly where it would wander off to if it could. Or I guess . . . *who* it would wander off to.

After the morning work and then a few hours at my desk, I typically swing by the restaurant to finish out the day, even though it's becoming increasingly clear how superfluous my presence there is. But if I don't go, I don't know what to do with my time, an embarrassing reality that I face as I stand in front of a closed restaurant, trying to decide how to spend my suddenly free Monday evening.

Ultimately, I head back to the house. Family dinner is in full swing, so I dip into the kitchen, planning to grab a bowl of the cheesy pasta on the island and hide away in my office.

"Memphis!"

I groan internally, turning toward where my aunt is sitting at one of the tables out on the patio with some of the crew.

"Hey," I say, giving her a tight smile as I approach the table. "I was planning to eat at my desk. Finish up some compliance paperwork."

My father, seated across from my aunt, is studiously ignoring me, his attention laser focused on scraping the last few pieces of pasta out of his bowl.

We haven't spoken since our blowup three weeks ago, when he bit my head off and stormed out of my office. In the few times we've needed to interact since, we've managed to get by mostly ignoring each other.

It might be childish, but if it works for him, it works for me.

"Oh, stop it," Sarah says, tugging out the chair to her right. "You've been working yourself to the bone. It won't kill you to take fifteen minutes to sit and eat with us."

As much as I'd rather go to my office, I acquiesce and take a seat.

Of course, the minute I'm settled, my dad stands. "I've gotta get back to work," he says, heading into the house with his plate.

"Yeah, I'll bet you do," I grumble, my words coming out with a nasty edge.

He pauses, turning back to look at me for a second before continuing inside.

I sit down to eat, but I can feel Sarah looking at me. When I glance her way, I find her watching me, the edges of her mouth tilted down, her wrinkles far more pronounced as she looks at me with obvious disappointment.

Instantly, the righteous anger inside me withers.

As much as I might be upset at my dad . . . for plenty of shit . . . I've never made it a habit of bringing my personal frustrations into an environment that affects the rest of our staff. And sitting at a table full of crew is not the place for me to vent my irritation.

Slowly, the people at the table around us get up to leave, but my aunt stays in her chair beside me. After I finish, I remain seated as well, the expectation that I stay behind an unspoken understanding between us.

Finally, when we're alone on the patio, she speaks.

"What is going on between you and your father?" she asks. "You two have been grumbly at each other for weeks."

I sigh, scratching at the beard that's been growing in. "I told him I was upset about the announcement at Harvest-Eve and he stormed out," I tell her, deciding to be brief but honest.

"Your father can be stubborn, but you two need to sort this out. When you have personal stuff going on, I try not to get involved. It's just between you two. When I *am* going to give my two cents is when it starts leaching into the crew." She pins me with a look. "The last thing any of these sweet kids need is to be working fourteen-hour days, and dealing with stubborn owners throwing rocks at each other."

I nod. She's right.

Sarah pushes out of her chair and kisses the top of my head as she passes behind me, leaving me with just my thoughts.

I don't want to "sort this out" with my dad. He can be hardheaded, and closed-minded, and refuse to see reason about things that are so small and simple.

But I respect my aunt too much to ignore her. After giving myself a few minutes, I go in search of my father. Eventually I find him in the garage, sorting through boxes that have been gathering dust in a corner for years.

Something tells me he likes to keep busy when he's irritated, too.

"Sorry for the dig earlier," I tell him, deciding to rip off the bandage. "I shouldn't have done that in front of the crew."

"No, you shouldn't have."

My jaw flexes, irritation rolling through me.

"But you're still young," he continues. "There are plenty of things you still clearly need to learn."

I scoff, my already thin patience withering. I extended an olive branch, and he decides the best move is to snap it in half.

"You're right. There *is* still plenty that I need to learn. Maybe you should have thought of that before you just . . . announced that I'd be taking over in front of the entire staff. Maybe we should have actually had a conversation about it first."

My father sends a glare my way.

"You know what, Memphis? Maybe I should have sold this place when I had the chance. It would have been a whole lot less of a headache than dealing with this bullshit."

"Maybe you should have. Because you made this place into a fucking mess that *I'm* having to clean up."

"Because I didn't know what the hell I was doing!" he shouts, his arms going wide, emotion rolling off him in waves.

My head jerks back in surprise.

"This place is a fucking mess because *I* was a fucking mess," he continues. "I never wanted to come back here. My life was in San Francisco, with your mother. But when she died . . ."

All his anger seems to drain away in a single sentence, and he trails off, looking to the side.

We stand in silence for a moment before he speaks again. This time his words are tense. Agitated. Brittle from years of resentment.

"I spent years working this land with my dad because it was my only option. That was the agreement. If I came home, if I accepted their help, then I was back."

My shoulders fall at his admission. It never occurred to me that there was some kind of . . . negotiation to my dad coming back to Rosewood with his three kids in tow. I assumed it was an accepted reality of life. That he'd come home, and the family would all work together.

That's what family does, right?

"The truth is that I have never really cared about this vineyard. Your grandfather cared about it, and your aunt. Your brother and you.

But not me. I never wanted any of it. The only thing I cared about was making sure my kids would be okay when I didn't know if I could hold things together on my own."

There's something that happens when you learn a new truth.

When information is shared with you that you didn't know before.

It shatters the old picture of what you thought the world looked like, distorting the previous version you've always known.

My father sharing *his* truth has now radically altered mine.

I loved my grandfather so much. In my memories, he was always kind and loving, somewhat gritty, his hands always covered in dirt. As a kid, I'd ride around on the ATV at his side and he'd share with me everything he knew about vines and grapes and the soil, about fermentation and acidity. Everything he knew, he shared.

That's the version of him that *I* know.

And while those memories are real, now I have to reconcile what my dad has told me. That the same man I knew and loved used my dad's grief and loss as a bartering chip to get him to come home and work the land.

"I didn't come back here so I could take over the vineyard, Memphis. I never *wanted* to take it over. I came back here for you. So that you and your brother and sister could have a good life. One that I didn't think I could give you without help."

He stands there for a long moment, his chest heaving like he's run a mile. Then he turns and kicks at a box on the ground, the cardboard denting slightly. The corner buckles and collapses, and the box on top of it tips over, the contents spilling out all over the floor.

"Fuck!" he grits out, staring down at it before he dips and begins to pick things up.

I cross to where he's crouched, dropping to my knees beside him to help. My eyes snag on a picture in a red frame, and I grab it, my finger streaking across the glass to wipe away the dust. It's a picture of my mom in a black dress and my dad in a suit, standing in front of a shiny red convertible.

"When was this?" I ask, my brows furrowed.

I can't remember ever seeing my dad in a suit before. He didn't even wear one to my grandpa's funeral. He just wore a button-up shirt and a nice pair of jeans.

My dad stops where he's picking things up and takes the photo from me, his lips tilting up at the sides.

"This was the night your mom got promoted at her job. We went out to this fancy steakhouse on The Embarcadero with her boss and his wife." He shakes his head, his finger touching the glass slightly. "God, I loved that dress on her."

It's weird to see my dad like this, reminiscing about my mom. Mostly because he so rarely does it.

I begin returning the other items that fell to the floor to the box—a handful of playbills, an envelope of ticket stubs, a few more framed photos of him and my mom or the four of us as a family in front of our house before Micah was born.

I push back one of the flaps and peer inside, taking in a host of memories that are from before my time.

"I thought you got rid of most of your stuff from before Mom died," I say, repeating back the line he said to me often over the years, any time I asked about things from before we moved to Rosewood.

There are a few boxes of her things in the attic, but this stuff looks like it belongs to Dad.

"I did. I sold the house, our cars, all our furniture, most of our belongings," he offers, dropping awkwardly down so that he's sitting on the dirty garage floor. "But there were a handful of things I've never been willing to part with."

He holds up the framed photo of him and my mom.

"Like a photo of your mom in this dress, when she's smiling like that." He looks back at it again, and something inside me pinches at the way he looks at it.

The evidence of his life *before*. The happy life that he wanted for himself. And suddenly, I feel like I understand him in a completely different way.

This was the life he and my mom wanted to live. Going out to nice dinners, a beautiful house in the city, family vacations.

Then, in a blink, it was gone.

And he was back here, the last place he wanted to be.

"I've never regretted that choice, Memphis. Coming back here," he says, breaking the silence, his voice quiet. Reflective. "It gave all of us a beautiful life. Especially you three. And that was always what was most important."

Something inside me aches at his words.

There's a truth I know now, not only about my grandfather, but about my father as well. The type of sacrifice he made for us . . . I get it in a way I didn't before.

Then I ask him something I've always wondered. "If you never wanted to be here, why were you so upset when Murphy left?"

He sighs. "Watching your sister leave . . . I don't know." He glances around, avoiding my eyes. "It was like losing your mother all over again."

We tuck the box safely on one of the shelves in the corner, then stand there, both of us staring at the boxes in silence.

"I struggled with the vineyard. Struggle," he corrects. "Still struggle, sometimes. But I don't doubt you're going to do right by this place. You're going to do with it all the things my father wanted *me* to do."

I huff a laugh. "I'm not so sure, sometimes."

My dad pats his hand on my shoulder and gives it a squeeze.

"You will. I believe in you." He pauses for a minute, licks his lips. "I should have checked in with you more. Or offered more support. I think I just . . . finally hit my wall. And when things kept getting worse, I thought maybe selling would have saved us all a lot of headache."

"Why didn't you ask for help when things started going south?"

My dad snorts a laugh. "We Hawthorne men are not the best at asking for help," he says. "I mean, look at you. You're working fourteen-, sixteen-, sometimes eighteen-hour days. When was the last time *you* asked?"

"I ask for help."

"With things that you don't need help with," he says, laughing. "Wine labels? That's a decision you can make on your own. You don't need my input. Or your aunt's. I'm talking about the day in and day out of running the vineyard, Memphis. It's exhausting and draining and shouldn't be all on one person's shoulders."

The truth behind his words resonates, as if it's something I've always known. My mind briefly revisits the conversation I had with Micah a few weeks ago, though I set that thought aside to mull over later.

My dad takes a step back, his eyes scanning the boxes along the wall.

"Maybe it's time to unbox some of these," I suggest. "Might be nice to see some photos of you and Mom around the house."

"Maybe," he says, then gives me a tight smile.

Then I realize, maybe he doesn't *want* a constant reminder of a version of him that no longer exists. Of a life that he can barely remember.

"Or maybe it stays right here," I offer.

At that his smile softens into one that's real, and he squeezes my shoulder again. "Or maybe that."

My dad and my aunt have both communicated things to me over the past few weeks that make me realize . . . it's time to really change things around here. Not just make some shifts to how we're managing the budget, but real, significant change.

So I put some finishing touches on my proposal, and then I call a meeting with my siblings. I know what I'm going to say will shock them—my sister, much more than my brother—but I think my ideas are going to move us in the right direction. I just have to hope they agree.

"Thanks for taking time to chat," I say, looking at Micah and Murphy, who sit across from me in the two chairs facing my desk.

"This feels very formal," Murphy jokes. "I don't think you've ever called a meeting for the three of us before."

"Well, hopefully, that's about to change."

Micah and Murphy look at each other briefly, then back at me.

"I've made some decisions about the vineyard. About the future and what I want it to look like. But it only works if we're all on board," I start. "With Dad announcing me as CEO, my first act as CEO is going to be . . . stepping down."

Murphy's head jerks back dramatically, and Micah's eyes narrow the slightest bit.

"This vineyard is something I love. Something in my blood. And I want it to succeed more than anything. But I think to really move us forward, it can't just belong to me. It needs to belong to all of us," I say, turning my computer so it's facing them.

Displayed on the screen is a mockup of a new organizational structure. It's mostly modeled after the one Micah created and presented a few weeks ago, but with a few adjustments.

"Does that say *I'm* in charge of the restaurant?" Murphy asks, disbelief on her face.

"Not just the restaurant," I clarify, pointing to some of the other elements. "You would be the hospitality director, overseeing the restaurant, events, the tasting room, and tours. All of the forward-facing stuff. And Micah, you would be vineyard management. So that includes winemaking, land and facility management, bottling, and the warehouse."

My eyes flick between both of them, trying to decipher by their facial expressions how they're receiving the information.

"And I would oversee business operations. So, admin, marketing, finances, human resources, and wholesale distribution."

Then I go on to highlight how that would impact our staff. Aunt Sarah working under Murphy with events, and Naomi in charge of the landscape and seasonal crew. Edgar overseeing the lab and how the rest of the full-time staff would then shuffle under me.

"I realize it's a lot to take in. It would be a big change."

"A *huge* change," Murphy interjects.

"I already have a feeling that Micah is on board, since the idea of a restructure was actually his."

I glance at my brother, who nods at me.

"It looks great, Memphis. Really," he says, giving me that quiet grin of his that says I have his approval.

"So, Murph. I want to be clear, there's no pressure here. I would love for this to be the three of us, managing it all together. But I know that songwriting is important to you, and I want you to be able to pursue your passions." I pause, trying to make sure I really drive it home. "But if you're interested, if this sounds good to you, I think you would do an incredible job. I've been watching you thrive in the restaurant over the past few months, and the truth is . . . I don't need to be there. You have it all under control."

I've never been the most eloquent person, so I hope I'm able to adequately express to my sister how proud I am of her and what a great job she's doing.

"What would you do if I said no?" she asks, still looking unsure.

"I can ask Sarah to step into that role instead," I offer. "Or I'm sure there are other ways to move forward. But I'll only do that if you don't want it."

She lets out a sigh, glancing at Micah and then at me.

And then her eyes begin to well with tears.

"You really think I can handle all of that?" she asks. "What if I mess it up?"

"You *will* mess up. Just like I have, and just like Micah has. But that's why we'd be doing it together. So when one of us struggles, we aren't facing it alone."

Murphy watches me for a long minute, then her eyes return to my screen.

"Murphy Hawthorne, hospitality director, *does* have a nice ring to it," she says, her lips tilting up at the sides. "I'm gonna be honest, Memphis. This terrifies me. But there's something inside me saying that this is the right move. I love writing music, and it's something that will always be part of me. As much as I haven't ever wanted to admit it, this vineyard is part of me, too. And I want to help. I want to make it better. So . . . count me in."

I smile, a sense of gratitude for my siblings and their big, incredible hearts coming over me. For their ability not only to believe in me, but to believe in each other and the possibilities ahead of us.

Letting out a long sigh, I decide that now is the time to be honest with them about the finances. Brutally honest. So that they have a full picture before they sign on.

"Before you get too excited, I want to share the realities of the finances," I say, watching the smiles dim slightly on their faces.

I click around on my computer and pull up the current financial spreadsheet.

"We've been in the red for quite a while, and in order to climb out of that, we have to continue making changes. But I think I have a vision that should get us out of that debt in the next five years. I've made a good first start. I plugged up a lot of the hemorrhages and cut operational costs, and I took out a personal loan to finance the restaurant. But there are still a lot of . . ."

"Whoa, whoa, wait a second," Micah interjects. He sits forward, resting his arms on his knees. "Say that last part again?"

I sigh, wishing I'd been able to gloss over it.

"Did you just say you . . . took out a *personal* loan?" he clarifies. "So none of that debt is from creating the restaurant?"

Shaking my head, I realize that if I'm going to be honest, I need to be fully honest. "Dad offered fifty thousand dollars toward the restaurant, and in reality, that wouldn't have even been enough to cover Wes's salary." I shrug. "I took out the loan so that I could give the vineyard the best chance of succeeding without further growing its debt."

"But now *you* have to pay it off," Murphy says. "How big was this loan?"

I pause. "Four hundred thousand dollars."

Her eyes widen, and Micah shakes his head.

"You're going to be paying that for the rest of your life."

I nod. "I know. But saving this place means everything to me, so I went all in." I pause. "And I think it's working. My financial forecasts are either meeting or exceeding the expectations. The restaurant is saving the vineyard."

My sister surprises me then, pushing out of her seat and coming behind my desk, wrapping her arms around me.

I'm not a big hugger, and it's always awkward at first. But eventually I give in and wrap my arms around her, too.

"The restaurant isn't saving us, Memphis," she says, her arms tightening around me. "You are."

A wave of emotion surges through me, a sense of pride hitting me square in the chest, possibly for the first time.

I pat her gently on the back, appreciating her words.

After a long moment, she returns to her chair, and we dive in. Looking at some paperwork and discussing our plans for how to move forward as co-owners. Scheduling our first full meeting to brainstorm and talk about next steps.

It feels amazing.

Incredible actually.

I always thought doing it on my own would be what made me proudest of this place. But it's not.

It's because we're doing it together.

Later that night, lying in bed, I do what I've been wanting to do all day. I pull up my lone social media account on my phone, go into the search history, and select the name I've checked almost every day since she left.

Vivian Walsh.

I've never been big into posting online. Mostly because my life is boring—nobody wants to see pictures of me sitting at my desk all day—but also because I don't have the time.

But Vivian posts daily.

Her feed is filled with photos of her with her guitar, her cat, the ocean. And ever since she left town, her stories have shown some of the behind-the-scenes stuff of her at the studio and sitting on her patio overlooking the water.

Each time I look at her page, I scroll back, looking at the static images she posted while she was in town.

Her notepad on the table at Rosewood Roasters.

An image of her sitting on the ATV by herself on the day Micah took her on the tour.

A photo of her and Murphy on the first night she came to town.

And then there's one I always look at for longer than I'd like to admit. The one of her legs stretched out in front of her, sunset over the vines in the distance, and me, seated on the edge of the porch with my legs dangling over the side.

It's an innocuous photo. There isn't really anything special about it. Except for the fact that we were together, and I often wonder what it was that she saw when she took it. Why she posted this one and not one of the many others she captured that evening.

I feel like an idiot checking her social media, trying to find deeper meaning in a simple photo.

She told me it wasn't worth it to try.

She told me that she wanted to go home, to her life.

To the things that matter.

That should be enough for me to let her go.

It should be.

God, it really should be.

So I click into her story one last time, watching the quick video of her cat rubbing up on the corner of her couch, and then the video of her singing into a microphone in one of those fancy recording studios.

And then I close it out, promising myself it's the last time.

Chapter Twenty

Vivian

I tuck my phone against my shoulder to listen to my voicemail while I scan my items through the checkout at the grocery store.

"Hey, Vivian, this is Gigi Wright. I was the announcer at the open mic night last month at The Standard?"

I pause, holding a bottle of wine over the scanner, surprise rolling through me at the idea I'm getting a phone call from Gigi. I try to remember when I might have given her my phone number.

"I hope you're doing well, sweetheart. I remembered you talking to Errol after your performance, and when I asked him he said you're pretty good friends with Murphy Hawthorne. Well, I saw her at Rosewood Roasters a few days ago and asked her for your number, because I've been reaching out to all the open mic performers over the past few months. Would you be interested in performing at our Fall Festival?"

My head jerks back in surprise, and I almost drop my phone. What?

"Originally, we had this band scheduled to perform. It's Shane Eldridge's son, Spencer, who is a really great country singer. You know, he went to LA once to perform on that *X Factor* show on TV?"

I glance around, confused about who Shane and Spencer are and thankful that there's nobody else in line to use the self-checkout machines. I seem to be really struggling to follow this voicemail and handle my groceries at the same time.

"Well, anyway, he broke his arm last week in some accident involving a horse drag race? I'm not really sure. I try not to ask too many questions. Anyway, he's not going to be able to perform on Saturday night, and I came up with the idea that we could do a big open mic night with some of our best performers over the past few months, and I just knew I needed to reach out to you and invite you to perform, if you're interested."

There's a brief pause, and I wonder if she ended the message without saying goodbye, but then she starts speaking again.

"Oh, and one other thing. I completely understand that you don't live in town. Murphy said you're in LA, but I figured I'd let you know that each of the performers will get a fifty-dollar stipend and a coupon to get a cinnamon and sugar pretzel at the festival. You know, just in case that sways you at all. Okay, dear. Give me a call back. Hope you're well. Bye now."

I chuck my phone into my purse and then swipe my card to pay for my order. When I finally make my way out of the little market around the corner from my condo, my mind is retracing over everything she said.

A part of me wants to say yes to Gigi's request. The idea of playing a few songs at a Fall Festival in the middle of wine country sounds incredible. All the wine and pumpkins and fall festivities, not to mention the excitement of being onstage.

That's not the real reason.

I sigh as I dig around for my keys, trying to ignore the voice in my head that's telling me I'm only interested because it means I might see Memphis again.

But unlike many of the other days when I've dismissed my thoughts, today it's not so easy.

I miss him. More than I thought I would. More than I want to.

Or maybe that's a lie.

Maybe I miss him just as much as I knew I would, and that's why it's so hard.

I thought that now, four weeks after coming home from Rosewood, I would have been able to move on. I heard in *Sex and the City* that it takes twice as long to get over someone as it did to fall for them.

I call bullshit.

Quite a few times I've found myself lying in bed at night and thinking back to the time we spent together. I've lost myself in memories of his mouth between my legs, bringing myself to the peak with my own fingers as a mediocre stand-in.

But I've also stared out at the water, thinking about that conversation we had sitting in the back of his truck after Theo came to town. Or about that time we spent wandering through the vineyard, the stupid grape game, and all the silly banter.

I've tried to convince myself that it wasn't as good as I remembered. That I'm waxing poetic about a fling I had on vacation, which is much easier to fixate on than the real problems you face in normal, everyday life.

Doesn't stop me from daydreaming about him.

Or imagining him coming down to LA, like a white knight, showing up to declare his love in some kind of grand gesture.

But it's a foolish dream.

I told Memphis I wasn't interested in things moving forward. I told him that I needed to come here and he needed to stay there.

I thought it would be foolish to try and turn us into something more. To allow the very big feelings I felt for him to continue once I left.

But it looks like it doesn't actually matter what I thought, because those feelings and emotions have continued anyway.

Leaving Rosewood was supposed to be enough to help me move on. But it wasn't.

Instead, I still feel all those things, plus the twinge of regret.

❖ ❖ ❖

"Look, I think if we can adjust the way you're singing that last word at a higher pitch . . . if you drop low instead, I think it'll be really killer," Richie says into the mic that pipes into my headphones.

I nod. "Yeah, let's try it again."

The music we recorded when I was in the studio last month filters through, starting a little bit before the bridge. I wait for the beat and when I hear my cue, I start with the same lyrics I've sung almost ten times now. But this time, I finish the last line on a lower note, dropping down instead of going up.

Richie cuts the music and puts both arms in the air. "That's it, baby! Perfect! I'm gonna send it over to Jonas."

I smile and tug off my headphones, thrilled that we're finally wrapping "Sweet Escape." I thought we finished it during my last few days in the studio, but Jonas said he felt like it was missing something and sent me back to rerecord.

"It doesn't have that same angsty *something* that you had when you sang it that first day in the studio," he told me. "Get that back."

Of course, after Gigi's call yesterday and spending my evening thinking about Memphis, about the connection we had that I still can't let go of, I finally broke down and did the thing I swore I wouldn't ever do.

I called Murphy, convincing myself it *wasn't* because I wanted to hear about Memphis.

I asked how she's doing. How the vineyard's doing. How things were going with Wes.

But my friend could see through the very flimsy conversation.

"Just ask me," she eventually said.

I sighed. "How's Memphis?"

"Really good, actually."

Something twisted in my gut. Not that I wanted him to be pining or depressed or anything stupid like that.

"I think he misses you, though," she added.

I laughed, shaking my head, surprised at how her words filled my heart with joy.

"Nah, he just misses the sex."

Murphy gagged, and we both laughed and moved on.

But her words stayed with me all night.

He misses you.

Once Jonas has had a chance to listen to the updated version, he gives me a call.

"It's perfect," he says, his voice coming in loud through the speaker on my phone. "Thanks for sending it over, Richie. Go ahead and wrap that. That's the final version."

Richie starts to press buttons on the soundboard. "Sounds good, boss."

I take Jonas off speaker and step out of the studio, heading into the hallway as I bring the phone to my ear. "Hey, before you go, can I ask a quick question?"

"Shoot."

Licking my lips, I debate with myself again, not even really sure why I'm asking, but still compelled to. Still wanting to know for sure.

"There's this Fall Festival. It's up in Rosewood, that place I went to write last month?" I push through the door that leads out to a long hallway, then rest my back against the wall. "How would you feel if I went up there and performed a few songs? Maybe got a little more inspiration?"

Jonas's response is quick.

"You know how the label feels about performances before an album releases," he says. "The official position is always going to be no."

I nod, though he can't see me. I knew that was going to be the answer. It's one of those realities you face when you sign with a label. Not everything is up to you anymore.

But part of me still needed to hear it. Still wanted confirmation.

Just on the off chance . . .

"But listen," Jonas continues, interrupting my thoughts. "Todd made it abundantly clear that visiting that town is what fueled you to create some of this new music that is just . . . so fucking good. And the reality of any hard-and-fast rule is that there are *always* exceptions, no matter what anyone says."

I swallow thickly, my lips parting a bit as I listen.

"So consider this my personal permission—no, my *encouragement*—for you to go back to that town and perform your little heart out."

My head falls back and thuds gently against the wall behind me as surprise fills me.

"Whatever muse of yours they've got hidden away in wine country up there"—he chuckles—"go back and let it speak to you."

He says a few more things before we get off the phone, and I sink down to the ground, wrapping my arms around my knees.

I don't even know why I asked.

I mean, it was a pointless question.

Of course I'm not going to go.

What real purpose could it serve?

You know why you asked. You want to see Memphis again.

I roll my eyes and go back inside to talk to Richie and make sure we're wrapped for the day before heading home.

But my thoughts about Memphis and returning to Rosewood stay with me long after I've left the studio.

Of course part of me wants to go back to Rosewood. Of course part of me wants to see Memphis. Listen to the warm cadence of his voice and feel him hot and hard underneath me. Hold him tightly in my arms and hear the deep rumble of his laugh.

It would be foolish of me to pretend otherwise.

I pour a glass of wine, sink into my couch, and stare out to where the sun has just dipped below the horizon.

But it's unrealistic.

My life is here.

His life is there.

And that's not going to change.

A knock on my door surprises me. Normally guests have to call up through the buzz-in. When I look through the peephole and spot Theo on the other side, my nostrils flare.

"What are you doing here?" I growl as I yank the door open. "All your shit is gone."

"Yeah, I know," he says stepping in past me without an invitation. "But there were a few things missing that I'm here to collect."

I roll my eyes and wave my hand toward the living room. "Take whatever you want, Theo."

"Don't be such a bitch, Vivian. I'm not here to rob you. I just want my Armani suit and the bottle of Macallan."

"I don't have your Armani suit."

"Yes, you do. It's in the dry cleaning from after that dinner at Nobu."

I walk into my closet and tug out the dry cleaning, seeing that he is, in fact, correct. His Armani suit and two dress shirts are tucked into the clear plastic alongside my pale-green dress. I pull out my dress and hang it back in the closet, then take the rest of the items out to where he's still standing in the entry.

"Is that all?"

"And the Macallan."

"A bottle of whiskey? That's important enough to come back for? Really?"

He shrugs and gives me that stupid smile. "It's good whiskey."

I grab it from the liquor cabinet and hand it to him, but when he reaches for it, I pull it back.

"Are you really going to never actually apologize?" I ask, suddenly overwhelmed with the righteous belief that I deserve an apology.

Not that it would change anything. But just because it feels . . . right. Like it might provide some sort of closure.

"I apologized when I came to Rosewood."

"That was a bullshit apology and you know it. You were only there to say whatever you thought would get you what you wanted."

"Why should I apologize, Vi?" he asks, chucking the dry cleaning over the couch and tucking his hands in his pockets, his posture easy even though his attitude is beginning to shine through.

"Because you slept with Amelia! Because you betrayed my trust and ruined our relationship."

He shakes his head. "You were checked out of our relationship months before it ended."

Crossing my arms, I glare at him. "You don't get to point the finger at me, as if I'm the one to blame for the fact you couldn't keep it in your pants," I volley back.

"Look, I cheated. It was a shit thing to do. And yeah, maybe I'm an asshole for it. But you act like you played no part in our relationship fizzling out. Which is bullshit. Fuck, sometimes I wonder if you ever even really wanted to date me in the first place."

My head jerks back at his claim. "What the hell are you talking about? Of course I wanted to date you. I loved you. I shared my life with you."

He shakes his head again, the move infuriating me.

"I'm not saying you didn't love me. I loved you, too. But you didn't share your life with me. You never got emotional with me, never shared your deepest fears or told me all your dark secrets." He picks up the dry cleaning and hangs it over one arm. "And I didn't, either. It was easier that way. But like I said, I may have played a part in this ending. But you did, too."

Then his eyes drop to the Macallan in my hand.

"Keep it," he says. "Have a nice life, Vi."

And then he's out the door, the soft snick of it closing behind him sounding like a loud boom with the way it echoes in my condo.

I stare at the bottle of whiskey in my hand for a long moment, suddenly having the urge to chuck it across the room, wanting to watch it shatter on the wall.

How dare he?

How *fucking* dare he?

I gently set the bottle on the counter in the kitchen and then storm out of my condo, nothing but my keys and phone in my hand.

The sky is fairly dark when I pull out onto the road outside my condo and onto PCH heading north, the highway that stretches from Orange County all the way up to somewhere in Northern California. Six-hundred-something miles of road.

Not that I want to drive six hundred miles, but late night on a Monday means Highway 1 is going to be mostly free of traffic and a great stretch for a mind-clearing drive.

I blast that stupid playlist that I found when I was in Rosewood, singing along to the songs I know and drumming along on the steering wheel.

I am enraged. Infuriated.

But as much as I try to drown my thoughts with music, they still manage to creep in. And eventually, I turn it down, roll down my windows, and give in.

Part of me is shocked at Theo's allegations that I'm equally responsible for the demise of our relationship. He fucking cheated. *He's* the slimeball. And placing blame on me is a cheap way for him to get out of feeling responsible for what he did.

Okay so . . . I know that to be true.

The problem is that I think there's another truth in there as well.

One I don't want to face.

But maybe one that I should.

Maybe he was right when he said I didn't share my life with him.

Growing up in a home like mine, that was what I saw. That's what I knew.

My parents didn't talk about their emotions and their fears. They didn't share with each other on a deep level. Hollywood is all about fake images, and that's what they portrayed. The perfect face of a perfect family.

The only person who truly knows me is . . . me.

And sometimes I wonder how well I actually do know myself.

Was I really not vulnerable with Theo?

I try to think back over our relationship. Three years of us dating and having sex and then moving in together at the end of last year. I mean, surely we were vulnerable about things with each other, right?

But try as I might, all I see when I look back are the same few things. Social outings with friends, semiregular sex, and maneuvering around each other in our home.

It's heartbreaking.

And almost unbelievable.

Which is why I dial Murphy's number. The dial tone ringing is replaced by the soft sound of a guitar in the background when she finally picks up.

I need more than just my own opinion on this.

"Hey, Vi. Two nights in a row. You must miss me, huh?"

"You got a sec?"

The sound of the guitar cuts off, and then Murphy's voice sounds closer.

"Everything okay?"

"You're my best friend. You know that, right?"

"*Awww.* Thanks, girl. You're my best friend, too."

"And as best friends, we're honest with each other."

"Right," she says, dragging the word out, clearly curious what I'm getting at.

"So I need you to be honest with me. Do you think we have a deep relationship?"

Murphy's silent for a minute before she responds. "I'd say you like to keep things close to your chest," she finally says.

"Don't be diplomatic."

"What is this about?"

I sigh. "Theo came by tonight."

"He's a prick. Don't believe anything he says."

At that, I let out a laugh. "Well, he told me that I never really let him in. That I don't let people get too close. So now I'm wondering if that's true."

Murphy pauses for a beat before she speaks again. "All right, if you want an honest answer, no. I don't think you let people super close. But there isn't necessarily anything wrong with that. And you shouldn't let him make you think there is. Not everyone likes to be an open book, and that's okay."

I chew on the inside of my cheek, considering what she's said. "So give me an example," I say. "An example of something I could share with you that would be . . . deeper. Letting you close."

"You could talk to me about Memphis."

"You really want to hear me talk about your brother's big penis?" I joke.

"See? Right there. When there's a chance to be honest about what's on your mind, you make jokes. It doesn't *have* to be about my brother's penis. We could talk about how he makes you feel or how much harder it was to leave than you thought it would be. Or the fact you miss him. *That* would be letting me close."

That same emotion wells in my chest from before. "But I don't want to talk about those things," I tell her, my voice quiet. "And why would you? Why would you want to hear about that?"

"Why did you listen to all the emotional, hard things I shared before I moved back to Rosewood? Or when I started dating Wes, why did you help me talk through the ups and downs? We listen to each other because we want to know each other, Vivian. And we share because we want to *be known.*"

My eyes well with tears. I bat them away, trying to keep my eyes clear as I drive. We continue in silence for several minutes, and I appreciate my friend so much for sitting on the phone with me while I battle that little thing in my chest that tells me if I'm vulnerable with someone, they're going to take advantage. That if I'm ever truly known, I'll be turned away.

But the thing that speaks louder than my fear is the voice that tells me I can trust Murphy.

"I miss Memphis," I tell her. "More than I was prepared for."

"I'm sure you do," she responds, her voice soothing and warm. "He misses you, too."

"You said that last night. How do you know that's true?"

Murphy snorts. "I caught him looking at your social media while he was at his desk," she responds, shocking me. "I've never seen a man close a browser so quickly. You'd think it was porn."

My mind scrolls back over the social media posts I've been sharing recently, trying to remember what I've put out there and what Memphis has seen.

"I wish I could tease him about stalking me," I say, giggling to myself.

"You could if you called him."

"He doesn't want to talk to me. I told him it wouldn't work and then left him after he poured his heart out."

"My brother poured his heart out to you?" she asks, chuckling quietly. "Jesus, Vivian. You two are so meant for each other. The way you draw each other out is just . . . wild. You're a watercolor, and he's an Excel spreadsheet. It doesn't seem like it's gonna work at first, but then it does."

"I think you need to learn better metaphors."

"Meh, I like it."

I laugh, my heart a lot calmer than it was a little while ago.

"He does draw me out," I say, deciding to share what's on my mind instead of keeping it to myself. Trying to do the thing that is so unnatural to me. "He makes me feel like I can be me, but like . . . an authentic version of myself."

Murphy hums. "That's so romantic."

I chew on the inside of my cheek, thinking it over. "Do you think if I tried, I'd be able to get him to forgive me?"

"As your best friend, my honest opinion is that he's madly in love with you and would forgive anything. But as Memphis's sister, I'm going to tell you that you better really fucking mean it if you try."

Blowing out a breath, I know what the right decision is. What the *only* decision is.

Doing whatever it takes to get Memphis to forgive me. To take back what I said in his driveway. To show him who I really am, and ask him to love me exactly like that.

Because that's the way I love him.

I would be a fool not to acknowledge that there are still very real hurdles in our way—his job and mine, the distance, my fears about relationships. But it feels even *more* foolish to give up on a man I've fallen in love with without ever really trying.

"Okay," I say, letting out a long breath, excitement beginning to simmer in my veins. "I have an idea. And I need your help."

Chapter Twenty-One

MEMPHIS

The weather is turning. Temps dip into the low fifties in the evening, and the fall foliage that makes wine country such a desirable place to visit during the autumn is emerging. October brings a boom to the vineyard and the restaurant, and with the surge of guests, we expand our tours and hire a few more waitstaff.

We've made it through the hardest part of the harvest, and now we're booking down the road at a steady clip.

Which should feel amazing.

And it does.

In some ways.

There are a lot of things to be grateful for.

My siblings' excitement about the restructure and how they've jumped in with both feet. The profit the restaurant is bringing in and the impact it's having on our bottom line. The positive energy around the vineyard that was missing for far too long.

Even though I still have a ton to do, there is a lightness to my work that I haven't felt in . . . maybe years?

Which is why it's infuriating to realize that the heaviness I'd been carrying around on my shoulders for so long has simply relocated to my chest.

I feel like a fool, still pining after a woman who made it clear that this was only ever supposed to be a bit of fun. That things between us could never work.

And I've tried every mental game possible to remind my*self* of the realities.

That it was just two weeks.

That it was just for fun.

That we didn't really know each other that well.

But those arguments are falsities. Like information that is completely out of context to the truth of what those two weeks were like, how those moments bloomed into something more, and how much deeper those feelings became.

It's a vicious cycle of regret. I stop wondering if I could have done or said something different to have truly convinced her that we could figure it out. That we didn't have to abandon our lives in order to create a new one together. That there was something here worth fighting for.

I didn't, though.

I didn't say any of those things.

Instead, I just let her go.

Just let her get in the car and drive away.

And my pride has kept me from calling her. Or texting.

Or fuck, driving down to LA and telling her how I really feel.

But she wouldn't want that.

Look what happened with Theo.

He went after her, didn't he? And she shut him down. Sent him packing.

Realistically, our situations are different. She communicated what she wanted, and I'm the kind of man who knows how to listen.

She wanted to say goodbye, so I let her.

If only I could fucking say it, too.

"I need your help tonight," Murphy says, resting her hip against the kitchen island.

I glance at her, but continue spreading mustard onto a slice of bread, intending on eating an early dinner and then heading over to the warehouse to look through some inventory.

We've settled on January as the transition timeline for the restructure. We don't want to rush things, but really give ourselves the time to brainstorm. Get through the busiest part of the year one final time before Micah and Murphy take on the full range of their new responsibilities.

As much as I'm looking forward to the day when we're sharing the joys and hardships of this vineyard together, I don't want to dump it all on them at one time. So for now, some of those tasks still rest with me.

Like inventory.

But I don't mind. The knowledge that we're in it together is almost enough to make it seem like I'm not working as much.

And my desire to keep busy and keep my mind off Vivian is definitely enough to make the continued work a nonissue.

"What do you need my help with?" I ask, putting the bread on the turkey sandwich and slicing it in half.

"I need to staff the booth at the Fall Festival."

My lip curls slightly at the idea. "No thanks. I hate that shit."

"I know you do. But we need two people—one to handle the wine samples and one for the game."

"Ask Sarah."

"She was originally who I asked, but she's not feeling good."

"Naomi."

"You want her to work the last shift at the booth and then do a harvest at two a.m.? Besides, she's covering crew dinner for Sarah."

I sigh. "Micah. Dad. One of your waitstaff."

"Micah's in San Francisco meeting with a distributor. Dad is also working the morning harvest. And our waitstaff are busy with the restaurant. I'm telling you, Memphis. You were my last ask."

Groaning, I take a bite of my sandwich.

I don't dislike the Fall Festival. I used to love it when I was younger. But now that I'm in my thirties, I struggle to jump into community events anymore. Everyone always seems so happy and carefree, and that's not the reality of my life right now.

Maybe it will be again. Someday.

I hope it is.

I believe it can be.

But not right now.

So the idea of handing out wine samples, or worse, managing whatever idiotic game has been set up, sounds like the exact last thing I want to do tonight.

"Fine," I grumble. "What time do we need to leave?"

"Probably thirty minutes?"

I give her a sarcastic thumbs-up and she laughs, telling me she's going to get ready and we'll head out soon. Then I'm left behind to enjoy my sandwich in peace.

About forty-five minutes later, Murphy and I are pulling into the dirt lot across the street from Rosewood High School. The bright lights from the football field are like a glowing beacon to anyone looking for a fun evening. It takes a few minutes to park, and then we're walking across the field, weaving between families and couples holding bags of popcorn and stuffed animals.

"Hey, guys! We're here to release you into the wild," Murphy says as we approach the booth with the big Hawthorne Vines banner across the top.

Mira and Enid wave and smile at us, then do a quick overview of how they have everything organized.

"How does the game work?" I ask, peering at the table with dozens of wine bottle corks sticking out of it, each with a red or black dot on the end.

"Okay, so it's ten dollars to play. Each person gets three rings, and they toss them onto the board. If it lands on one of the red dots, they get a standard bottle. If it lands on a cork with a black dot, they get to pick from the nicer vintages we brought."

"And if they miss on all three?"

"They get a ticket for a free glass of wine at the restaurant."

I smirk at Enid. "That's smart."

"It was Murphy's idea."

I glance at my sister, who is listening to Mira explain how she's been handling the wine samples and showing Murphy where the wines are boxed under the table. I need to stop being surprised by the things my sister does, by the mind she has and the things she's capable of handling. But for whatever reason, she keeps impressing me all the same.

Eventually, Enid and Mira take off, and then it's me and my sister, manning the booth and interacting with festival attendees. We stay pretty busy for about the first hour, doling out samples and encouraging people to play the cork and ring game. It's not as horrible as I thought it would be.

When there's a lull, we take a seat in the camping chairs set up behind the table, enjoying the break.

Murphy glances at her watch. "They're supposed to start the bands up on the stage soon," she tells me. "Apparently Gigi invited everyone who has ever performed at open mic night."

There have been some incredible performers over the years. The monthly open mic night is a beloved tradition in our small town. But of course, my mind immediately pulls up the memory of Vivian on the stage, singing that song she wrote while she was here. The sound of her beautiful voice filling the bar, everyone staring at her, enraptured. Including me.

I don't doubt I'll hear her singing on the radio someday. She'll take the world by storm and achieve all those big dreams she has for herself.

It's what I want for her.

Not that it matters what I want.

But still, a part of me is glad she wasn't willing to let go of the big things she's dreamed of for . . . some guy.

My chest still aches at the idea that maybe that's all I was to her, though, when she was so much more to me.

The music that's been pumping through the speakers comes to an end, and then we hear a familiar voice making announcements.

"All right, ladies and gentlemen, you're in for a treat tonight!" Gigi says, her voice echoing around the football field. "Tonight, we have a handful of incredible performers ready to bring this Fall Festival to life!"

I turn to Murphy as Gigi continues her announcement.

"Ten bucks says the first song is an off-key version of 'Indian Summer,'" I joke, referencing a Brooks & Dunn classic that I hear somewhere in town at the start of autumn like clockwork.

Murphy smirks at me.

"Welcome to the stage, all the way from Santa Monica . . ."

My head spins back toward the stage, my brows furrowing.

". . . Vivian Walsh!"

I blink, certain I've misheard. But sure enough, there's that familiar red hair as she walks onto the stage, a guitar slung around her shoulder. I push out of my chair and take a step forward, my hands on my hips as I watch her get set up, adjusting the height of the mic and plugging her guitar into the sound system.

"Hello, Rosewood!" she says, her voice ringing loud and beautiful and clear through the speakers as she steps in front of the mic. "Some of you might remember me from when I visited this incredible town last month and did a little performance at The Standard. Well, I'm back with a few songs, and I'm excited to share them with you. I hope you enjoy."

Then her fingers begin to pluck and strum her strings. I turn back to Murphy, finding her up and helping someone at the cork and ring game.

"Did you know about this?" I demand.

"Of course I did," she replies, laughing as she accepts cash from the couple standing, waiting to play.

I face the stage again, my ears soaking up the sounds of Vivian's voice as she plays that song she played at The Standard. "Sweet Escape," I think she called it. Listening to her play soothes something inside me in a way I didn't realize I needed. I watch her until the song finishes, and she begins playing another.

"Why is she here?" I call back to my sister, uncaring that she's supposed to be working.

"Why do you think?"

I look back at her, finding Murphy handing over a bottle of wine to the couple. She looks at me, a smile on her face.

"She's in love with you, dummy. This is her grand gesture."

I spin back around, my heart pounding at what my sister just said, wondering if it's really true. *Hoping* that it is.

I head toward where Vivian is on the opposite end of the field, leaving Murphy behind to handle the booth. I weave into the crowd surrounding the stage, getting close enough that I can see those freckles that I love so much.

God, she's a fucking queen up there. Commanding the stage and the attention of everyone listening.

And I can't do anything but drink it in. Bask in her presence.

Any attempt I'd made at moving past the feelings I'd begun to develop . . . is gone. Dust. Blown away in the wind of the storm that surrounds my heart when I'm near her.

She finishes singing, her eyes closed and her head tilted up on that last note, and then the crowd around me cheers and shouts, applause sweeping through the entire event.

That's when her eyes find me. Like she knew where I was standing the entire time.

"Technically, I'm only supposed to do two songs," she says, giving me a smile, "but I have one more. Something I wrote over the past few weeks. It's about that time in your life when your idea of home becomes less about a place, and more about a person. I haven't named it yet, but I'm thinking about calling it 'Where You Are.'"

Then she's strumming her guitar again, a folky-country sound that I find myself swaying along to, my fingers tapping lightly against my jeans as I listen.

She sings about running away, about not knowing what she was looking for, and I'd have to be an idiot not to understand instinctively that this song is about us.

And then she gets to the chorus, and her eyes lock on me, not straying for a moment as she launches into the lyrics.

I've been to the mountains, the valleys, the sea
Searching for something that might maybe set me free.
When all of that time all I wanted to be
Was home, home, home in your arms.
Home, home, home is where you are.

She hits another verse, this one about finding a place where she's known, and a shiver slides through me. I'm almost under a trance.

When she finally sings the chorus again, ending on that last line, the audience erupts in cheers. The people around me must surely know they've witnessed an incredible talent. A once-in-a-lifetime moment.

Gigi steps out onto the stage, thanking Vivian and making some announcements about whoever is next. But I don't hear any of that. All I can hear is the sound of my heart thumping in my ears as she walks off the stage, meeting me where I'm already waiting for her off to the side.

As confident as she was up there, now that she's on the ground, just a few feet away, I can see the hint of nerves in her eyes as we approach each other.

"Hi, Memphis," she says, her voice soft.

"You're here." I'm unable to hide my smile at that fact.

"I wanted to talk to you. To apologize. To . . . see if you'd reconsider what you said about us making this work . . ."

I step forward and pull her into my arms, cutting her off midsentence.

Her surprise is evident at first, but barely a beat passes before she melts into me, her mouth opening as I kiss her thoroughly. As I pour out every moment that I've missed her over the past month.

"I just really wanted to do that." I pull back slightly, resting my forehead against hers.

"I had a whole speech planned," she whispers, her eyes closed and her lips tilted up at the sides. "An apology and an explanation and everything."

"I don't need it."

Vivian laughs, wrapping her arms around my middle and tucking herself snugly into me. It's like a puzzle piece sliding into place.

God, I love you.

"I still need to say it," she says, her words coming quiet into my ear. "And you're a liar if you think you don't need to hear it."

I sigh, closing my own eyes and pulling her in even more tightly.

"Maybe I do," I finally say. "But not right now. Right now, I just want to enjoy that you're here, in my arms, where you belong."

She hums, rubbing her hands gently on my back.

"My home," she whispers.

I kiss her again, not wanting to miss the opportunity.

God, if it's up to me, I'll never miss a chance to kiss her again.

And then I wrap my arm around her shoulders, and we wander into the crowd.

◆ ◆ ◆

Vivian's body lies on top of mine, her chest heaving, both of us exhausted and thoroughly spent.

We stayed an hour or so at the Fall Festival. She helped at the booth for a little bit, and then Murphy shooed us away, telling us to go enjoy ourselves.

So we strolled along, hand in hand, until by mutual agreement, we left and came back home.

Where we lost ourselves in the physical connection that we so clearly have.

I know we need to talk. Vivian was right when she said I need to hear whatever she has to say. And I do want to hear it.

But I also wanted to feel her in my arms. Watch her writhe underneath me. See her fall apart at my touch.

Our physical connection is just as important as our emotional one, and I can't complain that that's the one we both wanted to focus on first.

She slides off my chest and tucks herself into my side. She draws lazy doodles along my abdomen as we sit in the silence for long moments before she finally speaks.

"I left because I was scared."

Her words are shy. Quiet. Filled with an emotion I'm not accustomed to hearing in her voice.

Fear.

"The things I feel for you are just . . . so much bigger than what I've ever felt before, and I was scared of what it would do to me when this eventually fizzled out." Her head tilts up, and she looks me in the eyes.

"Why were you so sure it would fizzle out?"

"Because everything does," she answers, her words quick. "Nothing lasts forever, right?"

"Of course not, but that seems to be an argument for taking what you want with both hands, not avoiding it altogether."

Vivian closes her eyes and tucks her face into my neck, and I wrap her up with both arms, knowing she clearly needs it.

"Talk to me. What's going through that head?"

"That's the thing," she whispers, not looking me in the eye. "I'm not used to sharing what's going on in my head. I don't . . . really let people in."

"Why not?"

She sighs. "I use my music to share how I feel, as a way to let people see parts of who I am. But I've always been afraid that if I let someone really see me—if I share the deepest, darkest parts of me, my fears and hopes and secrets—it'll be used as a list of reasons why I'm unlovable."

I push Vivian onto her back and bring a hand to her face, cupping her cheek, my thumb stroking down her jaw.

"You could never be unlovable," I tell her, my voice stern, wanting her to know how deeply convicted I feel on this very important point. "Ever."

Her lips tilt up at the sides, and she lifts up to press a gentle kiss to my mouth.

"You might be the first person I've ever really shared that with," she whispers. "And like I said, it's scary. Because it's me giving you all the tools to tear me apart if you wanted to."

I shake my head. "Not in any world could I ever take the things you tell me and use them against you."

She nods, something like resolve hidden within her gaze.

"I know that. I trust you. I trust you with the parts of me I've never shown to anyone before. With the things I'm scared to share." Vivian pauses, her hand coming up to my face, her eyes roving across it. "I want you to *know* me. I want to be known by you. I want this between us to be more than just . . ."

She trails off.

"More than just bene-mies?" I ask, grinning at her.

Vivian laughs, and the sound sinks into my skin, healing me in ways I didn't realize another person could.

My chest is tight, but I speak anyway. "It was never just a fling, you and me. Nothing I've ever felt for you has been small enough, or meaningless enough to have ever been a fling."

At that, she smiles, and that tightness in my chest settles.

"I'm sorry I left. I ran instead of giving this a chance."

"But you came back to me," I tell her, placing a kiss against her cheek, and then her nose, and then her lips.

And then I look her in the eyes and tell her a truth I know to be true.

"We can make it through anything if we always come back to each other."

Epilogue

Vivian

One Year Later

"Go! Go! Go! Go! Go!"

My smile is stretched wide on my face, my laughter loud as I run in place, my hands on the edge of the barrel, my feet stomping on the grapes at the bottom. The squishy, smushy sensation is strange and unfamiliar. But I keep going, unable to contain my wild cackle at how ludicrous this is.

To my left and to my right are several barrels, and other members of the Hawthorne Vines harvest crew are in each one, all in similar states of laughter and hilarity.

It's the End of Harvest Jubilee, a marker to declare that all the grapes have been collected and pressed and fermentation has begun. According to Memphis, the end of the harvest means the busiest, most difficult part of the year is behind them, which also means it's time to celebrate.

Apparently, some vineyards throw a big to-do, inviting the whole town out for a party. But the event at Hawthorne Vines is strictly a family affair with only the staff and crew present. There's food and wine and several competitions, including the grape stomping.

I wasn't in town for the Jubilee last year, so when I got my tour schedule and saw that I'd be free in November, I made sure Memphis knew I wanted to throw my hat into the ring.

I can safely say, I'll be a supportive spectator next time.

A loud cheer from the barrel two down from mine fills the air, and I look over in time to see Murphy with her hands in the air, her chest heaving, the bucket underneath the spout sticking from the front filled to the brim.

"Murphy advances!" Sarah announces into the bullhorn.

I laugh, panting and looking at Memphis where he's standing a few feet away.

"Advances? You mean she has to do this again?"

He grins, his hands coming to my waist as he helps me climb out of the barrel.

"Yeah, there are a few heats before the final round."

I shake my head, my purple feet settling into the grass. "I will gratefully take an L," I declare, then I turn and shout in her direction. "Congrats, Murphy!"

She laughs and waves, the glee at having won the first round clearly lighting her up.

"You did an amazing job."

I pin Memphis with a look that says I don't buy it. Then I look into the bucket sitting underneath the spout of my barrel, finding it only a quarter of the way full.

"You know, I don't need your false flattery," I say, my eyebrow high.

"You don't?" He smirks at me, that dimple I love so much becoming more prominent. "So I should stop telling you how good you are in bed," he says, his voice dipping low.

I bark out a laugh. "That's not false flattery. That's cold hard facts, my love. Cold. Hard. Hard. Very Hard. Facts."

"Keep saying *hard* like that," he taunts me, that sexy smirk still stretched on his face. "And I'll show you some facts."

Shaking my head at his absurdity, I drop down onto a bench and dip my feet into a bucket of water, then use a rag to try to lessen the purple hue of my skin. But something tells me it might be a day or two before this color fades.

"I'll scrub those for you later," Memphis says, pressing a kiss to the crown of my head. Then he wanders off, and I can't help the way my eyes follow him as he goes.

The way they always do.

If someone had told me that my trip to Rosewood last year would result in the relationship Memphis and I share, I wouldn't have believed it.

Yet, here we are. One year and some change later, and I've never been happier. I'd bet everything I have on Memphis feeling the same. And the reason I can say that is because it's something we discuss constantly.

We talk daily. Support each other's dreams and joys. See each other as often as we can.

Like now, my cat and I are in Rosewood for three weeks, give or take a handful of days here and there when I need to go down to LA for some publicity for a new single I'm releasing in January. Later this month, Memphis will be joining me at my parents' house in Brentwood for Thanksgiving—our first holiday with my family—and then I'll be back here for a week or two during Christmas.

Our lives are a little chaotic, but we both agreed on two things when I came back to Rosewood last year.

First, we love each other, and we're committed to finding a way to make it work.

Second, we would always support each other in the things that bring us the greatest joy.

Right now, that means pursuing my music. For Memphis, that means continuing to build back his family's vineyard into a successful, thriving business.

It also means that we aren't always together, which I'm sure some people find strange.

But it works for us. We are both people who are very dedicated to our work, and we would resent each other if we felt obligated to let our dreams go just so we could live someone else's version of happy.

This is our version, and it fits us perfectly.

After several more rounds of grape stomping, some delicious food, and a host of thank-you speeches and gift giving, Memphis and I finally take our leave, driving off to Main Street.

But when we pass by The Standard and I keep going, Memphis glances back, confusion evident in his expression.

"You remember where the bar is?"

I grin at him. "I know where The Standard is," I reply. "We can come back later. I have something to show you first."

We only drive for a few more minutes, and I turn left, then right, and then left again onto a cute little street about three blocks from downtown. Then I come to a stop on a residential street.

"Come on." Nerves begin to fizzle under my skin as I wave for him to join me.

If I'm honest, the nerves have been there since I signed the paper-work, but now that we're here and I'm going to share this with him, the anxiety is much more prominent.

It takes him a second to hop out and round the front of my car, but then he joins me on the little path leading to the front door of a dark-green Craftsman.

"What are we doing here?" He looks up and down the street.

"We're moving in."

His head spins quickly to look at me, and he blinks a few times. "What?"

I hold up the keys, the silver metal of the freshly cut set warm where I've been clutching them for the past hour or so as I imagined this moment over and over, rehearsing the things I wanted to say.

"I bought this house," I tell him, glancing at it again and then back at him. "For us."

His lips part in surprise, and then I slip my hand into his and we walk to the front door together, sliding the key into the lock and then pushing the door open.

It's an adorable three-bedroom with all the charm that Craftsman-style homes typically offer. Hardwood floors, original trim, built-in bookshelves, and a working fireplace. The kitchen was gently renovated by the previous owner, but care went into it, and it looks like a fresh take on an original style. But my favorite part is the cute little backyard, with the covered porch and swinging bench and the little bit of grass that extends out toward a small detached garage.

Memphis takes it all in, listening as I walk him around showing him everything.

"What do you think?" I ask as we take a seat on the porch swing.

I'm both excited and nervous to hear his opinion. I know there's a chance he might not like it. That he'll think the decision wasn't the right one. Or that I've moved too quickly.

There's always that chance.

But I know Memphis. I know his heart and his soul unlike I've ever known another person.

Memphis has been talking about moving out of his family's home for a while, looking to put some space between himself and the vineyard. Now that the new structure has been in place for almost a year, he's starting to feel like he has more time, and he'd like it if he was able to leave work and go home. Have a life outside the family business.

So when I saw this place for sale, everything inside me said that this moment was coming together at the perfect time. That the risk was worth it.

"I think it's amazing," he says. "But is this what you want?"

I slip my hand into his, our fingers twisting together.

"It's everything that I want," I tell him.

"What about your condo?"

"I sold it."

He blinks, his lips turning up at the sides. "When did you do that?"

"Todd hired someone to handle it while I was touring this summer."

"What about work?"

I shrug. "What *about* work?"

At that, he laughs. "What do you mean, *what about work?* You know what I mean."

"I know that I have a growing career that's important to me. But LA doesn't have to be my home in order for that to happen. I can fly in to record. I can travel as easily to other parts of the country for performances. And I can work on my music from here as easily as I could at my condo." Then I gesture to the garage. "Even easier if I convert that space into a studio."

He shakes his head, swallows thickly, and searches my face.

"I never want you to feel like I've clipped your wings, Vivian."

Emotion wells in my chest at his statement, the depth of his love for me something I always seem to underestimate.

"I feel very capable of spreading my wings as much and as often as I want to," I tell him, tucking in to his side and resting my head on his shoulder. "But when I fly home, I want to come back to a house we share together. Because *you* are my home, and I will always come back to you."

Memphis hums, places a kiss against my forehead, then rests his head on mine.

"I love you so much," he tells me, squeezing my hand.

"I love you, too."

We sit there for a long time, enjoying the moment, settling into the changes to come and the future that's right around the corner.

And nothing has ever felt so sweet.

ACKNOWLEDGMENTS

Always first and foremost, to Danny, for his relentless encouragement and belief in me. You are in every hero I write, and that will never stop. I am so thankful for you.

To Julie: for being such an incredible friend. To Andi: for always getting excited with me about each step of the process. To Meredith: working with you is so fun, every single time, and this was no exception. I can't wait for the next project. And to Kimberly, Krista, and Maria: for all the work that has gone into smoothing out our rough edges.

Enormous thanks to the dedicated teams at Montlake and Brower Literary for helping us bring this story into the world and for making it shine.

To Jillian, I'm so grateful that this little vineyard has brought us together. Thank you as always for your brilliance and for making every part of this journey that much sweeter.

About the Authors

Photo © Sean Murphy

Meredith Wild is a #1 *New York Times*, *USA Today*, and international bestselling author of twenty-three novels. Both traditionally and self-published, Wild's books have hit #1 on the *New York Times* and *Wall Street Journal* bestsellers lists. She has been featured on *CBS This Morning*, the *Today* show, the *New York Times*, the *Hollywood Reporter*, *Vanity Fair*, *Publishers Weekly*, and the *Examiner*. Her foreign rights have been sold in over twenty-three languages. She resides in Florida with her partner, her children, and many furry companions.

Jillian Liota is the author of more than fifteen contemporary and new adult romance novels. Her writing has been praised for depth of character, strong female friendships, deliciously steamy scenes, and positive portrayal of mental health. She has a master's in higher education and student affairs, and she is passionate about all things improvement, development, and organization. Jillian is married to her best friend, has a three-legged pup with endless energy, and enjoys traveling whenever she can. She currently lives in Georgia. For more information, visit www.jillianliota.com.